## DANCE OF HEARTS

Without being aware of it, Justin had danced Melanie onto the terrace. He slowed, then, as he turned her into deeper shadows, and came to a stop, his hand carrying hers to his shoulder while his other arm drew her tightly against his body. Her skin was blue-white in the moonlight; her eyes chips of copper fire.

"I have tried, Melanie," he breathed, his hand rising to touch trembling fingertips to the softness of her cheek. "From the beginning, from the first day I met you, I have tried. But I cannot keep from touching you . . . holding you . . . any longer."

"My lord—" Melanie gasped shakily, leaning into his strength.

"Justin," the earl urged her. "Please. Just for tonight, if that is all I can have, please call me Justin, Melanie."

Melanie was helpless against her own response to the earl's plea. Slipping her arms around his neck, she raised her face toward his and whispered, "Oh, Justin . . ."

Books by Jenna Jones

A MERRY ESCAPADE

A DELICATE DECEPTION

TIA'S VALENTINE

Published by Zebra Books

# A Delicate Deception

## Jenna Jones

Zebra Books
Kensington Publishing Corp.

http://www.zebrabooks.com

ZEBRA BOOKS are published by

Kensington Publishing Corp.
850 Third Avenue
New York, NY 10022

First Printing: July, 1996
10 9 8 7 6 5 4 3 2

Printed in the United States of America

*For my Camelback Mountain Wheezing Geezers . . .*
*Wil Passow, Woody Wise, and Ben Clevenger . . .*
*who adopted me.*

# One

*London, 1839*

Replete, Justin Mayhew, the Earl of Stonegate, lay upon soft down and pristine white satin, his gaze wandering aimlessly over the tasteful appointments of the bedroom. He was glad he had undertaken the furnishing of the small Bloomsbury house himself. Left to his mistress, his *pied-à-terre* would undoubtedly have shouted at his senses with red velvet, burnished gold, and mirrors; but as it was, the clean, crisp lines of several Sheraton pieces reposed against a background of white, gold, and blue. The room soothed him, and Justin Mayhew was a man in need of being soothed.

Beside him, the woman in his arms stirred.

"What, so soon?" he questioned as his mistress's delicately shaped toe began to trace an erotic path through the dark, dense hair covering his lower leg. "You give me too much credit, I think, Clarisse. I am, after all, only a mere man."

The woman responded with a throaty laugh. Tunneling one carefully manicured finger through the crisp hair covering his chest, she whispered, "Shall we see?"

Justin cast her a crooked grin, liking the feminine challenge sparkling in her eyes in the dim firelight. Taking a deep breath, he cupped his hands behind his head and shrugged his broad shoulders against the pillows.

"Do your damnedest," he replied.

Another deeply drawn breath controlled his response to the movement of Clarisse's mouth as she raised herself above him and suckled her way down the length of his body. Her hair trailed behind her, trickling over his sensitized skin in ribbons of soft auburn. His breathing stumbled as she touched, kissed, settled; one hand irresistibly drawn down to cradle and clutch as she began to work against him.

His head twisted to the side on a ragged sigh. Each time, it amazed him that his body could react in such contradiction to his thoughts. In truth, in spite of Clarisse's expertise, he felt nothing more than physical sensation. He felt no emotion. Only the coldness that irrepressibly enshrouded him.

He arched slightly as she took him deeper, his gaze coming to rest upon the slow flames sluggishly wavering in the fireplace across the well-appointed room. He might have been looking at a self portrait, he thought impassively. For two years he had borne the numbing weight of ice that incrusted his emotions, just as the fire was bearing its burden of cold, encapsulating Carrara marble, all its heat trapped inside. He wondered if it would be this way for him for the rest of his life, and, if so, how the deuce he was going to survive.

"You put me in mind of Oliver just then," said Clarisse, surging upward to blot her wet lips against his navel.

"Oh?" Justin replied thinly, still mesmerized by the dying flames.

"Yes. That was something he might have said."

Clarisse returned to her work, then, easing her hand between his legs to cradle his tightened orbs, flexing her thumb to stroke them. Justin thrust against her slowly, circling, fisting satin in his long, tapered fingers.

"I hardly think that unusual," he ground out through clenched teeth. "He was, after all, my brother."

"And my friend," Clarisse whispered. "More than a lover. More than just the man who came before you."

Peering up the length of his body, she held his gaze with a stare of piercing blue, her free hand rising over hard ridges of muscle and rib to circle his pebbled paps before returning to bury itself beneath his buttocks.

Justin closed his eyes, letting the sensations take him. His blood flowed stagnant and hot against the taut walls of his veins, coursing in a rhythm that echoed Clarisse's undulations. He writhed, his lips opening on a silent gasp.

Suddenly his eyes flew open, desperately seeking marble and flame. His body trembled. He was that fire, trapped within guilt-forged stone. He understood it fully, yet did not know how to escape. His hands swept down to tangle themselves in Clarisse's hair. His abdomen clenched; he shuddered, his hips driving against her again and again. The sweet tension built, boiled, overflowed; exploded in release.

Yet still there was nothing; no feeling, no abatement of the unrelenting ice.

Clarisse slid upward against the length of his side. Opening her robe, she nestled against the limp warmth of his arm.

"I shall never forget what he did for me," she murmured against his shoulder, raising his arm to cuddle it against her, brushing the softly furred back of it lazily across the tip of one breast. "If he had not taken me under his protection when Long Jake died, I think I would have been killed by the other women in his stable."

Justin smiled with great effort. "What could you possibly have done to make so many bits of muslin dislike you, Clarisse?"

"I never knew," she replied soberly. "Oliver happened by just when they were attacking, and rescued me. It was such a gallant gesture," she said, smiling sweetly, "sweeping me up into his carriage and driving me away. But since I never saw any of the women again, I was never able to find out why they wished to harm me."

"Perhaps they were jealous," Justin suggested, fingering a tangled strand of auburn. "You are quite lovely, you know."

"Am I?"

A new light flickered in the depths of Clarisse's eyes. Imprisoning his arm more tightly between her breasts, she reached across him for his other hand and drew it slowly toward her moist heat. "Justin . . ."

The earl kissed her, stopping her words while easily extricating his hand. "Not again, Clarisse," he murmured after a moment. "I must go." Dropping another quick kiss on her soft mouth, he slowly rolled to his feet.

"Oh, Justin, so soon?" Clarisse pouted, disappointment pooling beneath her brows.

"I am afraid so," he responded, strolling in a loose-hipped, masculine gait toward the mahogany stand where he had carefully hung his clothing earlier. "Angela is arriving in Town this afternoon with my niece and nephew. If I want to get any sleep before the bantlings descend, I need to leave you now."

After slipping quickly into his underdrawers, Justin donned his frilled white evening shirt, carefully closing it across his broad chest with a handful of gold studs set with diamonds. He then thrust his muscular legs into a pair of black pantaloons, tucking in the tails of his shirt before fastening them.

Clarisse watched him smooth his hands over his pant legs, chewing on the inside of her lip. "Shall your sister be attending the wedding?" she asked casually.

Justin stilled.

"Wedding?" His deep brown eyes shuttered, then searched her face. "And what would you know of that?"

Her reply came with a slow shrug. "I have heard rumors . . ."

Justin turned away from her again, beginning to wrap his neck in the narrow white silk of his cravat. "Tell me," he ordered gently as he tugged the embroidered ends into a small, neat bow.

"I have heard it said that you have offered for Lord Palmerton's daughter," she answered softly. "Is it true, then?"

Justin tugged his cream-colored waistcoat into place and fastened it, its thread-of-gold embroidery glinting in the firelight. "I have not yet done so," he replied quietly.

"But you will, will you not?" Clarisse asked again, her gaze sharpening.

"That is my intention, yes."

He heard the slither of satin against silk and knew that she had arisen from the bed. Coming to stand beside him, she took his diamond and gold cuff links from his hand and motioned for him to lift his wrists. Complying, his thoughts drifted, centering on stone and fire, easily conjuring an image of Eunice's golden hair and bright blue eyes.

She was everything that he could want in a wife. He had concluded that after only one evening spent studying her at the Hertford's ball. Not only had he been impressed by her beauty, but by her manner as well. She had been a pattern card of what was proper and correct, never laughing above a light, descending trill or speaking in anything but a voice that was soft and melodious. Her table manners, too, had been impeccable. He had specifically engaged her for the supper dance so that he might judge that aspect of her social training as well. He had not been disappointed. She had behaved with the utmost propriety. Even her gown had been well chosen; a tasteful confection of blue brocade, it had been modestly suitable for the event.

He had appreciated her attitude toward him as well. She had been respectful and subdued in his company as they had taken the obligatory stroll around the ballroom after their dance, and when he had returned her to her parents, she had been impressively obedient to their wishes. As he detested harping, raucous, giggling females, he had found in her a woman in whose company he thought he could rub along quite nicely over the span of his life. No, there could be no doubt. She was the perfect choice upon which to bestow the Mayhew name; and he was certain his father, were he still alive, would have agreed.

The late Earl of Stonegate had taught his son from Justin's earliest remembrance the duty that was owed his title and his name. Upon his shoulders, his father had often warned, would one day rest the welfare of the entire family. He must make himself strong, he was commanded. He must hold himself above reproach. And he must choose a countess to equal him. Only the most decorous of females could be considered for his wife. No taint must ever be allowed to touch Stonegate.

For six years, after his father's death, Justin had carried the burden dutifully. And then Oliver had died. Because of him. Because, in a moment of foolish irritation, he had let his responsibility toward his brother slide. Yet little had changed really. Oliver was gone, but he was still Stonegate, and he still had that damnable duty riding him relentlessly like a blue-blooded parasite.

And that was why he would offer for Eunice. She would

partner him in his duty superbly. He only hoped she never came to care for him. He would not be able to return her feelings. He regretted it deeply—remembering the love match his parents had made—but he could not return something of himself to anyone when there was only nothingness from which to harvest it.

There was only one thing that might interfere with his intentions . . . but, no, the betrothal had taken place over twenty years ago. Deuce take it, he had only been eleven at the time, and his second cousin a mere infant! His father had meant well, he knew. Out of his own strong sense of duty toward his family, he had tried to protect the child in the only way he could, forcing the arrangement on the girl's father, his own cousin, the Earl of Westbridge, because he had wanted to make sure that the child's future would be secure. But, as so many other ventures had been where the Earl of Westbridge was concerned, his father's effort had been foolishness.

He wondered where the girl was now. How long had it been since he had received the letter from her? Seven years? Perhaps eight. She had sent him three hundred pounds . . . recompense, she had written, for several vowels she had said she found in her father's vault owing to Stonegate. It had been the first he had known of her family's return from their long years in India, or of the Earl and Lady Westbridge's subsequent deaths in the cholera epidemic that had been sweeping England at the time. The girl had asked nothing of him, only thanked him graciously for being so patient about collecting on the debt that had been owed him, and politely bid him goodbye.

He had dropped everything to journey to Westbridge Manor, determined to do his duty by her. There had been no question, of course, of his going through with a marriage to her, but his obligation required that he bring her back to his home. When he had arrived, Westbridge Manor had been nothing but an empty shell. Everything of the Westbridge holdings that had not been entailed had been put on the block by a local agent to satisfy fifteen years of her parents' accumulated debts. The outcome had been just what his father had feared when his weak-minded cousin had followed his grasping wife's urging so many years ago. Westbridge's attempts to become a nabob in India had been ruinous. Of his cousin, his betrothed, there had been no trace.

He had looked for her; he had hired men to scour the country for some word of her for four long years. She had never been found, and he had finally come to accept that even if she were still alive somewhere, she had by now most likely ruined herself. No matter how he looked at it, she was lost to his family. Yet, even now, his sense of duty and obligation toward her sometimes tugged at him. When she had written her letter to him, the last and sole time he had ever heard from her, she had been a mere child of fifteen.

"What of me, Justin?" Clarisse whispered when she had finished her task and moved to hold open his black evening tail coat for him. "Will you still keep me?"

He paused imperceptibly, then continued to slip his arms into his sleeves before shrugging his shoulders all the way inside. When he had fastened the buttons, he turned toward her and took her face between his warm palms with great tenderness.

"I cannot think it right, Clarisse," he said quietly, "nor honorable. When I marry, my full attention will be owed my wife."

Clarisse's eyes hardened slightly, then grew soft once again. A slight smile played at the corners of her mouth as she smoothed his lapels with her warm hand. "Go then," she said with a disingenuous pout. "I shall not miss you a whit. Others have offered me their protection, you know."

Justin's brow elevated. "Indeed. Who, may I ask?"

"Oh," she said casually, flicking away a piece of lint from his sleeve, "Lord Ortby, for one."

Justin nodded. "You could do worse, my dear," he said pleasantly. "Ortby can elevate you in the circles of the *demi-monde*, and he will treat you well."

"Yes, I suppose so," Clarisse said thoughtfully, "but he is not as handsome as you."

"But as rich as Croesus," Justin countered, taking her arm and turning her toward the hallway. "See me to the door, Clarisse. I really must be on my way."

"Of course." Smiling as she linked her arm through his, she led him into the hallway and down the narrow descent of the stairs.

When they reached the entry, Clarisse retrieved Justin's black silk top hat, evening cape, and cane from the cupboard, as the housekeeper had long ago been sent to her bed. With practiced hands, she opened the cape for him, quickly wrapping him in its satin-lined warmth. After he had secured the frogs just under the collar, she turned him toward her and eagerly stepped into his outstretched arms.

"It will be a while before I marry, Clarisse," he said sincerely. "Oliver would not have wanted you to be forced into a situation you cannot like. Nor do I. Let's let things stand as they are for now, shall we? I shall let you know when it is time to cast your well-baited hook elsewhere."

Clarisse nodded slowly against the starched frill of his shirt. "As you wish, Justin," she replied quietly, almost in a whisper.

Justin raised her face to his with a tender nudge of the edge of his finger. "I shall see that you are well provided for, Clarisse. It is my intention, at the very least, to give you this house. Smile for me now, and do not despair."

She nodded, then, complying with liquid eyes. "Thank you, my lord," she breathed. "I shall await your pleasure. Take care."

"And you," he murmured, stroking her soft chin with his thumb. After a soft kiss and a brief smile, he turned from her and descended the flagstone steps into Blooms-bury Way.

He had taken no more than a few steps toward the cab stand waiting empty on the opposite corner of the street, when a rectangle of light suddenly flooded the walkway in front of him. Stopping abruptly, he turned to see Clarisse framed in the parlor window. He could not see her features, for the light behind her threw her face into shadow, but as he stood for a moment regarding her, he saw her lift a hand to her lips and then press her palm against the glass pane in a gesture of farewell. He smiled, then, watching as she tugged the draperies back into place, again shutting away the intruding light. Perhaps he would miss her after all, he thought as he resumed his walk to the cab stand. And then he dismissed her from his mind.

The cabbie liked to use Bloomsbury Way to get from the posh West End of the city to Gray's Inn Road. There was much less traffic that way, even at this hour of the night. And he was tired. He had just finished nearly twenty straight hours of driving, and had no wish to battle the more brazen who could always be found along High Holborn.

He wondered what awaited him in the Rookery, high in the attic rooms he shared with the Pollards and the Hicks . . . and Simon, of course . . . back in the twisting rat's nest of alleys that tangled in odd tangents away from

Portpool Lane. Had Bess safely made it through another night? He had promised her he would be there to help her when her time came. She was so frightened. But who would not be, after all six of one's babes had come into the world stillborn?

And what of Gran? He could tell the previous morning that her chest congestion was getting worse. He would try a poultice next time. He could probably find a recipe in one of the herbals in the lending library. And her son, Con, was no help, a man with useless legs. He needed just as much care as Gran sometimes, thanks to years spent in the mines. At least Maeve was strong and healthy . . . and Maudie. But then, they had to be. They carried the weight of all of them on their broad shoulders. The cabbie shifted on his seat, then, wriggling against the clutching ache in his lower spine.

He glanced about, when he had gotten himself more comfortable, taking in the view that unfolded as each block rolled slowly by. The street was deserted, its dark stretch broken only by the glow of a regimented row of gas lamps blossoming like dandelion puffs in the soot-dusted night. His sharp eyes missed nothing, scanning his surroundings restlessly, searching the hidden recesses of the alleys that ran like running sores between the buildings. After eight years driving first a hackney, and now his own hansom, he had learned to be alert at all times.

And then he spotted him, a man standing alone near the shelter of an empty cab stand a few blocks away. The cabbie cursed softly . . . a gentle curse, but improper just the same. Selfish thoughts began an insistent nagging to pass the man by and continue home to his pallet bed, but the cabbie knew that he would not. He could not afford to pass up any fare, no matter how much he ached for sleep. Simon would soon need every farthing.

The man was quality. He could see that quite clearly now. He was dressed in evening clothes tailored to skim his well-made form in a manner that bespoke elegance and expense. His hair was dark under the brim of his top hat, parted on the side and impeccably brushed into long waves that almost covered his ears. And, merciful heavens, he was handsome! Yet hard eyes gleamed from beneath his well-groomed mustache. The cabbie drew in a slow, settling breath, resigning himself both to another long, tedious trip back in the other direction toward the West End, and to yet another in a day-long series of collisions with a nobleman's impatient irritation.

Suddenly, there was a flicker of movement near where the man stood waiting. The cabbie was instantly alert, his weariness vanishing as quickly as his complacency. Jerking upright with a gasp of anger, he watched as two footpads spilled out of the shadowed maw of the alley nearest the cab stand and headed straight for the unsuspecting man.

They were upon him in seconds, spinning him around and laying into him with their fists until he staggered to his knees. And yet the man rallied, mustering a defense that caught the footpads off guard. Fighting back with a precise, well-trained counterattack, slowly, steadily, the man began to gain ground, hammering against the two attackers until their backs were flattened against the corner bake shop's bricks.

The cabbie began to breathe again. There was probably no reason to hurry, he thought, even as he whipped his hack to a faster pace. The mill, in fact, would most likely be over by the time he got there from the looks of it. Yet even as the thought formed, he dismissed it, his nostrils flaring on a quickly drawn breath. Within the charcoal shadows that hugged the wall, among the softly blurred reflections of relentlessly swinging fists, the cabbie saw the light from

the nearby gas lamp flicker over the silver-sheened blade
of a knife.

There had been no warning. One moment Justin was
impatiently craning his neck to watch the approach of a
distant hansom cab, wishing it to perdition for its slowness,
and the next, whatever sated lethargy remained from his
time with Clarisse was being quickly overwhelmed by a
flood of pure adrenaline. They were good, he thought as
he used the first of the blows they threw against his body
to take his measure of them. He might actually have to
work to get the best of these two.

Slowly, methodically, he counterattacked, using the
skills he had learned over the years at Witt's to weaken his
assailants and drive them back toward the wall of the building behind them, where he could trap them between bricks
and fists. He concentrated upon placing his blows intelli-
gently, hammering at vulnerable places, pulverizing flaccid
flesh.

And then, suddenly, a searing pain clawed at the side of
his neck. Almost immediately, another lanced through his
shoulder. He staggered back, clutching at the stinging ache,
cursing the sudden weakness that had him stumbling to his
knees, barely dodging another scythelike swing. Warm,
metallic wetness dripped between his clenched fingers,
darkening his shirt's starched frills.

Knives, he thought as he fended off another blow. Bloody
hell.

One of the footpads again lunged at him, taking advantage of his stunned paralysis. Justin was just able to wheel
away from the plunging thrust, but another caught his good
arm, biting into it with sharpened steel. Shutting out the
piercing pain, he summoned his remaining strength, strug-

gling to his feet just in time to seize the wrist of one of the men before his blade dug deeply into his chest. Willing himself to hold firm, he slowly forced the knife back, fighting with all his strength for each precious minute that remained of his life. He knew he did not have long. Locked within this struggle, there was little he could do to stop the other man. Out of the corner of his eye, Justin watched him approach, the footpad's battered face impassive as he readied himself for the kill.

There were only seconds remaining. Justin realized that fact with an odd sort of detachment. He was not sorry, but he found himself thinking that if he had to die in such an ignoble way, he really would have liked to have known why. He felt his arms weakening, his flesh beginning to shiver slightly. A light-spangled dimness began to infiltrate the edges of his vision as his grip on the attacker's wrist became tentative and sweat-slicked. It would all be over soon. He hoped it would be quick.

And then a soft whirr sounded above his head, followed by a solid thump. Immediately after, the same sound whisked past his ear. Justin started, then looked on incredulously as, in swift sequence, the two footpads stiffened and dropped limply to the cobblestones in front of him, amazingly, but undeniably, unconscious. Staggered by sudden relief, the earl wobbled drunkenly, clutching at his wounds as he collapsed to his knees.

He was vaguely aware that the hansom had pulled to a stop beside him, and heard a piercing whistle that he knew would summon the bobbies, yet he could not seem to focus his mind upon anything except the repetitive pattern of gaslit reflections cupping each rounded cobblestone, parading into the distance.

He heard windows opening in the nearby buildings, followed by the sudden sound of a pair of running feet. Voices called as if from a tunnel, and then there were strong, slim arms supporting him, worrying at his collar and frogs, and, close to his ear, a soft, husky voice.

" 'Ere now, guv'nor," the voice soothed, gentle and sweet. Justin flowed into the warmth of the sound. "Oi've got ye now. Lean against me. That's roight, milord. Ye fought a roight tappin' mill, sir, but yer done fer the day. Oi'll take care of ye now."

Like a flower seeking the sun, Justin slowly turned his head toward the voice. With even greater effort, he lifted his gaze. And then he stilled, amazed. His savior was no more than a boy, a lad not even old enough yet to shave, judging by the fine down that dusted his cheeks. Yet somehow the boy had incapacitated two streetwise footpads and saved his life. Or had he?

"Can ye 'old yerself up fer a minute, milord?" the voice asked gently.

Justin's eyes dropped drunkenly to regard lips that were full and beautifully shaped. As he watched, the lips opened in a smile that revealed even, white teeth. A nose rose above his upper lip, quite a handsome nose, he thought with some astonishment . . . slender and straight, and flaring delicately at the tip. His focus telescoped, then, taking in the wealth of short, midnight curls that peeked out from underneath the lad's unfashionable broad leather brim.

And then Justin saw his eyes. Surrounded by long, dark lashes, sheltered below finely sculpted, narrow brows, they were the exact color of copper, as bright as new pennies glinting in the gaslight. For some unaccountable reason, Justin's heart stumbled. He clutched at the lad's ragged coat.

"Does ye think ye can, sir?" the boy questioned again.

Justin wasn't sure, but he thought that he nodded.

The eyes smiled.

"That's awright, then," the lad said. "Them coppers'll

be here roight quick, Oi expect, but Oi wants to get yer
bleedin' stopped. Oi got clean rags in me cab, sir. 'Ang on
now, an' Oi'll go get 'em."

Justin watched the young lad scamper away, fumble
around under the driver's seat, then return just as quickly
carrying a small bundle under his arm. Flipping his frayed
tails out behind him, the boy knelt beside him and opened
his bundle carefully, glancing up at Justin as he did so with
another smile and the glint of warmth in his copper-colored
eyes. The glance caught, held; the two stilled, studied one
another, the clamor rising around them fading away unregarded. Something tugged at Justin . . . a memory, one
from long ago. He knew then, in that moment, that this
was not the first time he had seen those copper-colored
eyes.

And more. He knew that looking at them . . . losing himself in them as he now was . . . had shifted something inside
him. Gazing into their bright, welcoming warmth, even this
briefly, had melted just a fraction of that numbing, damnable ice.

# Two

"Who are you?" Justin whispered, staring intently into the cabbie's eyes.

The boy's smile widened. "Me name's Mel, sir," he replied in his soft, husky voice. "But ye oughtn't be talkin', Oi thinks. Just rest against me while Oi sees to yer cuts."

Justin nodded weakly, grunting softly as the cabbie shifted his weight to gently tug his coat from his wounded shoulder and unwind his silk cravat. Then, with swift, sure movements, the lad unfastened his studs and cuff links, dropping them one at a time into the earl's coat pocket before he laid the garment across Justin's lap. With great care, he rolled the earl's shirtsleeve up past his elbow, exposing the wound on his arm, then gingerly peeled the sodden shirtfront away from the seeping wounds in his shoulder and neck.

A series of shrill whistles sounded in the distance, followed by the squeak of wheels and the patter of approaching feet. Justin looked up to find himself suddenly surrounded by several uniformed constables of Robert Peel's Metropolitan Police. Called bobbies by some, peelers by others, they were the successors to the famous Bow Street Runners and were headquartered in offices in Whitehall which opened at the rear onto a garden area called Scotland Yard.

One of them, a rather large, florid-faced man in a blue uniform tailcoat and top hat, and with an air of onions about him, quickly took in the scene and then knelt with surprising agility before the earl. "I am Sergeant Hillman," he said brusquely, tapping the length of his wooden baton against one of his palms. "Are you all right, sir?"

"Cor," Mel muttered, spreading an herbal-scented salve upon a folded square of clean cloth and applying it to Justin's shoulder. "Awright? 'Course 'e ain't awright! Open yer peepers, ye twit! Only thing 'round here wot got more 'oles be yer 'ead."

Justin's right eyebrow soared disapprovingly at the lad's hostile, rag-mannered remarks, yet at the same time, he found himself oddly entertained by his brashness and the sergeant's irritated glare. Unexpectedly, a bit more of the ice melted. Dizzy from doing battle to keep his wits about him and from loss of blood, the earl could only wonder at it.

"I assure you that I am aware of your injuries, sir," Sergeant Hillman said stiffly, "and I regret having to cause you further discomfort, but I have an investigation to conduct. I'll have your name first, if you please."

"Ye'll 'ave nothin' yet," growled the cabbie in his rich, husky voice. "The guv'nor 'ere, 'e be needin' a doctor, so shut yer cake-'ole an' back off till Oi kin get him 'ome."

The sergeant's lips thinned. "Now see here, lad—"

Wincing, Justin held up a hand, then closed his eyes against the swirl of dizziness that accompanied his effort. "I am Stonegate," he answered wearily, putting an abrupt end to their bickering.

Behind him, the cabbie made an odd noise and grew rigid. Justin felt the change instantaneously, noticing, too, that the lad's seemingly competent hands had begun to discernibly shake.

The sergeant's eyes widened slightly. Immediately he assumed a more deferential attitude toward the earl. "Ah. I beg your pardon, my lord," he apologized. "May I assume that those two lying unconscious over there are the ones who injured you?"

"Yes," Justin replied, forcing himself to be helpful. In truth, he was much more interested in the sudden change in the cabbie's demeanor than in the sergeant's questions. "They attacked me when I was awaiting the lad's cab."

The sergeant nodded, then turned to catch the eye of one of his constables. In minutes, the two footpads had been bound in chains and dragged over to a waiting police van where they were quickly secured inside. As the three watched, the driver snapped his whip and the van lumbered away toward the jail.

"Do you know of any reason why you might have been attacked, my lord?" the sergeant continued.

Justin opened his mouth to respond, but did not. The cabbie's breathing, as it buffeted his bare shoulder, had quickened oddly. Ignoring the man beside him, the earl turned toward the lad, forcing him to meet his penetrating gaze. He saw the lad's eyes widen under his intense scrutiny, then soften and grow bright with wonder. Justin's gaze narrowed. Again they studied one another with an almost hungry curiosity. Justin could not understand the sudden tension that had arisen between the two of them at the mention of his name anymore than he could understand what it was about the lad that was so compelling. He only knew that the boy was somehow important to him. He did not know how it could be, but the certainty within him was overpowering.

The cabbie's lips moved.

"Stonegate . . ." he whispered with an inexplicable, yearning awe in his remarkable voice.

Justin shuddered as the soft, husky sound of his name rippled through him, feeling as if his whole being were seeping out of the confines of his body and flowing toward the lad.

"My lord?" the sergeant questioned again, abruptly loosening the strange, taut tether that had begun to weave between the two of them. "Do you know of a reason, sir?"

Justin returned his gaze to the man, almost angry in his reluctance to acknowledge him. Behind him, he felt his neck moistened by a shaky sigh. The action was unaccountable, but telling. He was not the only one strangely affected by the other's nearness. He found that discovery highly satisfying.

Ending his inner pause, he told the sergeant, "No."

"Then can you tell me, my lord, why you were at this particular location tonight?"

Justin dragged in a shallow breath. "I was . . . visiting in that house across the street," he replied, pointing toward his darkened *pied-à-terre*.

The sergeant followed his gaze. "Ah. It is quite possible, then, that its residents might have seen something important. As soon as I am through here, I shall call upon them for questioning."

"No," Justin stated quickly, wincing slightly as the cabbie wrapped a long strip of cloth under his arm and over his shoulder, tying it snugly to secure the bandage in place. "There is no need. The house is occupied by . . . a single woman. Her curtains had been drawn. She would have seen nothing."

"Ah," the sergeant drawled with understanding. "Then it is not unusual for you to visit the neighborhood."

Justin scowled slightly, glancing uneasily back toward the cabbie. "I fail to see what bearing that fact has on your investigation, Sergeant Hillman, but no, I visit my friend quite frequently."

The earl's skin tingled, sensing the touch and flow of Mel's gaze as it crept slowly upward over the contours of his face. He could not control the need to meet it, to restore their strange connection, and eagerly did so. There were spiderweb tracings of tension across the cabbie's well-formed brow.

"Not that I doubt your word, my lord," the sergeant continued, oblivious to the cabbie's whitened lips, "but in my experience, it pays to leave no stone unturned. With your permission, I shall still question your . . . friend."

Justin's lips tightened, but in the end, he relented. With an arrogant nod, he granted his permission, knowing that to object further would only place undue attention on a part of his life that he wished to remain private and which would soon be ended. As it was, when the tabbies got word of the attack upon him and the circumstances under which it took place, he would have enough indecorous behavior to explain to Miss Parkes and her family.

The sergeant turned his sharp gaze, then, toward the cabbie. "What about you, boy? Did you see anything?" he asked crisply.

"Enough," the lad confirmed, a tartness undergirding his soft huskiness. Keeping his gaze lowered, he placed another pad against the wound at the curve of Justin's neck and secured it with his cravat. "It were just loike his lordship said." Drawing his lips into a thin line, he glanced up at the sergeant before resuming his task. "Them two was waitin' fer him awright. Busted outta that there alley loike them 'ounds o' 'ell, they did."

"Excellent," the sergeant said, his gaze intensifying. "As a witness to the event, I shall need you to tell me everything you saw in detail. What is your name, lad?"

The cabbie's gaze suddenly slewed toward Justin, then dropped again to the hands bandaging the earl's wrist. His lower lip trembled minutely; he caught it between his teeth to arrest the movement.

"Well, lad?" Sergeant Hillman urged impatiently.

"Me name's Mel," the cabbie admitted warily.

"Mel what?" the officer pressed.

"There ain't nothin' else," the boy replied softly, hedging.

"I see," the sergeant said impassively.

"Oi ain't no butter stamp," the cabbie muttered defensively, "but that be all Oi'm gonna say."

The sergeant exhaled on a scowl. "Lad, there are consequences to impeding an investigation—"

But his next words were cut off abruptly. On a ragged gasp, Justin's head rolled against the side of the cabbie's neck and his long body convulsed with a violent shiver.

"Awright, that be enough talk," the cabbie said sharply, frowning with concern as he braced his arms protectively around the earl. "His lordship be needin' a doctor an' his own bed. 'E won't be tellin' ye nothin' if 'e takes a bad fever, an' neither will Oi. 'Elp me get his coat back on 'im. Oi ain't waitin' no longer. Oi be takin' 'im 'ome in me cab roight now."

Unable to dispute either the boy's words or the sudden pallid hue of the earl's skin, the sergeant nodded briefly and reached for the coat that still lay across the earl's lap. Quickly he eased it over Justin's shoulders and fastened it in the front, then wrapped him in his cape.

"I apologize for putting my investigation before your comfort, my lord," he said solicitously. "You must, of course, be taken to your home immediately. I shall send one of my men for an ambulance."

With effort, Justin shook his head. "No need . . ." he

said in slurred tones. "I shall go with the boy." Another shiver rippled through him even as he again acknowledged in the deepest part of himself his inexplicable unwillingness to be parted from the lad.

"Do you think that wise, my lord?" the sergeant asked, casting a glance toward Mel. "The lad seems a bit young."

"Oi ain't so young!" the cabbie cried hotly. "Ain't Oi the one wot dicked them rum dubbers in the nob?"

The officer looked at the boy disbelievingly. "You did that?" he questioned.

" 'Course Oi did," the boy insisted. "Just ask 'im," he said, motioning toward the earl with his chin.

"God knows how," Justin confirmed with a shaky nod, "but he did."

"You'll have to explain it, lad," the sergeant told him.

"Aw," the cabbie replied under a furrowed brow, "it weren't nothin' to get yer conks in a quiver about. Oi done it wiv this." Somewhat reluctantly, he reached behind him and brought forth a leather sling from the recesses of his coat pocket.

"Devil a bit," Justin said wonderingly. "So it was stones from your sling I heard whining past my head."

"Aye," the lad confessed with a single nod. "Dropped them bleedin' buggers loike 'ookers wiv the clap, Oi did."

Justin cringed at the lad's scandalous impropriety even as a sudden burst of warmth surged through him, almost blotting out his pain. He gasped from the force of it, incredulous that it should have happened at all. He had not experienced anything like it for a long, long time, so long he hardly recognized it for what it was. And yet he did know it, and was astounded. For the first time since Oliver's death, he had had the impulse to laugh.

"Where did you learn such a skill, lad?" the earl asked haltingly, equally as light-headed from the new sense of warming still curling deep within him as from his loss of blood.

"Well, milord," the cabbie replied, "Oi moight just tell ye some day. But not now. Now, Oi needs to get ye 'ome. Come on then, up ye go."

Carefully slipping an arm around the earl's bruised ribs, and with the sergeant's help, the cabbie lifted Justin to his feet and helped him walk unsteadily toward the cab. When they had reached it, the lad quickly opened the leather-covered door and jumped up past the seven-and-a-half-foot wheel into the small passenger compartment, turning back immediately to help pull the earl up the eighteen-inch distance from the street to the first step, and then up the next rise into his arms. With sure, gentle hands, he settled Justin into the padded leather seat and covered him with his own warm blanket. At last, after lighting the oil in both lamps fastened on either side of the carriage hood, the cabbie jumped down and scampered up to his own seat high and to the rear of where Justin sat.

The sergeant held up a delaying hand. Turning toward the earl, he said, "I shall need to question you and the lad further as soon as you have recovered sufficiently, my lord. Shall you be able to receive me in your home tomorrow afternoon?"

Justin shook his head slightly. "I have a previous engagement in the afternoon, sergeant, so I shall come to you."

Suddenly the small communicating door in the roof snapped open. "Mebbe ye ain't noticed, milord," the cabbie scolded, "but it awready be tomorrow!"

"Then we shall have to hurry, shall we not?" Justin replied with a tired grin. "It has been the deuce of an evening. I really do think I could use a bit of a rest."

* * *

"It be losin' all tha' blood wot makes ye so cold," the cabbie informed the earl through the communicating door in the hansom's roof. The boy glanced down at Justin worriedly. The earl was shaking uncontrollably now as he huddled in the corner of the seat; so badly, in fact that the cabbie had only a few moments ago stopped the carriage and climbed down to give the earl his own coat to wrap about his feet. "Makes ye thirsty, too," he said anxiously, afraid that the earl had sunk beyond hearing.

"How do you know such things?" Justin asked softly around his chattering teeth.

The cabbie started slightly, and then released a gust of pure relief. The earl had not fainted, thank God. He would keep him talking, he decided as he turned his cab from Bloomsbury Way into Oxford Street. He was sure it was important to keep him awake.

"Oi knows lots o' things," he said, trying to mask his worry.

"So it seems," the earl agreed, lifting his gaze to the communicating door, studying the cabbie with relentless intensity.

The cabbie smiled, unaware of the soft, touchable, flawless beauty the moonlight was imparting to his delicately formed features. He watched as the earl's fingers twitched against his leg, absorbing the sight. He wondered at the earl's scrutiny, only just kept himself from squirming beneath it, his eyes beneath his dark lashes glinting a compelling fusion of moonlit copper and fire.

"Oi knows fer instance that 'twould've been better to take ye across the street to yer mistress's 'ouse than to drive ye all the bloody way back to Mayfair," he said softly.

Justin flinched as if he had just taken an upper cut

straight into his self-concept. He swallowed thickly.
"You're a sharp lad, aren't you?" he said with some chagrin,
oddly disconcerted that the lad should know how he had
spent the evening. "I shall have to keep that in mind." Carefully, he reached up to tuck the blanket more closely around
his shoulders.

"Aw, ain't no need to keep yer mummers dubbed 'round
me, milord," the lad said in his unusual voice. "Oi been
drivin' a cab fer eight years now, takin' 'my lords' back an'
forth to their bawds. Ain't nothin' much Oi ain't seed."

"Eight years?" Justin exclaimed softly, again spearing
the cabbie with his sharp gaze. "Just how old are you, lad?"

"Me?" the boy replied, suddenly wary. "Oi be three an'
twenty."

Justin's chin lifted imperceptibly beneath narrowed eyes.
How could a man have three-and-twenty years in his dish
and not yet shave? "You don't look much past sixteen."

"So? Ye doesn't look much past thirty," the lad noted
cheekily.

Again the sudden warmth flared. Justin almost choked
with it, afraid to acknowledge that it had happened again.
He shook his head. "Four years past thirty, scamp," he finally, shakily responded, "and at the moment, I am feeling
every one of them."

The cabbie sobered, concern mirrored in a glance of tender intensity. "It ain't too late to turn back, milord."

Justin caught the glance and held it, helpless to keep
from doing so, incredulous as his whole being tightened
in response to the lad's constraining gaze. "No," he stated
more sharply than he had intended. Quickly he averted his
eyes. "I would prefer leaving Clarisse out of this. She
would not welcome having me underfoot, I think. She has
always belonged to Oliver, much more so than to me."

The cabbie's heart thumped irregularly. Clarisse. He had

not denied that she was his mistress. And her name was Clarisse. A fisting ache squeezed his heart. Suddenly he wanted to shout at the earl to be silent, to tell him nothing more of her. Yet, even as he wished for it, he pushed to keep him talking, hungry for anything he could learn about Stonegate.

Swallowing hard, he questioned, "Oliver?"

"My brother," Justin replied, staring into the nebulous shapes of the night.

The cabbie felt a tingling numbness pervade his hands and feet. A brother! He had never known of a brother. But, of course, Stonegate knew nothing of Simon, either. Again he forced a deep, relaxing breath.

"Oliver was Clarisse's protector before his death," the earl elaborated, fighting to understand his reactions to the lad. "It fell to me to tell her what had happened to him. I have never seen a woman become so distraught. It was obvious that my brother had come to mean a great deal to her. For his sake, I did what I could to help her . . . to offer her comfort and security over the next several months, and . . . she was grateful. She understood that I, too, acutely felt my brother's loss. Soon we began to comfort one another . . ."

"Oi be roight sorry, milord," the cabbie inserted quickly, his husky voice strangely dismayed, "about yer brovver, an' all."

Justin trembled. "My God," he whispered as the deep, inner ice suddenly coalesced, gripping him just as solidly as it had before. "I am so cold." The words were spoken as if by a stranger.

The copper eyes above him started with alarm. " 'Old on, milord. We be turnin' back," the cabbie vowed.

"No, Mel . . . no," Justin said when he felt the carriage slow. "It is not because of my wounds, lad."

The cabbie's brow furrowed with concern. "Why, then, milord?"

Noting the boy's worry, Justin felt moved to somehow explain. "It is something inside me, Mel . . . because it was my fault," he said on a ragged breath. "Deuce take it, why am I telling you these things?"

The cabbie sighed with compassion, knowing instinctively that Stonegate had never spoken of his brother's death before; sensing also the earl's desperate need to do so. With great gentleness, he urged him to continue.

"What were yer fault, milord?" he asked in that husky, mesmerizing voice.

Justin turned away, a wave of guilt tangling all that was sane and orderly within him. "My brother's death," he rasped. Then, hesitantly, he glanced up through the communicating door. He was met with acceptance, reassuring warmth flowing from the cabbie's copper-colored eyes. The tightness inside him eased.

" 'Ow did it 'appen?" The voice above him was low and sweet.

Justin swept a steadying hand across his face, closing eyes troubled by his sudden loss of control and the subsequent shameful breach of propriety. "It was two years ago," he began. "Oliver and I and two friends went to the South Bank to attend the dog fights at the Westminster Pits. It was Oliver's idea. I had no liking for such entertainments, but nothing was beyond the bounds for Oliver. He had always loved to stretch the limits of propriety." The earl began to breathe more easily. Calming, he relaxed his jaw, sensing his emotional equilibrium begin to level.

"I agreed to accompany them, as I always did, so that I could be a steadying influence if it should be needed." A corner of Justin's mouth twitched. "I remember how full of life Oliver was that night. He had worn his new bright green embroidered waistcoat for the occasion. He was preening like a peacock under his bows' admiration."

"Go on, then," the cabbie urged.

"The three of them were in high spirits by the time we had finished our dinner at the Carlton Club and were ready to leave. Against my advice, they had consumed far too much port and were flying rather high."

"No' you?" the cabbie questioned.

"No," Justin responded flatly, pleased to discover that he could hang on to a large measure of his concentration if he just avoided looking at the deuced boy. "I have never enjoyed quantities of strong drink. I do not enjoy the foolish behavior that results from overindulgence, nor do I admire impropriety."

The cabbie nodded sagely. "So you was cockin' a snoot whilst yer brovver shot the cat," he easily summarized.

Another surge of warmth rivered through the earl. A slight smile tugged at the corners of his mouth. Again his palm scrubbed his face. He could not deny it. In all his restrained, dignified existence, no one had ever before affected him so profoundly. The cabbie's brash freshness was fast becoming addictive.

"You could say that," Justin agreed when at last he could speak.

"So wot 'appened then, milord?" the cabbie asked.

"When the fights were over . . . it was early morning by that time . . . Oliver and the others wanted to go back to the Cock in the Haymarket to gamble and—" Suddenly, Justin interrupted himself to cast a quick glance through the roof hole.

". . . 'Oist some petticoats?" the cabbie suggested with an innocent grin.

Justin gritted his teeth.

"Don't say much fer Clarisse, do it?" the younger man smirked.

Justin scowled and shifted his position painfully. "They were pretty well under the hatches by that time," he offered by way of an excuse, and in defense of Clarisse.

Again the cabbie nodded. "Oi takes it, bein' a paragon, an all," and here the cabbie glanced pointedly at the earl, "that you refused to go along wiv their plans."

The earl tried to keep his gaze averted, but failed. He met the cabbie's glance with a raised eyebrow and tightened lips. "Yes," he admitted starchily, using pique to negate the strange emotions that consistently rivered through him when he looked directly at the lad, "and, as you have probably already guessed, all I received for my concern for their reputations was the accusation that I was a pompous prig."

The cabbie met the earl's unspoken censure with a broad, teasing grin. The earl groaned, passing his hand across his eyes again.

"Ah. So ye took yer toys an' went 'ome."

A short huff of air snuck past Justin's defenses. He swallowed quickly, thinking that the sound might have been a snort of laughter had he not known himself better.

"I think I would have attempted to make my motives seem a bit more noble, but, yes, that is essentially what happened. Are you always so blunt?"

The cabbie pursed his lips in thoughtful consideration. "Oi doesn't think o' meself as blunt, milord," he replied, "just honest. A bloke needs to see 'isself honestly, doesn't ye think? Else-wise, 'e ends up 'urt when someone makes 'im see the truth about 'isself, an' life's too short to spend it 'urt the 'ole bleedin' toime."

Justin drew in a slow breath, uncomfortable with the young man's perceptive intelligence. To his chagrin, he felt as if the skin over his hidden self had just been flayed. Yet as the hansom turned south into North Audley Street, he sighed reluctantly. The deuced cabbie was right. He was a pompous prig, and Oliver's accusation that night *had* hurt terribly. But knowing it did not change the fact that it was the way he had to be. He was still the Earl of Stonegate, and he still had an obligation to protect his family. And nothing changed the fact that Oliver had died because he had, in a moment of anger, shirked that responsibility.

"Wot 'appened after ye left yer brovver?" the cabbie asked, reminding the earl that he had not yet finished the telling.

Justin flexed his wound, wincing slightly. And then he smiled. Pain was good. It helped him know of a certainty that he was still a separate entity from the lad and had not yet been completely absorbed under the deuced boy's skin.

"Apparently, after I left him, Oliver received a message from the manager of the Pits informing him that his purse had been found there and requesting that he send someone trustworthy to get it. The note explained that the manager felt it best not to send the purse along with the messenger on the chance that the boy might prove to be dishonest and keep its contents for himself."

"It be loikely," commented the cabbie with a nod of agreement.

"Oliver thought so, too," the earl said. "He decided to go back for the purse himself, and, since his two friends had already obtained companionship for the evening, he went alone."

"Wot 'appened?" the cabbie asked, growing more intent in his listening.

"The wheel fell off Oliver's rented carriage while he was crossing Westminster Bridge. According to the police who investigated the accident, he must have gotten down from the carriage, probably to go for help, but was undoubtedly too cup-shot to navigate properly. They surmise that he fell over the railing and drowned."

"Cor," said the cabbie with soft sadness.

"There was very little left to recover by the time the body was found," Justin stated with a heavy flatness. "I was only able to identify him because he was still wearing that damned green waistcoat."

The earl glanced up then, helpless to prevent himself from doing so. Through the communicating door, he saw the lad's huge, pale eyes glinting with unshed tears. He stared, astounded; he could do nothing more. Then, disconcerted, he glanced away, sensing yet again a thickening in the intangible warp and weft of the bond that continued to weave between them.

"Well, Oi sees why ye says it were yer fault," the cabbie said a short time later, sniffing quietly. " 'Ow old were yer brovver when 'e died?"

Justin glanced up again in surprise. "Six-and-twenty," he quietly replied.

"Well, there ye 'ave it," the cabbie said with a brisk nod. " 'E weren't no moren'a babe, were 'e? No wonder ye 'ad to follow him everywhere, 'oldin' his 'and, an' all."

"I beg your pardon?" Justin said, tensing.

"Why, it be plain as a boil on yer bum, milord," the cabbie continued, ignoring the earl's building ire. " 'E were too young to be out an' about on his own. Why, a lad o' six-an'-twenty don't 'ave the brains to keep 'isself outta trouble. An' ye left a child loike that to spend a evenin' alone wiv his friends? Ye ought be ashamed, milord."

Justin bristled as he finally realized what the cabbie was doing. His brows lowered; his heated gaze intensified. "Why, you little scamp!" he gritted out between his clenched teeth. "Do you think to mock me?"

The cabbie's answering smile suddenly became tender.

"Aye, milord," he responded softly, "if it'll make ye see sense."

A long silence settled over them as the hansom passed through Grosvenor Square into South Audley Street. No word was uttered, not once did the earl's gaze leave the cabbie's face.

"I am Stonegate," Justin said finally. "It is my duty to protect my family."

"Cor," the cabbie breathed in astonishment. "Does ye run about 'oldin' *everybody's* 'and, then? When does ye 'ave time to go to the bleedin' privy?"

In the face of the cabbie's thoroughly endearing cheek, there was no help for it. A look of astonished exasperation claimed Justin's features, then faded from his face to be replaced by a wash of confusion and the inner warmth of more simple amusement than he could ever remember in the whole of his sober existence. The sound began soon after, rumbling around deep inside his chest before he could think to arrest it. And then it happened. Clutching at his wound, the Earl of Stonegate abandoned the last of his resistance. With not even a shred of the requisite decorum, he threw his head back against the squabs, and, quite improperly, filled the stillness of the night with shouts of cleansing, healing laughter.

# *Three*

"Devil a bit!" Justin uttered around the few remaining chuckles that still bounced across his abdomen. "Mel, you should be bottled and sold in every apothecary."

"Well, Oi be pleased ye think so, Oi'm sure," the cabbie replied with a broad grin.

"I do indeed," Justin asserted, reaching up to wipe the remnants of tears from the outer corners of his eyes with the edge of his cape. "Deuce take it, I feel almost . . . I had not realized . . . Do you know, lad, until tonight I had not laughed since Oliver's death."

"Not much more afore that neither, Oi'll wager," the cabbie responded softly.

"No," Justin admitted. "My father rather frowned on frivolity. Especially in his heir."

"Mmm," the cabbie returned thoughtfully. "Well, fair's fair, Oi s'pose. If one brovver gets to sew enough scapegrace oats fer the two of 'em without no worry, it be only roight that the other brovver should 'ave to carry around double his guilt."

Justin's eyebrow soared. "More mockery, scamp?"

The cabbie chuckled softly. "Aye. But only so's ye can see the truth, milord. Yer brovver's death weren't yer fault, ye know. Oi thinks mebbe it be time someone told ye so."

The earl's eyes glistened as he nodded. "You must be

right, Mel. Just hearing the words makes me feel as if I have dropped fifty stone."

"Well, there ye 'ave it, then," the lad said cheerfully. "Things be roight an' toight again. Now ye'll have a new bounce in yer bum to go wiv that 'andsome laugh."

Justin chuckled again before shaking his head wonderingly. "Damme, Mel, it has been so long since I have felt anything but a cold hollowness inside, I am almost lightheaded with it. I feel as if anything might be possible. Do you know, I am almost persuaded that I might even be able to develop a genuine affection for the woman I intend to marry."

The cabbie's lips parted against a quickly fading smile. The very air seemed to thicken and still. "So ye wants to get leg-shackled, eh?" he asked with an alert breathlessness. "Wot about Clarisse?"

Justin shot the impertinent young man a censorious glance. "That, scamp, is none of your affair. However, since I am deeply in your debt, I shall tell you that just tonight I began preparing Clarisse for the time when I shall give her her *congé*. It is my intention to offer for Lady Eunice Parkes after I have paid proper court to her, and I cannot think it seemly to keep a mistress at the same time."

Stonegate was to be married. The cabbie grew weak-kneed.

"But ye sounds loike ye doesn't care fer this laidy," the lad commented with a frown.

The earl chuckled softly, absorbed in the uniqueness of the sound. "A man in my position does not marry for love, Mel," he explained. "He marries to join himself to a family of equal or greater status and wealth so as to increase his own family's stature in Society."

"Cor," the cabbie muttered disgustedly, "Oi'd wish ye

'appy, milord, except it seems Oi'd do better wishin' ye 'aughty."

Again Justin burst into healing, cleansing laughter. "Thank you," he replied with a chiding grin, "I think. However, save your good wishes for now. I have not yet made my declaration. Perhaps the lady will not have me."

"Aye, she will," Mel murmured.

"That is my fondest hope, of course," Justin commented, ignorant of the hint of despair in the cabbie's unusual eyes. "She will be the perfect wife for me, Mel . . . gentle, biddable, above reproach. She will be a credit to the Mayhew name."

With unconscious skill, the cabbie turned right from South Audley into South Street, heading west toward the dark, shadowed verdancy of Hyde Park only a few blocks ahead. Dawn was just beginning to soften the evening's stark blackness to a colorless wash of gray, but the lad was oblivious to the somber, muted beauty of the scene. Cherished fantasies were crashing down around his head.

"She sounds a roight tappin' laidy," he finally said as the hansom straightened and the earl's town house came into view.

"I do not yet know her well, but I believe her to be."

Mel breathed deeply, and then nodded, letting go of the last of his dreams. "That's awright then," he said after a soft sigh, and a moment later he reined in his hack before the earl's softly lit town house.

As soon as the cab had come to a stop, Mel opened the carriage door for the earl by working the levers and chains near his seat, and then cautiously helped him climb down onto the damp cobblestones. Carefully supporting him by his uninjured arm, he escorted him through the wrought-iron gate.

"Shall you be driving again later on today?" Justin asked

when they had covered the short distance to the columned portico and stood before the earl's gleaming mahogany door. He was reluctant to bid the lad good night. The thought of their imminent separation nagged at him. The tether still existed, and it tightened.

"Aye," the cabbie replied with a nod. "I be always on the streets, milord."

Justin released the breath he had been holding. "Good," he said, relaxing a series of tensed muscles. "As long as we both have to make more detailed explanations of the night's events to Scotland Yard, we may as well do so together. I shall expect you to take me up here again in the early afternoon."

The cabbie's rather delicate jaw dropped slightly. Releasing Justin's arm to plant his fists firmly upon his hips, he turned to face the earl, scowling fiercely. "Ye'll not be goin' nowhere but yer bed, me fine lord. Not wiv them cuts, an' all."

"I shall," Justin countered, sagging against the doorjamb with a tired, but stubborn grin, "and you shall carry me. As a matter of fact, I shall hire you for the entire day. No, better still, for the entire week."

"For the week?" the cabbie parroted, intrigued.

"Exactly so," Justin replied with satisfaction, his eyes gleaming brightly at this perfect method of keeping Mel near him. As much as the connection disconcerted him, the growing bond between the two of them was pulling at him like a puckered scar. "It is an excellent plan. Why did I not think of it before? I do not keep a carriage in Town, you see," he went on to explain. "I prefer to rest my bloods at my country estate during the Season. When I need a carriage larger than a hansom for transportation, I rent one from one of the jobbers. But there is no reason why I cannot hire you for a longer period, too, is there?"

"Well, no . . ." the cabbie said hesitantly, "Oi doesn't s'pose so, milord."

"Excellent," Justin said hurriedly to cut off the cabbie's further argument. "I shall pay you ten pounds for the week. You shall begin this afternoon . . . shall we say around two o'clock? That should give us time to finish at the Yard before I must pay a call on Miss Parkes."

Ten pounds! The cabbie swallowed hard to stifle a gasp. And, as the length of a swallow was all the time Justin needed to slip into the house, by the time Mel looked up again to resume his argument that the earl should remain in bed for the rest of the day, he found that he was standing alone.

"Aw, dish me!" the disgruntled lad muttered as he walked to the hansom, climbed back up on the seat, and turned his hack toward the Rookery.

And then he brightened. He would have one week, he thought as his heart began to kick against his breast. One week before all his solitary yearnings had to be forever banished from his thoughts. One week with Stonegate.

By the time the cabbie had made his way back to the stable on Gray's Inn Road, where he boarded his hack and hansom when he was not plying his trade, and had paid the washer three shillings to clean his cab and another three bob to the proprietor to turn his tired horse up "gassy" before he took him out again, the sun had settled the first and faintest of its rays over the Rookery in a swirling, pale ochre ether that peeked timidly into the shadows of early morning, giving to nearby Saffron Hill a prospect that echoed its name.

The cabbie peered about himself cautiously as he rounded the corner gin shop and entered Portpool Lane.

The area was known as Thieves' Kitchen for good reason. There, amid the malignant, urban forest of towering tenements, unending ranks of children were continually being trained as cracksmen and pickpockets, awaiting their chance to be disgorged into the city. Anyone who happened by was fair game.

A soft moan brought the cabbie up short just past the gin shop's entrance. Sitting on the curb, huddled against the blackened bricks of the building, a woman slowly sagged to the side and emptied the contents of her stomach onto the cobblestones, barely aware of how close she had come to defiling her sleeping child.

The cabbie winced visibly. "Aw, Susan," he whispered, dropping to his knees beside her. "Mind the babe. Aw, lass, ye mun mind yer babe." With gentle hands the cabbie reached beyond the gin-sotted woman and took the infant into his arms. Cradling the sleeping child against his breast, he gave the woman a firm shake. "Come on, now, Susan, wake up. Come on. Time to go 'ome."

The woman moaned again and peered up at the cabbie with half-lidded eyes. "Mel," she murmured on a soft puff of fetid air. "So 'tis you. Wot ye want wiv me?"

"Oi wants ye to go 'ome, Susan," the cabbie replied gently. "Come on, now. Up ye go."

With care, the lad tugged on the woman's arm, shouldering her weight until she could rise and balance upon her own feet. She leaned heavily upon the cabbie's chest, swinging her gaze to his, her head lolling against his shoulder.

"Yer a good lad, ain't ye, Mel," she breathed. "Always sees to me an' the babe, doesn't ye? Well, Oi kin pay ye fer yer trouble, lad. Owd Susan, she knows wot a young lad loike you be wantin'. 'Ere now, no one be 'round now. Just lift me skirts—"

"No, Susan," the cabbie interrupted quickly, a red stain creeping up the length of his neck. "Oi wants ye to go 'ome, that's all. Ye mun take care of the babe."

The woman peered questioningly at the cabbie and then shrugged. "Suit yerself," she said, patting his shoulder haphazardly. "Bu' when ye wants it, lad, see that ye comes to me." Pushing herself away from the cabbie with a strength that made him stagger, she took her child into her arms and stumbled away unsteadily into the noisome depths of the alley.

The cabbie hurried the last few blocks to his own tenement. He was late, and Simon was no doubt already waiting to ring a peal over him. Pausing only long enough as he thundered up the stairs of the eight-story building to call a greeting to Bart Pollard and his twin sister and brother, Evie and Jack, costermongers who were leaving to buy their day's wares at Covent Garden, he quickly wound his way to the top story and entered the apartment shared by the Hicks and the Pollards, two families who let the garret above their two tiny rooms to him and to Simon.

"Ho!" he called when he burst breathlessly through the door. "Oi be back! An' how's me Bess this mornin'?"

A slight, fortyish woman, bending over the meager heat of a small brazier, looked up at the cabbie's entrance and then glanced toward a large, mounded form lying motionless on a pallet in the corner. "Still asleep, no thanks to you," she scolded. Then, pushing a graying string of hair back into the loosely wound knot at the nape of her neck, she turned toward the lad slightly and grinned at him. The small, close room stank of urine, bacon, and yesterday's onions.

"An' stubble that Cockney flap-jaw," she added gruffly. "In this 'ouse, ye'll talk loike ye was born to."

The cabbie laughed brightly and bent to give the woman

a loud kiss on her weathered cheek. "Veddy well, madam," he said, bowing low enough for his knuckles to scrape against the rough planks of the floor, "your wish is, as always, my command. I shall henceforth become the perfect pattern card of proper speaking." Seizing an empty jar from a nearby shelf, the cabbie quickly positioned the bottom against his eye and, elevating his nose, peered at the woman haughtily.

"Go on wiv ye," the woman giggled, retrieving her precious jar. "Oi ain't got time fer yer foolishness. Me man George be gone to the dust yard awready. Oi should there workin' meself, but some'un had to cook fer Con an' Gran."

"Is Gran worse, Maudie?" the cabbie asked, sobering instantly.

"Aye. It be my thought she don't 'ave much time," the woman said, shaking her head as she stirred a small pot of gruel.

"I thought a poultice might help," the cabbie responded. "I intend to go to the library at my first opportunity to see what English plants might serve."

"That be good o' ye, dearie," Maudie replied.

"I just wish I could discover something that would make her well. Here now," the cabbie said, taking the spoon from Maudie's heavily jointed fingers, "I can finish that. Do go on and join George, Maudie. I saw Bart and the twins on the stairs as I came home, but has everyone else broken their fast?"

"Aye, all bu' those two," the woman answered, giving up her possession of the spoon. With a smile of thanks, she shuffled over to a peg near the door and tugged a plain, black straw bonnet onto her lank hair. "An' Maeve did get Con settled on his platform afore she left fer her milk route, so ye doesn't 'ave to fret about that."

"And the children?" the cabbie inquired, lifting the spoon to her lips to taste the barley potage gingerly.

"Well, now," Maudie summarized, placing a finger aside her cheek, "Annie be awready at Covent Garden buyin' her oranges, and young Fred be out sellin' Gran's matches today. Then, o' course, there be wee Ben an' Tom . . ." she chuckled softly as she fitted a black shawl around her bent shoulders, "they is most loikely 'avin' the time o' their little lives gettin' dirty."

The cabbie frowned slightly. "I cannot like that those babes are mudlarks, Maudie. It is far too dangerous. All sorts of things have been washed down the Thames. One day they will step on something sharp when they are scrounging in the mud flats, and if that happens . . . Oh, Maudie, children lose limbs when their wounds turn putrid. And the boys are but six and four."

Maudie's gaze hardened imperceptibly. "Aye, but that ain't up to us, now is it? It be up to the lads' parents, Con an' Maeve. Besides, to my way o' thinkin', the banks o' the river ain't no worse than the Rookery streets. They be as safe as any other babes their ages 'round 'ere. Safer, Oi be thinkin'. At least they ain't got a Pa an' Ma who be drownin' in blue ruin."

The cabbie dropped his gaze. "I know, Maudie. I apologize."

Maudie grinned, then, revealing several gaping holes between her stained teeth. "Shut yer gob, now," she scolded softly as she opened the door and stepped into the hall. "Ye just got to remember, dearie, we all got to live our lives as they come to us, whether it be in Portpool Lane or Bond Street. It don't do no one no good to forget it," she called as she started down the hall. "We all got our appointed place."

The cabbie stilled, staring at the empty doorway for several heartbeats. The thought would not leave him: except for me, Maudie. Except for me.

"Mel?"

At the sound of the soft, sleep-sated voice, the cabbie turned instantly, a warm smile displacing the anxiousness etched between his brows. In moments he had crossed the room and knelt beside one of several pallets that were scattered about the room.

"Good morning, Bess," he said gently. "How did you pass the night?"

"Better," the young, round-faced woman replied. "Oi 'ad some crampin', but Bart rubbed me back an' eased it some."

"Good for him," the cabbie nodded. "Only a month or so, now, Bess, and then you shall swear that all this trouble will have been worth it."

Bess's gaze dropped. The cabbie knew that she was thinking of all the other births that had gone before this one. Bending forward, he helped her awkwardly lever herself into a sitting position around her heavily pregnant abdomen, then moved away as she rose from the rumpled pallet to seek the chamber pot.

"That bacon smells good," she called from behind a small screen. "Oi be roight gutfoundered, Oi am."

"Oh, no you don't," the cabbie replied with a bright smile. "Until this babe is born, you shall break your fast as I have instructed you . . . with gruel, fruit, and vegetables."

Behind him, the woman laughed, then rose to wash in a nearby basin of water. After a few more steps, she seated herself upon a bench tucked beneath a roughly hewn table. "Ye know, Mel, when ye first told me about them things wot ye'd read in the birthin' books," she told him, nodding her thanks when the cabbie set a plate of food before her, "Oi thought ye was dicked in the nob."

The cabbie laughed softly. "I know," he replied.

"But Oi does feel better this time," she admitted with a tinge of wonder in her voice. "More spry-loike. Oi be that grateful fer wot ye done, Mel, an' fer yer promise to be wiv me when me time comes."

The cabbie smiled. "You couldn't keep me away, Bess. I have read every birthing book in the lending library, and already prepared everything I shall need. You and Bart had better start choosing names, my girl. What will Father Laughlin think when you have nothing to tell him at the christening?"

As Bess chuckled gently, the cabbie filled two more bowls with gruel and rashers of bacon. Then, casting one last teasing grin toward Bess's tear-softened eyes, he took the bowls through the connecting door into the Hicks's room, setting one bowl down on the low bench used as a table by Con when he was seated on his rolling platform, and the other on the floor beside the pallet holding the wizened form of Gran.

"Good morning," the cabbie said brightly.

"The same, ye rummy jehu," muttered Con, scowling as he used his knotted knuckles to push himself and his platform over to the bench.

"Mind yer mouth, Conrad 'Icks," Gran wheezed from her corner.

"Never mind, Gran," the cabbie said gently. "Your foul-tempered son's setdowns have not turned me into a watering pot for years. What is hurting you this morning, Con?" he called, reaching down to touch the parchment skin of Gran's forehead. A spate of coughing rattled against his arms as he helped her to sit up, and his own brow wrinkled with concern.

" 'Oo says anything is?" the man groused, biting off a bit of bacon and chewing it as if it personified his pain.

"No one has to," Mel responded cheerfully. "You are grumbling like the loser in a bare-knuckle mill with Black Richmond."

"Aw, stubble it, ye poxy—"

"Con . . ." warned Gran, arresting her son's next epithet with parental efficiency.

The cabbie's grin broadened. With a slow wink, he began lifting spoonfuls of the nourishing gruel to the woman's thin lips. "You may as well tell me, Con," he cajoled. "I shall keep after you until you do, you know."

Con shot the cabbie an irritated glare. "It be me back," he muttered. "An' me good-fer-nothin' legs."

"Do they ache?" the cabbie asked.

"Aye. Loike bloody 'ell."

The cabbie's eyes warmed with concern. "Have Bess brew you some willow bark tea as soon as she is able, Con," he ordered. "She has some packets in her room. It should help until Maeve comes home. I shall send down some comfrey oil with Simon, too, when he goes out to sweep streets. Have Maeve massage it into your soreness. It should give you some relief."

Con's gaze lifted to hers, abashed. "Mel . . . Oi thanks ye. An' about them other things wot Oi said—"

"Cut line, do, Con," the cabbie laughed heartily. "I shall hardly know what to do if you cry peace. Why, I should probably go all vaporish if you are not constantly ripping up at me."

A half-smile softened the deep grooves of Con's be-whiskered mouth before he muscled it into a tight line accompanied by a fierce scowl. "Awright then, ye mutton-brained, bottleheaded—"

The cabbie laughed merrily. "Finish feeding your

mother, you rag-mannered, scapegrace smoke-merchant. I still have to see to Simon." Dodging Con's outstretched arm as he swept past his platform, the cabbie deftly scampered to the ladder leaning against the frame of the attic entrance and swiftly climbed it, turning back just once to stick his tongue out at a grinning Con before disappearing through the trapdoor at the top.

The young man who turned away from the small brazier and, smiling widely, crossed the tiny garret to take the cabbie's whip, coat, and hat, was almost his perfect copy. Coal black curls framed a face that was only just beginning to hint at the firm jaw, straight narrow brows, and vibrant hazel eyes of the adult he would one day be. He was taller than the cabbie, and lean. And his gaze, when he looked at the tired face before him, warmed with concern and love.

"You are late, Mel," he said in gentle reprimand. Hanging the cabbie's things on a nearby peg, he crossed to a chipped earthen pitcher and poured water into its matching basin for him.

"It was an eventful night," the cabbie replied with a weary half-smile. Rolling up his sleeves to the elbow, he used a bit of their precious tallow soap to carefully scrub away the day's grime.

"The explanation, if you please," the young boy ordered with a grin, returning to the brazier.

Drying his face and hands, the cabbie crossed to a small, rude table bracketed by two chairs and sat down in the nearest of them. "I came to the rescue of a nonpareil who was being attacked by two men outside his *pied-à-terre.*"

"The deuce!" the young boy exclaimed, whirling eagerly around to face the cabbie.

"Your language, please, Simon," the cabbie chided

tiredly. "And, as long as you are facing this way, put the white cloth on the table before we eat. And the potted plant."

"Devil a bit, Mel!" the boy grumbled. "You act as if we live in Buckingham Palace. What difference does it make?"

The cabbie lifted his gaze and looked at Simon steadily. "A great deal, Simon," he stated firmly. "Good manners will need to be so ingrained within you that you will practice them without their even crossing your mind if you are to be successful when you begin to go about in Society."

Simon sighed deeply and then nodded. "I am sorry, Mel. I know you are right. And considering everything you have given up for me, the least I can do is set a proper table." Giving the cabbie an attractive, masculine grin, the boy reached into a small metal cup on the shelf above the brazier and brought down a handful of worn silverware. "Were you hurt during your little foray?" he finally asked, spreading the cloth and beginning to position the plant and silver upon it.

"No," the cabbie answered, "and it was hardly a 'little foray,' Simon. The footpads were using knives against the man."

"What about the lord?" Simon asked, laying bowls and fruit plates in their proper places, his intense interest again piqued.

"He was stabbed three times . . . once quite deeply."

"The deuce!"

The cabbie's gaze dropped to fidgeting hands. "Simon . . ." he said hesitantly.

One glance at Mel's anguished face told the boy quite quickly that he was not about to be taken to task for his language again. "Tell me, Mel," he urged, pausing in his ladling of gruel into their bowls. "What is it?"

"The lord . . ." the cabbie whispered, bleak eyes seeking his. "He was Stonegate."

Slowly, Simon sank into the other chair. "Bloody hell," he breathed.

The cabbie broke into a soft chuckle. "Simon, please!"

"Did you tell him?" the boy asked, ignoring the cabbie's reprimand.

"No, of course not! Besides, what is there to tell?"

"A great deal, if you ask me," Simon exclaimed.

Reaching over, the cabbie took the pan of gruel and finished filling their bowls. "Simon, I made my decision years ago. I can never go back. What I was in the past no longer exists for me. But it will again for you, and that is what we are working toward."

"But it isn't fair!" Simon cried, cutting viciously into an orange.

"That's as may be, Simon," the cabbie said softly. "But you did not force me in my choice. The decision was mine."

"What did he look like?" Simon asked, his mind flitting to another subject with youthful mobility.

The cabbie smiled gently, staring into his gruel. "He was handsome beyond belief."

"Oh, Mel . . ."

"And soon to be married."

Pained silence eclipsed any further curiosity.

"Well," the cabbie said sometime later as they finished the last of their breakfast with swallows of small beer. "Let us see how you have done with your lessons, shall we? Clear the table and I shall begin with your geometry."

The cabbie was soon immersed in a parade of proofs and theorems. Simon used the time to wash their dishes and lay a blanket over a rope that had been strung between opposite walls. When that had been accomplished, a partition had been created which gave privacy to the side of the room containing their sleeping pallets. As soon as he had finished, he returned to his place at the table.

"Oh, Simon, this is very good," the cabbie proclaimed, tapping the essay he had been reading. "You have shown real insight into why Chartism failed. I especially appreciated your understanding of the underlining apathy that prevailed among workingmen at the time. Now for tomorrow, I want you to solve the geometry problems on the next five pages, study another section of Debrett, and translate this essay into Latin and Greek."

"Both?" cried Simon as his broad shoulders collapsed.

"Both," the cabbie grinned. "But don't look so Friday-faced, little brother. At least I am not asking you do it in French as well."

Simon shook his head around a rueful grin. "Go to bed, Mel. Now. Please. Before I forget how much I am supposed to appreciate all you are doing for me."

The cabbie laughed delightedly. "I rather think I shall." Turning toward the blanket partition, he added, "Oh, and Simon . . . when you go down, will you take that vial of comfrey oil to Con for me?"

"Yes, of course," he replied, moving about the tiny room to gather coat, hat, broom, and vial. Sharpening his gaze as he cast one last glance toward the cabbie, he said, "Get a good rest, Mel. You look so tired this morning."

The cabbie smiled warmly. "I will. Good night, Simon."

The boy made as pretty a leg as was ever seen in the most lofty of the *ton's* drawing rooms and answered, "Good night to you, Melanie."

# Four

It was the socially ordained hour for the *ton* to do its visiting. Stonegate, however, was not in the mood. His shoulder hurt like the very devil and he ached all over. He was certain he was coming down with the fever. Bloody nuisance, this courting. Bloody disconcerting, too, to find out one has been the target of an attempted murder. He shivered slightly. Bloody hell.

"Mel!" the earl called impatiently, thumping on the hood of the hansom with the silver head of his cane. Instantly the communicating door slid open.

"Aye, milord?" the cabbie questioned softly.

"Those bastards wanted me dead," he repeated for the third time since they had boarded the hansom outside Scotland Yard and wedged their way into the thick traffic along Whitehall. "What reason could they have had?"

"Moight nivver know, milord," the cabbie said, shaking his head, "since they be dead, too, an' all."

"Deuce take it," cursed Justin as he grimaced and shivered again. "Cyanide. Administered to them right in their cell. Even I could detect the almond odor about them. But why? Why would they attack me, and why are *they* now dead?"

"The stews be a hard place, milord," the cabbie said

softly, flatly. "Ye fails in yer hugger-mugger, ye comes a cropper."

Stonegate's gaze slewed toward the cabbie, noting the grim resignation residing in the lad's coppery eyes. His hands fisted against the sudden realization of what the boy must have to contend with each and every day of his life. The thought of the cabbie, this lad who was so inexplicably necessary to him, battling for his existence in the midden that was the Rookery, clenched at his insides.

"You are implying that someone hired those men to attack me," Stonegate said finally, drawing his coat lapels closer together in spite of the warm afternoon sun.

"Aye," Mel nodded, monitoring the earl's unconscious movements closely, "that be me thinkin'. There ain't no other explanation fer why them two footpads was killed. A bloke can't tell the coppers nothin' if 'e be dead. Nor can a 'my lord' be 'oistin' his pinky at some poxy tea party if his spoon be stuck in the wall. Just look at yerself. Ye looks loike 'alf-boiled puddin'. Oi be thinkin' that Oi should be drivin' ye 'ome to yer bed, not to yer laidy."

Justin gave the cabbie a chiding half-smile and then groaned slightly as he adjusted the position of his wounded shoulder. "Believe me, Mel, I should like nothing better, but I must keep this engagement. Lord Palmerton has no doubt already heard of last night's scandal broth, and, as a suitor for Miss Parkes's hand, it is only proper that I present myself to him to explain."

"But ye be 'urt, milord," the cabbie insisted. "Wouldn't that Lord Palmerton understand if ye was to beg off fer one day?"

"Probably. But I am not in so much discomfort that I cannot do what is proper, Mel," the earl replied. And then he smiled up at the cabbie. "If it will ease your mind, lad, I shall only stay the required half hour, and I shall even beg off the ride in the park I promised Miss Parkes. Would that satisfy you?"

"Not in a stone's lifetime," the cabbie muttered grudgingly. Then, in a darting move, he thrust his thin arm through the connecting door and laid his cool hand upon the earl's forehead. "You got the fever, milord."

An instant tremor skittered through Justin at the lad's soft touch. He inhaled sharply, very much aware that this new trembling was not fever-induced. His heart raced. Cautiously, disbelievingly, he peered up through the communicating hole, watching while the cabbie bent to retrieve his bundle from beneath the seat and then spread it out upon the roof. What the deuce was happening to him now?

" 'Ere, milord," the lad said, fumbling around in the bundle's contents until he brought forth a small blue bottle. Innocent of the earl's dismay, he jabbed the bottle toward him and continued, "Take summat o' this."

"What is it?" Justin asked, mentally shaking himself before uncorking the bottle and sniffing suspiciously.

"A tincture o' catnip an' meadowsweet," the lad responded. "It be just the thing fer the fever. Go on now, take a swallow."

Justin did. It was not so bad as he had thought it might be. "You made this, Mel?" he asked after the liquid had hit his stomach like an herbal nine-pounder and begun to warm him from the inside out.

"Aye."

"And it works?"

"Aye," the cabbie said over a small giggle.

"What is so amusing, then, you scamp?" the earl asked as his eyes narrowed with suspicion. "Am I about to turn as blue as this bottle and see all my hair fall out?"

"Nay, milord," the cabbie chuckled, "but Oi would keep me mummers dubbed if Oi was you."

"Oh? And why is that?" Justin asked, chuckling now, too.

" 'Cause once ye starts blowin' about wot's on yer breath, you'll be up to yer watch fob in cats."

The earl burst into laughter. When he chortled, "Just so long as I can keep my hair," the cabbie joined in, too, and the hansom jiggled and shook into Green Street.


"He will come up to scratch before the Season is over, I tell you," Lady Palmerton declared in the ornately cluttered drawing room of her Green Street mansion. A wide sweep of deep burgundy floral wallpaper competed with unmatched, overlapping Oriental rugs to overwhelm the eye. Knickknacks of every value and description covered the surfaces of the tables. "But you will have to be very careful, my darling. Stonegate is the highest of sticklers. He will not tolerate the least impropriety in his intended."

"Quite right," agreed Lord Palmerton, tugging some order into his pink embroidered waistcoat as he nodded his head and paced. "Best thing in my opinion is to just stay mumchance. No man worth his salt wishes to hear a lot of female drivel anyway."

"But should I not be able to converse with him about his interests?" asked Miss Parkes, smoothing the belled skirt of her soft green, shot-silk carriage gown over her slim legs.

"Egad, Eunice," her brother, Stanley, Viscount Nesbitt, sneered. "He has his acquaintances and his clubs for that. Try not to be such a ninny."

"I am not a ninny!" Miss Parkes declared hotly. "I merely wish to be certain of doing nothing that might displease him. I do so want him, Stanley. Already my friends are over the boughs because of my good fortune in gaining his interest." She smiled coyly. "I know for a fact that Sarah Manning is green with envy. Elizabeth Wilmington told me just this morning that she is so full of spite she is telling everyone I dye my hair! Can you fancy it? I told Elizabeth that we would be driving out today. I cannot wait for everyone to see me in his company."

"Mmm. Well, you must be careful not to rush your fences, my darling," her mother warned. "He is interested, but he has not yet reached the point of dropping the handkerchief. And until his ring is on your finger, you must be the pattern card of propriety. Conduct yourself with modesty and circumspection at all times."

"And put a period to that infernal, giggling gossip your friends get up to," her father ordered with remembered irritation. "No man wishes to be the object of such disagreeable attention."

"Of course, no one would think to put a period to Stonegate's goings-on, would they?" Stanley inserted waspishly.

Into the silence that followed, the earl lifted a chiding brow to his offspring. "If you are referring to the episode in which Stonegate found himself embroiled last evening, Stanley, you are to say no more about it."

"Devil a bit!" Stanley cried, rising to his feet. "The man was wounded coming out of his light o' love's house, deuce take it!"

Both ladies gasped.

"Hold your tongue!" the earl commanded, glancing apologetically toward his stricken wife. More mildly, he continued, "We must be realistic, Stanley. The man is four-and-thirty years old. And it is unhealthy for a man to . . . well, you know. Damnation, we all know a man has needs!"

"Is it true, Papa?" cried Miss Parkes. "A mistress! What am I to do? What shall I say?"

The earl seized his daughter's shoulders in a tight grasp.

"Look here, girl," he growled, "do you truly want this man?"

"Oh, yes, Papa," she breathed through tiny tears. "I shall be the envy of every woman in the *ton*. I should like it above all things."

"Then we say nothing about it, do you understand?"

"I daresay you would not be so understanding if the impropriety blotted *my* copybook, would you, Father?" Stanley stated petulantly.

The earl glared at his son. "No, I would not. But then, I am not trying to secure a leg-shackle to someone you are desperate to marry. Now cease this incessant jealousy, Stanley. It does not serve."

It was into the midst of this tension and scowling hostility that the butler stepped, wisely keeping his gaze fixed upon the fireplace across the room as he informed his lordship that Stonegate had arrived.

"Ah, Stonegate," the earl cried in a startling change of demeanor as Justin appeared at the drawing room entrance. "Do come in, my boy."

Removing his gray silk top hat, Justin crossed to the earl's side, resplendent in a dove gray coat and matching peg-topped trousers, a starched, rolled-collar shirt setting off his wide emerald cravat. Taking Lord Palmerton's hand in greeting, he then made his leg to the ladies and nodded to the viscount.

"Please do sit down, my lord," Lady Palmerton cooed. "I have rung for tea. You will take some with us, will you not, before you spirit our dear Eunice away for your drive?"

Justin settled himself rather stiffly upon the edge of a heavily carved, velvet-upholstered settee. "I shall indeed be happy to take tea with you, my lady, but, unfortunately," he said, as he turned toward Miss Parkes, "I must ask to be excused from our drive. I have taken a wound . . ."

"Yes, yes, we heard all about that," the earl interrupted solicitously. "Most unfortunate, my boy."

Justin gazed at the earl, straightening slightly. "I feared that you might have heard of the attack against me before I could see you," he confessed. "If I might explain—"

"No need, my boy," the earl cried magnanimously. "Accidents will happen, don't you know. Do not concern yourself with apologies, Stonegate." And then the earl gave Justin a knowing grin. "I would be less than honest if I did not admit that it could have happened to any of us, what?"

Throwing himself into a chair near the gaming table, Stanley fumed silently.

Somewhat nonplussed, Justin smiled weakly. "Just the same, sir, I do owe an apology to your daughter. Miss Parkes, may I extend to you my deepest regrets. I did promise you a drive, but, as yet, I find it difficult to manage the ribbons."

"La, sir," she breathed, smiling with tender sweetness, "you must not concern yourself with me. You must of course give the greatest possible care to your condition." Demurely, she lowered her gaze and brushed nonexistent lint off the cool shot-silk of her bodice.

"I do hope you are not too disappointed," Justin said, leaning forward slightly so that he might more easily hear her gentle, feminine responses.

"Oh, no, sir," she whispered softly, plaintively. "However . . . oh, pay no attention to me. I am sure I shall be able to send messages to my acquaintances in time. My friends were so anxious to meet you. I fear I must make haste to cancel the tentative arrangements I had made with them to join us after our drive and perhaps take an ice at Gunter's if you were agreeable."

Justin began to feel quite the consummate cad. "My dear Miss Parkes," he responded contritely, "I can see that I have truly inconvenienced you. I assure you, if it were not for my wounds . . ."

"Oh, please say no more about it, sir," Miss Parkes soothed, laying a soft, white hand on Justin's coat sleeve. "I am persuaded that you came today at great risk to yourself. You must be in great pain."

Justin smiled warmly. "Not so much at the moment. My cabbie . . . Well, never mind. It is kind in you to be so caring."

"I am only glad and most relieved to hear that you are recovering so well, sir," she said softly. "But you should not be visiting today, I think. You should be in your own home where you might rest and heal completely."

Justin chuckled at the thought. "My niece and nephew arrived in Town today," he explained when she regarded his laughter oddly. "I misdoubt there is a moment's rest to be found in my home just now." Miss Parkes laughed delicately. "I shall have to disappoint them, too, I fear. I had thought that an evening at Vauxhall would take some of the devilment out of them after their journey here, but . . ."

"Ahh, Vauxhall," Miss Parkes breathed with a flutter of lashes, her lovely eyes rounding with what, for her, were uncharted heights of animation. "Such an entertaining place. I am ever amazed at how much there is to see and do. I had heard that there was a new equestrian act in the Rotunda. I should like to see it above all things. And what a delightful entertainment it would have been for the children."

"Yes," Justin replied hesitantly. "I had thought so, too."

"What a shame to disappoint them," the lady sighed. "But, of course, you are right to refuse their treat, my lord. You must consider only yourself now. You owe it to yourself to rest and heal. And, as Mama tells me, children recover from their little disappointments so easily. So, of course, do I."

Justin gritted his teeth through a heavy, sinking surge of all-too-familiar guilt. "Miss Parkes . . ."

"Yes, my lord?" she replied, eyes dripping solicitude.

"Perhaps if I rested this afternoon . . ."

"Oh, no, my lord," the young woman replied with a firm shake of her golden curls. "We must not take advantage of your kind, generous nature. Until you are completely recovered, you must consider only your own needs."

"Yet I am sensible of your disappointment, Miss Parkes," Justin responded, regretting every word that came out of his mouth and appalled that he could not stop the flow, "and I cannot be so self-absorbed as to deny you what pleasures I can provide. I am sure that with an afternoon's rest, I shall be fine. We shall make a party of it, shall we? We shall ask Angela and the children, of course, and . . . how about you, Nesbitt? Will you join us?"

Stanley's gaze slewed slowly toward Justin. "Equestrian act, eh?" he replied flatly. "Hoorah. I would not miss it for the world."

Justin's jaw tightened, curious as to what burr had become lodged under the young man's saddle, but not so much that he really wished to find out. "Very well," he replied, turning back toward Miss Parkes, masking by his movement a sudden chill that rippled over him. "I shall procure a brougham, then, and take you up later this evening."

"Rubbish, my boy," Lord Palmerton interjected magnanimously. "No sense in doing that when my own carriage will be sitting idle this evening. I shall have Stanley and Eunice take you and your sister up instead. It would be better for your wounds, too, I vow, since you shall in no wise have to drive."

Justin bowed slightly and wavered to his feet. "You are most kind."

"Not at all, dear boy," cried Lady Palmerton, setting down her teacup as Stonegate made his leg. Quickly, she seized Eunice about the shoulders and, casting a glowing benediction upon her daughter's face, continued, "Why, who in the entire city would we entrust more with our precious things?"

"Who, indeed?" beamed Palmerton, settling his arm around Justin's wound as he escorted him toward the drawing room door.

"Yes, who, indeed?" murmured Stanley, turning his face toward the fire to seek solace in the sleek undulations of the flames.


Mel jumped down to stand beside the hansom when the earl emerged from the mansion, waiting to help him up the awkward steps and settle him comfortably into the carriage. The look on the earl's face as he accepted the cabbie's aid bespoke resigned dismay. The cabbie shook his head reprovingly. Saying nothing, he touched gentle fingers to the earl's forehead and then tucked a blanket around his broad shoulders. Then, determining to take the earl nowhere else but home to his bed, he jumped quickly into the driver's seat and snapped his whip over his hack's head, soon turning the hansom south into Park Lane.

The cabbie once again considered the plans he had formulated while the earl had been inside taking tea. There could be no denying that Stonegate was in danger. It was also obvious that he needed to discover who it was that was threatening him, and why. The cabbie was certain that the earl was not a man who would be satisfied without all the answers. An unknown of that magnitude could eat at a man, weighing down upon him like a fresh fifty-stone load. Such a thing could not help but detract from his ability to make a success of his marriage. And the cabbie was only too aware that Stonegate wanted a loving relationship with his chosen bride.

And that was why the cabbie had made the decision that he had. Well, one of the reasons, anyway. It would be his wedding gift, he had thought happily. He would spread the word around the Rookery grapevine that he was looking for information about the two footpads who had attacked the earl and the person who had hired them. He would soon learn the truth of their identities. And, in the meantime, while he awaited the news, he would keep the earl safe by plastering himself to the heedless looby like a dollop of spilt gruel to Maudie's brazier grate.

"Bloody hell."

The earl's epithet was muttered, spat in frustration, and audible in the driver's seat.

Instantly the communicating door snapped open, and the cabbie glared down at Stonegate's tired face.

"Awright, me fine lord," the lad said with a reproving smile, "ye been lookin' loike ye ate summat o' Maudie's black puddin' ever' since ye comed out o' that door. Wot 'appened wiv them nobs?"

Justin grinned up at the lad wearily. "Who's Maudie?" he asked.

"A friend wot lives below me," the cabbie replied. "Now answer me question. Wot 'appened?"

Stonegate sighed. "I am still trying to figure out what happened myself," he said. "One minute I was telling Miss Parkes that I could not drive out with her today, and the next I was making arrangements to take a party to Vaux-hall."

The cabbie gaped at the earl.

"Bloody 'ell."

Justin chuckled and relaxed back against the squabs, wonderfully content to be in the cabbie's company again. "Just so. Therefore, it seems, my lad, that I shall not need your services for the rest of the day. If I am to have any chance of survival, I must go home, bar my bedroom door against the demands of my energetic niece and nephew, and get what sleep I can before I have to play the charming host at this deuced engagement tonight."

The cabbie's glare hardened, his copper eyes glinting in the lowering sunlight. "Oi changed me mind about you," he muttered.

"Did you?" Justin replied, peering up at him with a grin.

"Aye. Oi used to think ye 'ad some sense, bein' one o' them 'my lords' an' all. But ye ain't more'n ninepence in the shilling."

Stonegate laughed heartily. "You'll get no argument from me, lad."

"It ain't no laughin' matter!" the cabbie cried, his husky voice unknowingly sending wavelets of pleasure over the surface of the earl's skin. "There be the smell o' rain in the air, an' ye still got the fever. Wot ye gonna do?"

Justin responded swiftly, his strong, masculine hand suddenly thrusting through the communication hole. "Catnip and meadowsweet, scamp," Stonegate said on a heavy sigh. "Better give me the whole deuced bottle."

# Five

The predicted rain began that evening as a cold, settling mist that gradually solidified during the first act of entertainment at the famous pleasure garden, a concert of music, until the moistened Rotunda appeared molten under the warm glow of its hundreds of lights, and the Grand Cascade—the water spectacle that followed featuring a waterfall with a mill and a bridge with a succession of vehicles crossing over to the sounds of rumbling wheels and rushing water—seemed almost an anticlimax. Umbrellas ballooned intermittently, forming black canopies that cupped huddled shoulders and blocked the view. Caught between chair backs and ribbed black blooms, children squirmed.

"Uncle Justin, shall we have to go?"

Justin glanced down at the young girl tugging on his sleeve. She had inherited her father's soft blond hair, her mother's beauty, and a smidgen of her Uncle Oliver's taste for impish impropriety.

"It seems so, Fanny," he replied, adjusting her damp cloak. "This looks to be a long, slow drizzle. Even if enough of the audience remains to view the equestrian act, the rain will certainly prevent displaying the fireworks."

"But I wish to see fireworks!" declared the future Viscount D'Antry from the earl's other side.

Justin grinned widely.

"Edward, do not badger your uncle," the Viscountess admonished. "He was good enough to provide you with this entertainment in spite of his being unwell. He cannot help it if it rains." Turning toward her brother, she again begged him, "Justin, do let us leave. You are positively whey-faced and I, for one," and here she glanced pointedly at the sedately seated Miss Parkes, "am becoming concerned for you. Why, even Nesbitt has already sought the protection of his brougham."

Justin gave his sister a warm half-smile. "Thank you, Angela, but I am not yet preparing to stick my spoon in the wall. Besides, I have some medicine that has been helping."

"Yes, I have seen you swigging it periodically," his sister grinned. "What is it?"

"Herbs," Justin told her. "I was given it by a cabbie."

"Ah, the lad you told Mama and me about. But really, Justin," Angela stated firmly, "herbs or no, you need to be home in bed. Why you thought to attempt this evening is beyond me, especially after all Mama and I said to try to talk you out of it."

Justin's glance flickered toward Miss Parkes. "It seemed necessary at the time," he responded. "Shall you be too disappointed if we must leave, Miss Parkes?" he asked, allowing himself a long enough, but still proper, amount of time to admire the perfection of her attire and coiffure. Even in the swirling, heavy mist, the clusters of ringlets that were gathered above her ears remained tight and springy.

"La, sir, what a rag-mannered baggage you must think me," Miss Parkes exclaimed prettily. "How shall I be disappointed, knowing that you are suffering?"

Justin's gaze warmed. "Nevertheless, I must again

apologize. I fear that the rain will only worsen, Miss Parkes, but I do not care to see you unhappy."

"Well," she commented, shrugging daintily, "it hardly signifies at this point. I have seen none of my friends since we arrived, and everyone else is beginning to leave anyway."

Slightly disconcerted, Justin masked his emotion by assisting both her and his sister to her feet. "Then let us leave as well," he said, taking Miss Parkes's arm. "We shall plan to repeat our visit another time when the weather is clement. Edward, take hold of your mother's hand. Fanny, you walk up ahead."

"But I want to see fireworks," Edward demanded.

"Hush, Edward," his mother said.

Viscount Nesbitt awaited them in the Palmerton brougham just on the other side of the turnstiles. "I am relieved to see that you have come to your senses," he stated indolently after a bedraggled footman had opened the carriage door for their entrance. "I am hard put to recall a more ill-conceived evening."

Miss Parkes, the first to enter, scowled at him, a silent chiding. "Lord Stonegate was all that is thoughtful, Stanley," she stated for Justin's benefit. "I, for one, am most grateful for his efforts." Carefully smoothing the back of her skirts, she seated herself across from her brother, facing front.

"No harm has been done," Lady D'Antry said rather acidly as she took the seat next to Miss Parkes and settled Fanny between them. "And do not forget, sir. Due to the selfless consideration of my brother, we have had the pleasure of enjoying *your* charming company this evening. That fact alone should give us all reason to be grateful."

Last into the carriage, Justin rolled his eyes at his sister's pointed remark, well aware of the stony stare Nesbitt was returning in her direction. Angela, he knew, was not a woman to let her own go undefended. He hoped they would not come to blows before the evening ended. Deuce take it, he was trying to court the man's sister! Taking his seat and pulling Edward into the space beside him, he braced his legs as the coachman called out to his team, wincing a bit as the carriage started forward.

Once away from Vauxhall, there was little traffic on the rain-slicked streets to impede their progress, a good portion of the London populace content to remain inside and avoid the nasty weather. Therefore, as they approached the river, the coachman had no trouble maintaining a fast pace that carried the brougham smoothly over the cobblestoned streets and onto Westminster Bridge.

They had traveled nearly halfway across the bridge when, suddenly, without warning, just as the carriage reached the slight downward slope leading to the opposite side, it veered slightly and then jolted.

"What the deuce was that?" the viscount exclaimed over his sister's frightened gasp.

Justin heard the coachman curse viciously. Seizing Edward by the shoulders, he braced himself as another jolt shuddered through them and the carriage again careened, one wheel rolling over an obstacle large enough to pitch them all to one side. From somewhere nearby, a horse released a squealing cry of agony just as the body of the coachman flew past the window on Nesbitt's side. Miss Parkes, seeing him, clutched at her brother and screamed. And then the carriage began to shudder arhythmically, jarring them with teeth-rattling tremors.

"Dear God, Justin, what is happening?" Angela cried, pulling Edward into her lap.

"Nothing good, I think," Justin responded, his brow tightening as he felt the carriage begin to pick up speed.

"Stay seated, all of you. I shall try to find out what is going on." Ignoring the thrumming ache in his shoulder, Justin angled his head out the window and surveyed the scene.

The carriage had been abandoned. Even the horses were no longer bound in their traces. Strands of the leather harness were tangled and tossed aloft, returning time and again to spank the cobblestones passing swiftly beneath the carriage. Looking ahead, Justin saw one of the horses some distance away, bolting in panic across the remainder of the bridge. The other was lying behind them, twitching and blowing in his agony. Justin quickly reasoned that the poor fellow must have stumbled and been caught beneath the wheel, and most likely was the large object they had rolled over. Averting his eyes, he forced aside his regret.

Both the coachman and the footman had jumped to safety as soon as the trouble began. Narrowing his gaze on the road ahead, Justin soon understood why. A part of the traces had caught on the splinter bar in such a way that the tension was pulling the carriage pole slightly off center. It did not take much of the earl's considerable intellect to determine that if something were not done in the next few moments, the carriage would soon reach the edge of the bridge, crash through the balustrade, and tip over into the Thames.

Justin immediately tucked his broad body back inside. "The harness has broken," he informed them evenly. "But I—"

"Oh, Stanley, do something!" Miss Parkes cried, burying her face in her brother's frills.

The viscount reacted instantly. Wrapping his arms tightly around his sister's waist, he shouldered his way to the carriage door, threw it open, and jumped with her outside. Angela clutched her children to her bosom and stared after them in astonishment, biting her lip as she heard them thump against the cobblestones and cry out in pain.

"My God, Justin . . . should we . . . ?"

"No, dear, we are moving too fast. As I tried to say before, I shall attempt to climb to the front of the carriage and use the harness to steer it. But don't do anything foolish, Angela. You and the children remain inside."

"But, Justin, your wound . . ." she cried, clutching at his elbow when he moved toward the door.

The earl shot her a quick smile. "It does not signify. Given the choice between a little pain and an early demise, I would choose pain every time." Pushing the door back against the body of the carriage, he lithely slipped outside.

The earl moved as quickly as possible, but the rain-mist had slicked the carriage's surfaces until trying to catch hold of the wooden panels and brass appointments was like trying to cling to glass. To his frustration, when he reached the driver's seat, he saw that he would not be able to accomplish his plan. Much of the harness was slapping against the cobblestones out of reach, even the long, trailing strands of the reins. Immediately deciding upon another tactic, Justin cautiously climbed over the footrest, gripping the angled panel with his upper arm while, stretching down, he tried to seize the pole with his other hand.

He cursed roundly. The distance was too great, and time was quickly running out. Straightening, he used both arms to grip the panel and tried to hook the pole with the top of his booted foot. But just as he had managed to angle his toes beneath the long shaft, the splinter bar at the end of the pole caught on a section of balustrade and bounced free, sending a violent jolt through the brougham. Justin's legs flew outward and swung into space, dangling before first one spinning wheel and then the other as the carriage continued its wild careen.

The earl's shoulder felt imbedded by splintered glass. He writhed, barely hanging on, feeling himself weaken. He looked down at the pavement racing by beneath his tossing legs. His fingers loosened.

And then suddenly a hansom was beside him, pulling close, wheel to wheel.

" 'Ang on, then, guv'nor," came the familiar husky voice as the hansom pulled ahead.

Justin almost laughed with relief. Mel.

With great skill the cabbie maneuvered his cab slightly to the front of the brougham and close to the remains of the carriage's shattered splinter bar. Then, forming a wide loop with his long whip, he leaned far to the side of his cab and slipped the loop over the bouncing pole, drawing it up quickly, taking care to swing it free of his hansom's huge wheel. With a soft snick to his hack, he then increased his speed just enough to lever the pole behind him and lodge it against the solid body of his cab. Then, with a gentle, measured tug on his reins, he soon brought both carriages to a standstill.

Justin was waiting for him when he jumped down from his elevated perch behind the hood. He had never been so glad to see anyone in all his life. Using his uninjured arm, the earl gripped the cabbie's shoulders and exuberantly crushed the lad against him, knocking his broad-brimmed hat to the pavement beside them. The top of the lad's head only reached his shoulder. Justin grinned, tucking midnight curls under his chin.

"Mel, you little scamp! Where the deuce did you come from?" With unbridled joy, the earl buried his nose in the lad's midnight curls.

They were fragrant with rose.

Justin jerked with surprise; his senses reeled. He clutched at the cabbie's frayed clothing as his breath deserted him. He weakened, feeling his head drop forward of its own accord to bring his cheek into contact with the flawless softness of the cabbie's. The touch of his skin against the lad's was like a jolt from an electricity machine.

Justin pushed away, stung.

"I must see to my sister," he husked in confusion.

"Aye," the cabbie replied, eyes round with wonder, his breath coming in short little jerks.

Justin noticed. If he had not been so disconcerted after their incredible embrace, he might have taken great satisfaction in the fact that the lad was every bit as discomposed as he. He wondered if his wits had gone begging. He had lived for four-and-thirty years and never once even considered backgammon play. So why . . . ? Deuce take it, what was it about the boy?

It was hardly a haughty prig of the first stare who reached inside the brougham to hand out his sister a few moments later. Far from it. From what Justin could determine, it was a mere shell of the man he had recently been . . . either that or a mass of quivering nerve endings. And it was all the fault of the cabbie. He had been perfectly fine until he had met the deuced lad. Now he wasn't sure whether or not he would own the same name from day to day.

Yet he did know one thing. He needed to get some perspective back into his life. And soon. He was glad he had not rushed to put a period to the most significant of his bachelor pleasures. He obviously was not meant for abstinence. Judging by the appalling turn of his thoughts lately, he most definitely needed Clarisse.

"Oh, darling, are you all right?" cried Angela after he had opened the door and she had flown into his arms.

"Quite," Justin responded with a calm that belied his state of mind, helping the children down and handing them to their mother. "Come with me a moment, Angela. I want you to meet my cabbie." Oh, Lord, where had that come from? "My cabbie," indeed!

"So you are Mel," Angela said with a warm smile, crossing to where the cabbie stood before seizing both the lad's hands. "The one his lordship has told us so much about. How can I ever thank you for the aid you have rendered my brother . . . and not once, but twice."

The cabbie's eyes misted, studied the woman, Stonegate's sister; stared. His lips trembled slightly. "Aw, Oi just be 'appenin' by," he said softly, huskily.

Nearby, the siren sound wrapped around Justin's spinal cord and strummed. He trembled.

"Nevertheless," Angela insisted, "I assure you that I am sensible of what you have done for my brother. I shall see that you receive a reward."

The cabbie's eyes widened. "Oh, nay, milaidy," he cried, shaking his head and pulling away. He could not take guineas from Stonegate for his own wedding present. Yet there was no way to make the lady understand that.

"I insist," Angela replied, motioning toward Stonegate with the unmistakable gesture all women possess to signal a convenient man to draw forth his purse.

"Nay," the lad said stubbornly, backing up against the huge wheel of his cab. "Besides, Oi mun carry them other two toffs 'ome. Oi picked 'em up when they jumped outta yer brougham."

"You have Nesbitt and his sister in your hansom?" Justin queried quickly.

"Aye," Mel responded, crumpling a bit as he noted the leap of concern in Stonegate's eyes. "The young miss, she be awright except fer some scrapes. But the milord, 'e got a broke arm." As he spoke, the cabbie's face sank into studied resignation.

"I must talk with them," the earl said worriedly. "Please excuse me a moment, Mel. Angela."

With a wide stride Justin hurried to the hansom and rounded it, his eyes searching the passenger compartment. "Are you all right Miss Parkes?" he asked softly.

Peering out from the hooded shadows, the lady stretched out a hand and answered with sweet, feminine appeal. "Yes, I am fine, sir. I have only taken a few bruises. But Stanley . . ." Tearfully she gazed at her brother whose twisted features revealed his pain.

"I am more sorry for the accident than I can say," Justin told her, taking her hand to comfort her, but hard put to muster any sympathy for the man who had abandoned the rest of them, endangering not only himself, but his sister. More sharply he added, "Nesbitt, you must, of course, have a doctor attend you as soon as possible. I believe it would be best if you remained here in the hansom and let the cabbie take you the rest of the way home. It will no doubt take a while yet before the bobbies ascertain what caused the accident. I shall stay here to deal with them, and to see to your brougham's removal if you like."

"So generous in you," the viscount gritted out.

"Oh, indeed, sir," Miss Parkes echoed. "It is most kind. We should like that above all things."

"Then rest your minds on that score," Justin said, managing a smile. "I shall call upon you tomorrow to let your father know where he might find his carriage and to see how you fare."

"You would be most welcome, sir," Miss Parkes said, squeezing his hand meaningfully. "Until then."

Justin bowed over her hand and kissed the tips of her fingers. Looking up into her eyes, he echoed, "Until then."

The cabbie was bent over the carriage pole when Justin's boot scuffed against the cobblestones behind him, telling him of the earl's return. "Will ye be takin' yerself 'ome now, too, milord?" he asked quietly.

"Just as soon as I talk to the police and deliver the brougham to be repaired."

"That's awright then," the cabbie replied. "Ye needs to be where ye kin be safe." Turning, he held forth two sections of the leather traces and put them in the earl's hands. "It be 'appenin' again," he said with low intensity.

"What do you mean, Mel?"

"Oi means that them traces was cut, milord. This 'ere weren't no accident."

Justin glanced toward the brougham where Angela, Fanny, and Edward awaited, concerned that they might overhear the conversation. Then, consideringly, he turned the pieces of leather in his hands, fitting the sharply severed edges together. His gaze meshed with Mel's in complete understanding.

"This is beginning to put me in a bad skin," he said with a quick grin.

The cabbie made a noise of disgust. "Ye ain't takin' this serious, is ye?" he scolded.

"Of course I am," Justin countered more soberly. "But what would you have me do?"

"Take up embroid'ry."

Justin broke into laughter, the unusual sound drawing the attention of his sister as she supervised a skipping game for the children on the cobblestones. Her jaw dropped slightly, amazed.

"And that is supposed to keep these 'accidents' from happening to me?"

"Nay, but it'll keep ye off the streets," the cabbie replied. "Ye be a menace, y'know."

Justin chuckled again. "Perhaps I shall take up *papier mâché!*"

The cabbie hid an answering smile. "Ye moight try Puxley's fer the carriage. It be where Oi stables me 'orse. They be open all night." The lad bowed then, scraping his battered hat against the sodden cobblestones; a strange poignancy lit his copper-colored eyes. "Watch yer back, milord . . . ta."

In only moments, the lad had expertly mounted the hansom and smartly tooled away.

"How much did you give him?" Angela asked, joining the earl after the cab had disappeared from sight.

"How much?" Justin parroted.

"Yes, Justin," his sister said with an exasperated laugh. "How much of a reward?"

The earl's jaw dropped. "Devil a bit," he cursed, angry that the distractions of Miss Parkes and her brother, not to mention finding out about this latest murder attempt, had kept him from doing his duty to the boy. "It slipped my mind."

"Well, you can give it to him tomorrow, I suppose."

Justin flushed uncomfortably. "Perhaps not. In all the excitement, I neglected to tell him to resume his duties."

"Then perhaps you had better go after him now, Justin," Angela laughed. "Given your state of mind lately, I rather imagine you have no idea where the boy lives either."

"I confess I do not," Justin agreed, growing a bit ruddier, "but I cannot leave you alone, and the lad is already out of sight. He did mention Puxley's stable, though. As I recall, it is in Gray's Inn Road. No doubt I can find out his direction from there."

"See that you do, darling," Angela said, patting her brother's sleeve before walking back toward the brougham. "That young man saved my babies' lives."

\* \* \*

Justin threaded the tangle of narrow courts and alleys to the south of Portpool Lane just as predawn began to rub at the soot-black night, cleansing its shadows to lifeless gray. He decided, as his senses reeled with the stench of free-flowing ordure, a hovering, stagnant miasma of spoilage and rot mocked by the overriding floral bouquet of gin, that he now believed in hell.

Already the street arabs were about . . . those legions of children who swarmed throughout the Rookery, working, stealing, doing anything they could to put food in their mouths for one more day. To a child, they halted in their tracks when he passed them by, eyeing him suspiciously, judging his strength and dexterity, their stares cunning and yet wrenchingly bleak.

"I am looking for Mel," he said to several he passed before they scampered away, "Mel, the cabbie. Might you direct me to his place?"

Finally, after receiving more hollow-eyed stares than he could count, one very small girl stopped long enough to jab a tiny finger toward another narrow alley. Justin smiled and rewarded her with a coin, then rounded the corner, passing between a dingy chandler's, whose soot-streaked window displayed samples of his wares . . . of candles, puddings, cat's meat, tripe, cow heels, and coal . . . and an already bustling gin shop.

A bundle of moving rags blocked his way. Looking down, he only just managed to check a gasp.

"Ye be lookin' fer Mel, eh?" the bundle said, shifting before his eyes until it resolved into the shape of a woman. "Wot ye want wiv the lad?"

Justin fought to mask his distaste. "I have something for him."

"Summat good?" the woman asked hopefully, weaving to her feet and steadying herself against the wall.

Justin held himself ready, having no idea how to respond. If he said that he did not, the woman might not tell him how to find Mel, yet if he agreed, the woman might possibly try to take it from him, or at least call someone else to do it for her. In the space of a few seconds, he decided that he had no choice but to be truthful. Otherwise, he would be helpless to find the boy.

"Yes, madam, it is something good," Justin said with a slight smile. "Can you direct me to his home?"

The woman revealed teeth clumped with yellowed masses. "Aye, Susan knows. It be over yonder . . ." she replied, pointing with an emaciated finger, ". . . the one at the end. Ye mun tell 'im Susan sent ye since ye got summat good, an' all. Lad's good to owd Susan . . . Won't take a woman's reg'lar pay . . ."

"My thanks, madam," Justin interrupted, drawing a coin from his pocket and placing it in the woman's scaly hand. Then, anxious to escape, he bowed his head slightly and turned away toward the building.

"Cor," the woman breathed with delight, "God bless ye, sir! An' Mel, 'e's all the way to the top, 'e is," she called after him. "Tell 'im owd Susan sent ye on the way."

Justin skirted a pig noisily snuffling in something unidentifiable at the foot of the entry steps and entered the building. He barely held back a shudder, his thoughts filled with the horror of what he had just seen, with the obscenity. Floor after floor passed beneath him, anyone entering the hall as he pounded by being almost forced back against the wall in the face of the earl's focused, determined stride.

At last Justin reached the top floor. Breathing deeply to steady his heartbeat, he cast a searching glance at his surroundings before striding purposefully toward the last rooms at the end of the hall. He knocked brusquely. The door was opened by a broad, barrel-shaped man who quite efficiently parried his advance.

" 'Ere now, 'oo're you?" the man bellowed belligerently.

"Wot is it, Bart?" a soft voice said from behind the man.

Bart's eyes scanned the earl, top to toes. "Some toff by the look o' 'im," he responded. "Go on back to yer pallet, Bess. No need fer ye to get up yet. Mam's fryin' the bacon."

Justin realized that he had better do something to intimidate the man or he would most likely soon be tossed down the stairs. Summoning all the hauteur he could muster, he looked down the length of his nose and said, "I am Stonegate. I have come to see Mel."

The change that came over the burly man was instantaneous. Breaking into a wide grin, he said, "Well, why'n't ye say so?" Then, seizing Justin's coat sleeve, he all but dragged him into the room.

" 'Oo be it, Bart?" came a thin, gravelly voice from the next room.

"A reg'lar nob, Gran," Bart answered with a shout. " 'E's come to see Mel."

"Mel?" came the question from beside him. Turning, Justin saw a middle-aged woman cease stirring something pastelike on the brazier and turn to study him. "Wot 'e be wantin' wiv Mel?"

"Oi doesn't know, Ma," Bart said with some exasperation, "Oi ain't been gived the chance to ask. Bess, Oi tol' ye to get back into bed."

"Husband, ye can't just let a 'my lord' keep on standin'," Bess scolded. "Ye has to offer the gent a seat." Slowly the younger woman toddled over to the table and pulled out one of the roughly hewn chairs, gesturing toward it with a smile. Justin did not want to give offense, though the seat looked none too clean. Nodding his thanks, he sat down.

"Now," pronounced Bart, glancing around the room

meaningfully, "so's we doesn't have no more interruptions, Oi'll introduce us all. Con!" he shouted toward the adjoining room. "Get Jack an' Evie to carry you and Gran in 'ere." As soon as they were settled, Bart stated, "Now over 'ere be us Pollards," he said. "Them two is George and Maudie, our parents, Oi be Bart, an' the younger two is me sister and brovver, Evie and Jack. An' this be Bess," he said pulling the heavily swollen woman proudly to his side, "me wife."

"How do you do?" Justin responded, somewhat overwhelmed.

"Now over there," Bart continued, sounding for all the world like a barker at a country fair, "be the 'Icks. That be Conrad an' his ma, Gran. Con's wife, Maeve, ain't 'ere roight now. She be a milk-seller so she has to get an early start on the day. Now over 'gainst the wall, lined up loike a bunch o' sawed-off stumps," he pointed with a grin that was eagerly returned, "be Con and Maeve's brood. That be Annie, Fred, an' the little ones, Ben and Tom. Them last two be mudlarks, so scuse them muddy feet."

"I am delighted to meet you all," Justin stated politely, unaccountably warming to the families in spite of his aversion to his surroundings, "but I am rather anxious to locate Mel."

"Why?" came the soft sound, as faint and rasping as wind-rustled paper.

Justin's eyes slewed toward Gran's. She was terribly ill, he saw instantly, yet there was a strength, a wisdom, in her ancient eyes.

He smiled, acknowledging to her her right to question him. "Twice the lad has saved my life. I wish to reward him."

The faces around him suddenly beamed, their joy in Mel's good fortune astonishingly apparent. They were close, Justin realized suddenly, the lad and this odd collection of people. They genuinely cared for Mel. A bit of the tension drained from his shoulders and he drew a deep breath.

"Not many nobs'd bother to do that," the old woman commented, her rheumy eyes boring into his. "Fewer still'd come theirselves into the Rookery, no matter what they thought they owed."

"I suppose not," Justin replied honestly. "But there is something very special about Mel. My reactions toward him . . . There is a bond between us, Mrs. Hicks . . ." The earl laughed self-consciously then. "This is most difficult to explain."

Gran's sagging lips wrinkled into a knowing grin. "Not so difficult as ye moight think. Mel strikes most people that way. Been wiv us nigh eight year now. Come to be one o' us, an' all. Ain't one o' us who don't want to see Mel get the reward 'e deserves, ain't that roight?" she asked her enlarged family. A dozen heads murmured their agreement and nodded vigorously. "So Oi'll tell ye wot, milord," she told him with an intensity in her old eyes that set Justin's heart beating faster, "because ye wants to reward our Mel, Oi'm gonna reward you. There be a ladder in my room wot leads to the attic. Mel be there."

Justin rose slowly, his gaze intent upon Gran's. He nodded, saying nothing. In truth, he could not. He did not yet understand, but he knew without question that he had just been given a very special gift. Astounded by his own actions, he walked over to where Gran sat, bent to her skeletal, feverish cheek, and tenderly kissed it.

"Thank you," he whispered, and then he strode toward the adjoining room.

The trapdoor opened soundlessly. Justin stepped higher into the attic, supporting the door as he came to a halt half in, half out of the room. The chamber reposed in semidarkness, a single candle burning on a rude table on the far side. Justin's gaze first centered on the candle, and then widened to encompass two people who huddled over it, working with great concentration, one on either side.

A woman dressed in a plain blue gown with slim white-cuffed sleeves, a round, white, turned-down collar, and a fitted bodice that emphasized her slender figure was sitting at the table, poring over something that lay before her. Across from her was a young man; Justin grinned and took another step up, thinking at first glance that the lad was Mel, but then he hesitated, realizing that something was different about him. He looked more closely. The boy's eyes were not copper, but hazel.

"Is there something wrong with the tense?" the boy said to the woman with perfect diction and a good deal of exasperation. "Deuce take it, you know I hate Latin declensions!"

Justin frowned. A young man of quality? Here? Doing lessons? And he was studying Latin?

The woman laughed softly.

Justin's whole being clutched at the familiar sound. He gaped, astounded. No. It could not be.

"Simon, I shall scrub your tongue," she chided in her low, husky voice. "Yes, you have written the wrong tense. The word should read, *portaveram,* 'I had carried.' You needed the pluperfect there."

The trapdoor slipped from Justin's limp fingers and crashed back against the floor. Instantly the boy was on his feet, his chair banging against wall, his hands fisting as he stepped forward in challenge.

"Who are you, sir?" he demanded. "What are you doing here?"

Justin could not speak. His eyes fixed on the woman and raked her. He hardly dared draw breath.

"Get out, sir," Simon said when he received no answer. "Get out before I—"

"No."

Melanie's low, husky voice stopped him cold. Simon waited, tensed, glaring between the intruder and his sister with heated, hostile eyes. "Who is he then?" he finally demanded.

Slowly, the woman rose to her feet and walked to Simon's side, her copper gaze never deserting Justin's, supporting him, holding his disquiet at bay. Linking her arm through her brother's, she said, "Simon, may I present your cousin, the Earl of Stonegate."

Justin's awestruck gaze slewed to the boy's, saw it warm and glint with recognition, then slid back again to lock with Melanie's. His head thumped with questions, yet every one stuck in his throat. Instead, on a ragged breath, he uttered the only thought his lips seemed capable of forming.

"Bloody hell. It's you, Mel."

# Six

The impressions came at him quickly. Skin that was merely soft and flawless on the boy now appeared translucent on the woman, glowing with an inner fire. Hair that was once dark curls now grew soft, crushable, scented with rose. Lips that were once well-shaped now beckoned his own with a siren call. A voice that had strummed his senses, even in its coarseness, now tuned itself perfectly to his ear, echoing his own perfect diction. And her eyes . . . once merely copper-colored, now they glistened as swirling pools of molten metal drawing him down . . . down.

She was beautiful. His gaze swept her form, lingering appreciatively on once-hidden curves before returning to feast again upon her face. How had he not seen it before? Desire rivered through him, but for once, he almost laughed with relief. Days ago, his body had acknowledged what his mind had not, it seemed. Slender, delicate, completely feminine . . . how had he ever thought her a boy?

"It is a pleasure to meet you at last, cousin," Simon finally said, closing the distance between them and helping Justin up the last few steps before shaking his hand.

Cousin? Justin wondered, racking his brain. How could that be? And the cabbie . . . his cabbie. Who the deuce was she?

"You must forgive me," the earl managed to say, "but I was not aware that I had any male cousins."

"Then allow me to complete the introduction, my lord," Mel replied. "May I present Simon Baxter, the Earl of Westbridge."

"Westbridge?" Justin echoed, stunned. "But he was my father's cousin, nearly eight years dead."

"And this is his son, my lord," Mel said quickly, "born fifteen years ago in India."

"My God," Justin whispered, briefly closing his eyes.

"If you doubt our word, sir," the cabbie continued in her mesmerizing voice, "I assure you we have documentation."

The earl's gaze slewed to hers. "It is not that I doubt . . . no, perhaps I had better see it." Immediately, Mel turned and crossed the room, dropping gracefully to her knees before a small trunk that had been placed against the wall. Opening it, she removed a packet of papers tied with a yellowed silk ribbon from which she took several sheets.

Gesturing toward the table, she said, "Do sit down, my lord. No doubt meeting Simon is something of a shock to you." When Justin had complied, she rose to light another candle before handing him the papers.

Justin studied the documents, laying them on top of the boy's—damme, his cousin's!—Latin lesson when he had finished. "The documents could be forgeries," he said, looking up to see a quick frown make the woman's eyes grow even more molten. "I would need to have them looked at by experts before I put my trust in them. But the letter from my father's cousin telling him of Simon's birth is indeed genuine. It is adequate proof for me. I remember my uncle's handwriting very well, as well as his manner of speaking. But why was the letter never posted?"

"Papa suffered some rather serious business losses just

after I was born," Simon explained. "He was embarrassed for your father to find out how accurate his predictions of Papa's financial ruin had been. He was afraid your father would travel to the ends of the earth to celebrate the birth of his cousin's heir, and would witness his circumstances."

Justin nodded. "He would have made the visit, and done it gladly. Family meant everything to my father." His dark eyes sought the cabbie then. "And how do you fit into all of this . . . Mel? Damme, I hardly know what to call you!"

"I should think that would be obvious, cousin," Simon said, laying a hand on Mel's shoulder with a wide smile. "Do we not resemble one another? This is my sister, Melanie."

Justin's gaze tightened. "Of course," he breathed, his eyes boring into hers, a smile beginning to grow. "Melanie." Reaching out to take both her hands in his, he squeezed them tightly. "Your eyes . . . I knew I had seen them somewhere before! Dear God, woman, I looked for you for four years."

Melanie's delicate brow furrowed. "You did?"

"Yes!" Justin cried. "After your letter telling me of your parents' death arrived, I traveled to Westbridge to bring you home, but you had sold everything and disappeared. I hired men to search the country for you, but you were nowhere to be found. And now I see why. You and Simon were in London all the time, were you not? Practically under my unsuspecting nose. But, my dear cousin, how did you come to be here?"

Melanie glanced up at her brother, and then nodded. Without speaking, Simon crossed to the small trunk and dragged it over to the table, seating himself upon it.

"It is a rather long story, my lord," she finally replied.

Justin grinned impishly. "I have been commanded by my cabbie to stay inside and take up embroidery. Just between the three of us, I would much rather listen to your tale."

Melanie blushed furiously.

Justin swallowed hard, aching to kiss each softly rounded stain.

"I fear that Simon and I lived rather more independently than most children in the English quarter while we were growing up in India," she began. "My mother controlled Papa's business affairs, much as, I understand, your father did before we left England, though certainly not as successfully. Papa's pride was hurt immeasurably by her rather cavalier usurpation of his duties. He began to drink quite heavily not many years after we arrived, and Mama did nothing to give him more of the responsibility that might have restored his confidence until she was with child and there was no help for it. Simon has already told you what happened as a result of that."

"Yes," Justin said with a soft smile and intense eyes. "Please go on."

"We became virtual outcasts among English society," Melanie continued. "Because of Mama's insistence on running Papa's affairs, she became *de trop,* and Papa's weaknesses . . . well, we did not see many of our countrymen socially. Simon and I were quite literally on our own. Mama was always busy and had little time for us, and Papa . . ."

"We began to go about the countryside," Simon said, giving his sister a moment to compose herself. "We found an old cart and fixed it up, and hitched it to my pony. We lived in the villages with the native people more of the time than in our own compound. They taught us whatever we asked to learn of their ways."

"Like the sling," Justin stated, a light going on in his eyes.

"Yes," Simon replied. "I was in leading strings at the time. Melanie needed to have some way to protect me."

"And the herbs?" he continued, searching Melanie's face.

"We were quite on our own, my lord," she answered softly. "I had to learn what was necessary to keep Simon safe."

"So you became his nurse, his nanny," Justin said, fingering the Latin lesson, "and now his tutor as well."

Melanie smiled, then, rather mischievously. "The Jesuit priests caught Simon and me listening at the window of their school one day when I was nine," she told him. "When they found out I could repeat back the Latin lesson they had assigned their students the day before, they began to let me come to their classes. I have quite a good education as a result, my lord."

Justin sat back in his chair and rested his palms flat upon the table. His mind was reeling with what Melanie had so far revealed. With determination, he mentally stepped back a pace, shaking himself, telling himself that this beautiful woman before him was Mel . . . his Mel . . . his cabbie.

"I assume that your father's financial situation never improved. Is that why you finally returned to England?"

"Yes, and within the year, both Mama and Papa were gone."

Justin slammed the table in a release of emotion. "Why the deuce didn't you let me help you?" he cried suddenly, the sound almost squeezed from his throat in his frustration. "Deuce take it, Melanie, you sent money to *me* instead!"

"There were many reasons, my lord," she said softly, each sound thrumming against his senses in the way that her words always did. "I thought at the time that your father was still alive. I knew nothing of Papa's relationship to him except that Papa did not wish to see him or communicate with him, fearful that such an occurrence would be too degrading, and I could not find it in myself to go against his wishes, even after his death. And then, Simon and I had always been on our own. We had learned to take care of ourselves. When I was confronted with the staggering debt my father owed, I knew only two things: I must do all I could to see the debt paid, and then I must find a way to keep us alive."

Justin sat forward again, scrubbing a hand across his face. "And so you became a cabbie."

"Yes," Melanie replied, regarding him with no hint of shame. "I was quite good with horses by the time I left India, and driving a cab seemed the ideal solution. I purchased used men's clothing in Houndsditch and learned from the Hicks and Pollards to speak Cockney like the lower classes in the Rookery. Then I drove a rented hackney until I could save enough to buy my own hansom cab."

"But a man with his own cab earns a fair living, Mel," Justin argued, "so why remain in the Rookery? Why did you not take a small house in a modest neighborhood?" His exasperated gesture swept the tiny room. "Why are you still living like this?"

"It is because of me," Simon interjected softly, gazing at the top of Melanie's head. "Melanie has given everything up for me."

"No, Simon," Melanie interrupted, placing her hand upon his.

"I will say it, Melanie," Simon insisted. "She has given up her life, her rightful place in Society, for me."

Justin stiffened, and then nodded again. Simon had spoken the truth, and he was well aware of it. As much as it repelled him, he had no choice but to acknowledge it. Gritting his teeth, he breathed, "Why?"

"So that I can regain what was lost to me," Simon told him, swallowing hard, his Adam's Apple bobbing helplessly. "She saves every farthing she can so that I can go to university. It is the only way we could think of to put me in the way of earning enough money to restore the Westbridge properties and some measure of honor to my title and name."

Justin stared at the lad for long moments, nodding with perfect understanding. He knew only too well the imperative of an unimpeachable honor and an untainted name. Suddenly he rose to his feet and began to pace, his thoughts settling, rejecting, settling again; finally coalescing around the solution. They were his cousins, second cousins to be precise, but still they were of his family. He could not deny his responsibility toward them anymore now than he could have when they had first returned home from India. And, yes, Melanie had put herself beyond the pale, but he believed there was a way . . . Deuce take it, he would make there be a way . . .

The earl stopped in his tracks and wheeled around toward the table, fixing the two with determined eyes. Gesturing toward their surroundings, he said, "In the first place, this cannot continue. You are my cousins, of my rank. No matter what plans you have made for your future, they are over as of this day. You, Melanie, are no longer a cabbie, and you, Simon, no longer—"

"Sweep street crossings," the boy said, grinning sheepishly.

"The deuce," the earl muttered on a heavy sigh. "No, you definitely no longer sweep street crossings. You are the Earl of Westbridge. From now on you shall comport yourself accordingly."

"And when our savings run out," Melanie countered tartly, "what do you command us to eat?"

Justin's gaze snared hers, glittering. "You shall not be spending a farthing of your precious horde, cousin," he told her with a triumphant grin, "for, in the second place, I am taking you both home to live with me."

Unexpectedly, Melanie shot to her feet, her eyes fairly blazing with copper sparks. Justin absorbed them, caught fire, reveled in the heat.

"I agree that Simon should go with you, my lord," she stated tensely, "but surely you realize that I can no longer go about in Society. Even the hint of how I and my parents lived our lives in India would be enough to not only put a period to any social aspirations I might have, but also to your standing in the *ton*. It does not bear thinking of, should anyone discover I was a cabbie! This must be my life now, my lord. I made my choice long ago. I shall stay."

"Make another decision, Melanie," Justin replied through gritted teeth. "That one does not please me."

Melanie laughed softly. "I do beg your pardon, my lord, but that does not signify. I have always known that when Simon took his rightful place among his peers, I would have to separate myself from his life. I thought to have another year or so with him, but . . . but it is right that he be with you. I give him into your care gladly."

Simon, too, bolted to his feet. "Deuce take it, Melanie," he declared hotly. "I am too old for you to be deciding my fate for me. As long as you stay here, so shall I."

"Simon—"

"Cease trying to sway me, Melanie," Simon scolded. "I shall not leave you alone."

"Simon, this is ridiculous—"

"Cease, please, both of you," the earl interrupted, rubbing his thumb and finger over the bridge of his nose. Returning to his chair, he looked long at Melanie, then took her hand, pulling her into her seat again. "You have sacrificed everything for Simon," he stated softly, his gaze warmly intense. "Sacrifice one more time."

"What do you mean?" she breathed, jolted as she always was by his touch.

"I think perhaps that, having grown up outside the country, you might not quite understand the *haute monde,* my dear."

"In what way?" she asked quietly.

"To your way of thinking, an education is the solution to Simon's problems, and in many respects it will help greatly, but the truth is that the *ton* is, on the whole, a shallow, self-absorbed, ignorant bunch, who consider someone who has earned his wealth in trade, even if titled, as rather beneath the rest of them."

Melanie's gaze dropped to their clasped hands and then rose again slowly. "Tell me plainly, my lord," she said with enticing huskiness, "what are you trying to say?"

"That Simon will be at a far greater advantage if he is under my aegis and is introduced into Society by me."

"But I know that already, my lord," Melanie asserted. "I do not object to his going to live with you."

"Ah, but he will not go without you, my dear," Justin said with a soft smile.

"My final sacrifice?"

"Yes."

Melanie's copper-colored eyes grew liquid. "But what of my past?" she whispered.

Justin surprised her with a mischievous half-smile. "Quite simple really," he stated impishly. "We lie."

Simon burst out laughing.

"Lie?" Melanie cried.

"Well, only a little," Justin grinned. "It is not a lie that you are my cousins, nor that you were brought up in another country. It is also true that you have a legitimate title, Simon, and a perfect right to go about in Society. As to what you have been up to for the past eight years, well . . ." the earl said, rubbing his early-morning stubble.

"We could have been living on our father's sugar plantation in the West Indies!" Simon offered.

"I think not, cousin," Justin said, shaking his head with a smile. "Best to keep our lie as simple as possible. How about our saying that you have been residing at one of my smaller estates all this time?"

"They will wonder why you have not given me a Season," Melanie stated tersely. "I *am* three-and-twenty, quite on the shelf as far as the *ton* is concerned."

"Damme, I forgot about that."

"Well, then, we shall say it was because of me," Simon offered. "That is not far from the truth either. We could say that I was so blue-deviled at the loss of our parents that Melanie felt compelled to stay with me."

Justin glanced at Melanie and smiled at the oddly hopeful look in her eyes. "Very well, my poor, Friday-faced Simon, that is what the story shall be. And I shall see to your education. You are not to worry on that score. And from now until your majority, I shall personally guide you in learning to invest in the 'Change wisely."

"Devil a bit!" Simon responded enthusiastically. "I shall need to know that most of all if I am to restore our properties."

"Simon," Melanie said, laying a restraining hand upon his arm, "do not rush your fences, little brother. We only have our savings. It is quite a paltry sum to invest."

Justin's eyes gleamed above his broad smile. "But not when you add it to the funds I am holding for you," he said. When his two cousins merely stared at him in astonishment, he laughed. "Have you forgotten the money you sent me, Melanie? Your three hundred pounds has compounded quite nicely over the past eight years."

"But—"

"It is yours," Justin told her softly. "You see? Even after all these years, I have never really stopped hoping to find my cousin. Come now, gather your belongings. We shall leave for Stonegate House immediately."

Melanie flushed, overwhelmed. She turned slightly and cast a quick glance at Simon. His face was wary. It came to her then. They neither one of them had a stitch of proper clothing. A look of understanding passed between them, and then she smiled supportingly. "It will be fine, Simon," she urged softly. "Go behind the blanket and dress in your better clothes."

He nodded hesitantly, then turned and disappeared around the makeshift curtain. Melanie rose gracefully, glancing up at Stonegate before crossing to the small trunk and opening it. With great care, she placed two miniatures of her parents inside along with a small, precious collection of books. After she had done that, she took her cabbie's clothing from the pegs near the door, folded each item neatly, and lay them, too, inside. Her white tablecloth came next, followed by her carefully hoarded silverware. And last, after Simon emerged from behind the blanket in strapped, lavender-gray trousers, a violet satin waistcoat, and a black long-skirted cutaway, she took his street clothing from him, placed it, too, inside the trunk, and deftly latched the lid in place.

Justin suddenly smiled ruefully. "I am sorry, Melanie," he said kindly. "Had I known ahead of time who I might find in this garret, I would have brought extra packing cases. It does not signify, however. We shall send someone for your other things as soon as we arrive at Stonegate House."

Melanie smiled sweetly. "What is left belongs to the Pollards and the Hicks, my lord," she explained. "They loaned us many things."

"But your clothing . . . ?"

Melanie flushed crimson and dropped her gaze. Then, proudly, she raised her head. "What I own, my lord, I have already packed or am wearing."

Justin stilled, comprehension coming suddenly. "I see."

The earl's heart kicked against his ribs. Seeing his cousin standing before him so filled with pride, so strong and brave, melted something within him. Not the coldness. Not the ice. That had disappeared days ago when he had first met Mel, the cabbie. No, this was different. He could not put a name to it, but it felt as if his heart had swelled. At that moment, he wanted nothing more than to draw Melanie into his arms, tuck her soft, midnight curls under his chin as he had done before, and, for the rest of his life, keep her there, warm and safe.

But nothing was more impossible, he knew, reality lancing through him on a pang of bitterness. She had put herself beyond the pale. She was ruined. He could never link her past to the Mayhew name. And yet he wanted her, craved her, more than any woman he had ever known. He could acknowledge that fact to himself now. She stirred his senses with every glance, every touch, every word she spoke. But, unless he was willing to make her his mistress, she was lost to him.

Even as the thought came, he dismissed it. She was his cousin . . . family, deuce take it! After all she had given up for her brother, she deserved a home and children of her own, and even though it would probably destroy him, he knew it was his responsibility to see to it. He would have to endure the torture of countless courtships, a betrothal to someone worthy but less hampered by propriety, and in the end, give her into the hands of that other man. The thought twisted knots into the muscles of his abdomen.

And then it occurred to him. Bloody hell.

She was already betrothed to him.

# Seven

Perhaps she was never told of the betrothal, Stonegate pondered seven days later as his gaze once again drifted toward his cousin with the dogged tenacity of iron filings seeking north. She was seated across from him in the rented brougham, happily chattering away with Angela as if a gaggle of geese had taken up residence in her mouth. He smiled slightly. She couldn't know how he detested female chittering. Yet, somehow, coming as the irritating noise did from a voice that coated his nerve endings like warm, husky honey, he did not think the sin quite so bad. She was nervous, of course. In a very few minutes they would arrive at the Fremont's ball . . . her first brush with polite society . . . and the ruse into which his entire household had readily entered would at last be put to the test.

At least she should show to advantage, he thought, and then he chewed his inner lip at that plumper. Show to advantage? She was an Incomparable. Dressed in a new gown of pale rose satin whose waist-hugging bodice, wide, puffy sleeves, and belled skirt were overlaid with yards of filmy, delicate lace in a rich shade of burgundy, she had so stunned him when she had come down the stairs earlier that he had hardly been able to speak. The uncertainty in her eyes had told him that his aloof reception had shaken her, but he had been powerless to reassure her. The struggle to maintain a proper distance from her had become almost more than he could handle. Even now, seated so that their knees occasionally jostled against one another, his whole body still tingled with the need to touch, to caress.

Perhaps her father had forgotten to mention the betrothal. *She* certainly had, he thought with chagrin. He had been on tenterhooks the entire week since her removal to his home, waiting for her to demand her proper place in his life as his intended. Yet she had said nothing. A part of him felt immense relief. A larger part of him wanted to shake her soundly, crush his mouth against hers, and demand every right their betrothal gave him.

She had no idea what her presence in his house was doing to him . . . soft laughter that seeped into his study from the morning room next door when she, Angela, and his mother were enjoying tea together, ensorcelling his brain; molten eyes that would catch the muted candlelight in the dining room and burn a path straight to his groin when she suddenly looked up at him; and that voice . . . a bedroom voice that entwined in and around his nerve endings until he was nearly reduced to whimpers, a voice made to be unleashed into a man's mouth when he had brought her to her completion and was buried deep inside her. She was driving him insane.

Perhaps he should be the one to bring up the subject of the betrothal to her. He was, after all, the man. And they had to discuss it sooner or later. He knew she would understand why he could not honor it. She had acknowledged her state of social ruin herself. But what if she really had never been told of the arrangement? If that were so, then his dredging the whole matter up and then rejecting her might hurt her doubly. Deuce take it, she had had enough suffering!

He would wait. Yes, that was the only decent thing to do.

Of course, it would mean delaying his plans for marriage, but he had not made a commitment in that direction yet. Later . . . yes, much later . . . when Melanie had found a new and proper direction for her life, he would explain everything to Miss Parkes. As sweet and kind as she was, he had no doubt that she would understand.

Things were going well for Simon, at least. Justin had almost immediately enrolled him in the coming Michaelmas term at Oxford, then introduced him to several of his acquaintances' younger brothers who would soon be his classmates. Simon, a much more mature and accepting friend than most of his peers, had taken well; so much so that it had become a common lament that if one wished to see him, one had to be prepared to keep watch in the pantry, the one place in the house where he appeared with any regularity. But that was as it should be. Justin could not complain. Simon had missed so much that his title should have secured for him; yet he was a healthy, well-favored lad. Because of Melanie.

Melanie. The delicate scent of roses came to him subtly, from under and around Angela's heavier fragrance. Again his gaze lifted, drifted, locked with hers . . . heated coal fused with liquid copper. He watched as her lips parted, sticking slightly to each other, slowly released. Melanie.

Suddenly the carriage jolted to a stop, scattering Justin's musings like the puddle of ordure splashing under its wheel.

"Ah, here we are at last," said Angela, turning toward her cousin. "Melanie, pinch your cheeks just a bit, dear . . . that's right. And bite your lips . . . good."

"What is that for?" Melanie asked as her features grew flushed and kissable. Justin swallowed. Hard.

Angela eyed the earl consideringly. "I believe I shall let Justin tell you," she replied, grinning widely. In spite of his sudden scowl, she continued, "Now, brother dear, if you would be so good as to hand us down, we shall proceed to take the *ton* by storm."

Shaking his head to clear it, Justin collected his scattered wits and did as he was told.

The ballroom of the Fremont mansion in Upper Brook Street had been decorated to suggest a summer scene at Brighton. Gaily colored murals depicting the houses and walks along the Steyne had been fastened along one wall, while another held a representation of the Chain Bridge, its huge pulley wheel converted into a device for carrying champagne to the dancers. At the far end of the room was a depiction of the Royal Pavilion built by the old Prince Regent, situated so that when entering the supper room, it appeared as if one were entering the Pavilion itself. Carrying through with the theme, the supper room had been decorated in the Chinese style that had so fascinated the Prince and had influenced so much of the Royal Pavilion's own interiors.

"Ohh!" gasped Melanie as Justin paused at the entrance while the major domo announced them. "How lovely it all is!"

Justin smiled indulgently, then escorted her and Angela through the door. "Melanie, my dear, poke your beautiful eyes back inside your head. You are a lady of the *haut ton* now. Such open admiration must be beneath you."

"Never say so!" Melanie exclaimed in an expression she had readily picked up from Angela over the past week. "Does no one praise the hostess for all her efforts?"

"Of course," Justin responded, "but with great subtlety."

"Oh?"

"Indeed yes," Justin said knowledgeably. "One might glance casually about the room and say, 'Charming. Quite charming,' to one's hostess, or perhaps request to meet the caterers for the event. But if one wishes to give the highest of compliments, one asks the hostess for the name of the man who did her decorations."

"Why is that the highest compliment?" Melanie asked, genuinely intrigued, and completely oblivious to the rapt stares of most of the men present.

"Because the decorations require the greatest expense," the earl answered, quite sensible of the spellbound male interest. Drawing Melanie's elbow against his side, he frowned quellingly at the deuced upstarts. Then, letting his gaze sweep the room, he located Lord Palmerton and his family standing near the punch bowl and immediately nudged the two women in their direction.

Melanie's gaze grew thoughtful. "I see now why you name Society as shallow, my lord," she commented softly.

"Mmm," Justin agreed, scowling away several more young men who called out to him for introductions as they passed by.

"Justin, if you are squeezing Melanie's elbow as tightly as you are squeezing mine," Angela whispered with an uncontained grin from his other side, "we shall both be black and blue."

"Oh, sorry," he apologized, loosening his clenched fists. "But have you seen the leers on these bounders' faces?"

"Of course I have," Angela chuckled. "It is wonderful. It means that Melanie is taking."

"Damn it, Angela, I do not want her tak—!"

Justin's feet stopped moving. He stood silently, rigid with dismay.

"My lord?" Melanie inquired softly from his other side, turning toward him.

"Go on. Say it, Justin," Angela urged quietly. "The word is taken."

"Is something wrong?" Melanie asked more firmly.

Justin looked at her, breathing deeply for control. His very soul leaned toward her. Finally, at great cost, he replied, "No, my dear, nothing is wrong. Come, I wish for you to meet Miss Parkes." Walking like a condemned man, Justin closed the distance between himself and the woman to whom he would soon offer himself up like a sacrifice on the altar of marriage, a noble, duty-bound offering to the damnable god of propriety.

"Ah, Lady D'Antry," Lord Palmerton said, making his leg to her as they approached, "and Stonegate. How good to see you this evening. I say, you are looking quite fit after your ordeal, sir. Cannot say the same for Stanley, however. Poor lad has had to give up Society for the nonce. His arm must remain braced for another week at least."

"Yes, I should imagine that a broken bone would take a bit longer than a mere flesh wound to heal," Justin stated as he made his bow. "May I present my cousin to you, sir . . . Lady Melanie Baxter."

"Miss Baxter," Palmerton replied with a courtly bow, "and may I present my wife, Lady Palmerton, and daughter, Eunice," he finished, gesturing toward each one in turn.

"I am delighted to meet you," Melanie replied, curtseying politely and trying very hard not to focus her gaze upon Miss Parkes.

She was so lovely. Dressed in a gown of honey-colored satin embellished with bands and bows of blue satin and wide flounces of ecru lace about the hem and neckline, she was a vision of elegant propriety. Melanie stole a glance at her placid, smiling face. Smooth, clear, and unlined, she looked like a perfect, dew-kissed bud about to unfurl. So different from Bess's complexion, craggy and careworn far beyond her years, though she was sure the two were of an age.

Her thoughts turned to Gran and Bess then. She had

visited them earlier in the day in spite of Stonegate's injunction that she and Simon must never return again to Portpool Lane. She knew that if anyone ever saw her and recognized her it would be the end of everything, but she had promised Bess to attend her during her laying-in, and the time was fast approaching. And Gran was worsening. She had to take the risk. She could not turn her back on any of the Pollards or Hickses. They had done so much for Simon and her when they were in need. They were not merely landlords; they were the dearest of friends.

"I have been most anxious to meet you, Miss Baxter," Eunice said in an almost inaudible voice, drawing Melanie's thoughts back to the present. "Lord Stonegate has told me much about you and your past circumstance."

Melanie glanced quickly up at Justin, wary of what he might have said. His gaze remained resolutely upon Miss Parkes. She wondered at that, felt slightly hurt, but dismissed the feelings quickly. This was the woman he would marry. And she was beautiful. Of course he would want to look at no one but her.

"That was most kind in him," she replied, her own gaze returning to Miss Parkes. "My cousin is aware that I do not care to speak of my past. How thoughtful of him to tell my tale for me." She felt Justin's glance flicker toward her then. She smiled sweetly, feeling oddly smug in his startled attention.

"Then, of course, we shall say no more about it," Miss Parkes vowed kindly.

"Would you care for refreshment, Miss Parkes?" Justin offered quickly, a bit wary of the present course of the conversation.

"Why . . . yes, thank you, sir," she replied. "A glass of lemonade, perhaps?"

"Of course. But I have one remaining hand," Justin told

the rest of their party, glancing around with a grin. "Would another of you ladies care for something?" He received three negative replies. "Very well, then, please excuse me."

"Do hurry, Stonegate," Lady Palmerton called after him. "They are beginning to form up the squares for the opening quadrille." The lady glanced pointedly, then, at her daughter. "I am certain that you have not yet signed your name to any young lady's dance card."

"Mama, please," Miss Parkes cried softly, blushing. "You are the one who told me not to rush my fences!" She glanced toward Melanie then, suddenly conscious of the other's presence and somewhat suspicious.

Melanie flushed and glanced away, edging more closely to Angela's side. Subtly, amid the voluminous folds of their gowns, Angela reached over and took her hand reassuringly. "She is a sweet child, is she not?" she observed only to her.

"Yes . . . quite the loveliest woman at the ball," Melanie agreed, squeezing Angela's fingers in return as she glanced about the room.

"Mmm, would you care to make a wager on that, cousin?" Angela grinned, letting her gaze rove the room as well before returning to Melanie.

"What do you mean?"

"Look about the room once again, Melanie," she whispered. "The young men have just been waiting for my brother to leave your side so that they might have their chance at you."

"At me?" Melanie breathed in astonishment. "Oh, no, Angela. Surely their gazes are directed toward Miss Parkes. She is standing quite close to me."

Angela laughed softly. "You may think what you will, of course," she told her. "But if were you, I should brace myself for the onslaught, my dear. It is not Miss Parkes they are about to inundate. It is you."

Melanie's eyes widened. Every male eye in the room seemed to be focused on her. She turned slightly to look behind her, sure that a diamond of the first water was standing there, and Angela laughed brightly.

"Cousin," Melanie breathed, "what do I do?"

"You dance, Melanie," Angela whispered, slipping a supporting arm about her waist. "Tonight is your night. For once in your life, be selfish, my dear. Allow yourself to enjoy all of it."

Almost before she could nod, Melanie was duly inundated.

Justin returned from the punch table to find Angela waiting for him alone. "Where is everyone?" he asked, feeling somewhat foolish standing with a glass of lemonade in his hand.

Angela nodded toward the sedately moving squares. "Here, give that glass to me. You look a bit discomposed."

"Melanie is dancing?" he scowled. "Deuce take it, I made no introductions!"

"No, but I did," his sister grinned. "It was the most amazing thing, Justin. Her card was filled within minutes . . . nay, seconds, I should say. Miss Parkes is also dancing, by the way."

"Filled, you say?" Justin responded. "She did not save a dance for me?"

Angela bit her inner cheek with glee. "Why would you think she would, Justin?" she asked. "You have been frowning at her since she stepped into the hall earlier. Were I her, you would be the last person I would think would care to dance with me."

"What rubbish!" he growled. "All she had to do was ask."

Angela barely stifled a giggle. "I do beg your pardon, Justin, but it has always been my impression that it is the gentleman's responsibility to do that."

"Drink your lemonade, Angela," replied Justin, his frown softening into chagrin.

The ball became interminable. Justin could count on the fingers of one hand the number of times he danced that evening: twice with Miss Parkes, twice with Angela, and once with Lady Palmerton. He drank; he paced. He stared hotly while scoundrel after scoundrel pulled Melanie far closer to their obvious erections than was proper during waltz after damnable waltz.

He all but dragged Miss Parkes over to the table next to hers during the supper break, consuming a plate of something he could not have named if the Inquisition had asked it of him, while he watched her laugh with her partner and flirt. Flirt! He excused himself with poor grace when the dancing began again and took himself off to the card room, thinking that if he just did not have to watch her he could throw off this insanity, but by the time he had lost a pony at whist, he knew that it was no use. He could stand it no longer. He listened for the last strains of the ending gallop, pushed away from the card table, and strode back into the ball room with a determined gleam in his eye, immediately spotting her among the milling dancers by the masculine horde that enveloped her.

"My dance next, I believe," he forced out from between clenched teeth as he came to a halt by her side.

Melanie started slightly, and then gaped up at him. Quickly regaining her composure, she replied, "I am sorry, my lord, but this waltz is promised to Lord Cuthbert. He is coming this way now."

"Indeed," Justin replied, elevating a haughty brow. Immediately, he whirled around to stare coldly at the approaching gentleman, unleashing upon the hapless fellow all the raw, primitive challenge of a powerful male animal protecting his preserve. The man's stride faltered, came to a slow halt. He blinked twice, then smiled placatingly, slowly raising his palms as he backed away. Again the earl turned to face Melanie, giving her that same possessive stare.

"It seems you are free," he told her quite distinctly, and then escorted her onto the ballroom floor.

Melanie's heart began to thunder from the moment Stonegate placed his warm palm at her waist, took her other hand in his, and began to sweep her in slow, sensual swirls around and around to the strains of the newest offering from Strauss. His warm brown eyes pierced into hers, holding her gaze captive as, behind him, the ballroom melted into a kaleidoscopic blur. She was stunned by her reaction to his nearness, fought against it. She felt frightened and vulnerable.

"Why are you doing this, my lord?" she cried softly.

Moved by her obvious distress, Justin gentled his hold. "What, dancing?" he replied, trying for lightheartedness.

"Yes! With me! I thought you were angry," she told him quietly.

Justin breathed deeply. "No, not angry," he said. "Confused, perhaps, but not angry."

"Because of Simon and me?" she questioned softly, her eyes a firestorm in her vulnerability.

The earl shook his head. "Because the things that I wish for are not always the things I may have," he confessed obliquely.

"It is the same for me," she told him with a tender smile. "For everyone I should think."

"And what do you wish for, Melanie?" he asked her, slowing his turns.

"For Simon to resume his rightful place," she answered quickly.

"Ah, but that has already been accomplished," Justin reminded her. "I am interested in what you wish for yourself."

"I cannot say," she responded, tucking her bead almost beneath his chin.

"Cannot or will not? he prodded.

"Will not," she stated firmly, again lifting her copper-colored gaze to his. "It does no good to dwell upon what cannot be, my lord."

The earl stared into her eyes for long moments, his jaw muscles moving, rolling. "Why do you never call me Justin?" he finally asked.

"What?" Melanie gasped, thoroughly disconcerted by his change of direction.

"Why do you never call me Justin?" he repeated. "Simon does."

"I cannot," she responded, her breath soft against his neck.

"Cannot or will not?" the earl teased with a grin.

Melanie answered his smile. Justin's abdomen tightened. "Both," she responded after a short time.

The earl's grin faded. "Why?"

"Because we are not equals, my lord," she responded quietly.

"What rot!" Justin said with irritation. "You are the daughter and sister of earls. Your rank matches mine perfectly."

Melanie's gaze softened and she drew back slightly. "I am a cabbie, my lord," she whispered evenly.

Confronted once again by the truth he wished desperately to deny, Justin's pulse began to pound against his throat. His hand tightened at Melanie's waist, drawing her almost against him as his other hand squeezed hers painfully. He began to turn, then, swirling her around the floor faster and faster, his eyes never leaving hers, filled with all the hopelessness they both knew stood between them. The lights around them dimmed, and still they spun relentlessly, round and round, until darkness enshrouded them.

Justin came to his senses quite suddenly as a cool breeze touched his face. Without being aware of it, he had danced Melanie onto the adjoining terrace. He slowed, then, as he turned her into deeper shadows, and came to a stop, his hand carrying hers to his shoulder while his other arm drew her tightly against his body. Her skin was blue-white in the moonlight; her eyes chips of copper fire. His body clenched with his wanting, his discipline dissipating like mists on an autumn morning as he looked at her.

"I have tried, Melanie," he breathed, his hand rising to touch trembling fingertips to the softness of her cheek. "From the beginning, from the first day I met you, I have tried. But I cannot keep from touching you . . . holding you . . . any longer."

"My lord . . ." Melanie gasped shakily, leaning into his strength.

"Justin," the earl urged her. "Please. Just for tonight, if that is all I can have, please call me Justin, Melanie."

Melanie was helpless against her own response to the earl's plea. Slipping her arms around his neck, she raised her face toward his and whispered, "Oh, Justin . . ."

On a groan, the earl's lips covered hers, gently at first, teaching her, tasting, then, dissatisfied, growing more and more ardent until his tongue pressed between her teeth and she was filled with him, her body vibrant, taut with her burgeoning response. Melanie clung to him as the world receded and the only awareness remaining was focused at each sensitized place on her body where it touched against his. Instinctively, she pressed closer, trying to meld with him, to become one with his trembling essence, to soothe his desperate need.

He gasped at her offering, arching over her, his mouth moving against hers with an almost mindless passion. His hands formed her flesh, discovering hip, breast, possessing greedily, gentling to caress with solemn reverence. At last, when he knew that to go further would dishonor her completely, he summoned what few shreds remained of his honor as a gentleman and loosened his hold on her.

"Oh, God, Mel," he said, his forehead pressed to hers, his breath buffeting her face. "I love you. God help me, I love you."

"Oh, no, Justin," she whispered in agony, beginning to cry, "you cannot. You must not."

"But I do," he said with a rueful half-smile. "Oh, love, do not cry," he pleaded, wiping her tears away with his thumbs. "Instead, tell me you love me, too."

"Oh, no, I can never . . ." she responded, shaking her curls violently.

"Say it," he commanded. "I know that you do."

"No! It can never be!" she cried desperately.

Justin released her, stung. Stepping back a pace, his handsome features hardened and clenched.

"I know," he said finally. "But that changes nothing of how I feel, how I shall always feel about you. I shall always love you, Melanie. You may reject my feelings, my own dear heart, but at least I had the courage to admit them to you."

Melanie turned away, then, swallowing back her sobs. At last, when she was again able to speak, she turned and faced him again, her eyes a flood of copper fire.

"These feelings are not new to me. I have always loved you," she said with soft poignancy, "since I was but a child in leading strings. You . . . you were my hope through all those bleak years, a prince charming who would one day rescue Simon and me. And you did, did you not, my lord? But too late . . . God help us both, you came too late for me."

Justin's head dropped back, his chest heaving with the effort to control his own emotions, with his need to rage at the wall of convention that stood between them, at his father's mandate which would keep them apart forever. His hands fisted impotently at his sides. "I never felt anything until you came into my life," he rasped. "God, how I wish for more of that damnable ice!"

Melanie reached toward him, then let her hand drop back to her side. There was nothing more to be said. Perhaps too much had been said already. Rubbing the remaining dampness from her cheeks, she said, "We should go back inside."

Justin looked at her and then nodded, his eyes dark with defeat. "Yes. I have kept you out here alone far too long, have I not?" A short, mirthless laugh escaped him. "How unlike me to overstep the bounds of propriety." Taking her elbow gently into his warm palm, he gave her one last speaking glance, and then turned her toward the lights of the ballroom.

Moments later, fingertips pressed to whitened lips, Miss Parkes traced their steps.

# Eight

"How am I to bear it?" Eunice sobbed into her lace-edged handkerchief during breakfast the following morning in the Green Street dining room. "Stonegate is paying court to me, but he is in love with her!"

"There, there, now, darling," Lady Palmerton soothed, stirring milk into her tea. "I am persuaded it was quite dark on the terrace. Perhaps things were not as they seemed."

"I am quite sensible of what was going on between them, Mama," Eunice insisted adamantly. "He was kissing her like—like—"

"A mere cousinly kiss, perhaps," her father offered.

"It was not!" Eunice vowed hotly. "And I know what I heard. He told her again and again that he loved her. What am I to do?"

"Cease making a cake of yourself, Eunice," Stanley ordered indolently from his position across from her. "Undoubtedly, Stonegate is enjoying the chit's charms while she resides under his roof. Obviously, for high sticklers such as he, a single mistress is not enough."

Lord Palmerton shot a quelling glance toward his son. "Try not to let your ignorance show quite so often, Stanley, if you please. No man of Stonegate's reputation would take a member of his own family into his bed, and certainly not with both his mother and sister in residence."

"Papa, please!" cried Miss Parkes, sniffing prettily. "Have a care for my sensibilities!"

"Give over, Eunice!" the earl reprimanded. "You are not fresh out of the schoolroom. A man of Stonegate's age has women in his life before he marries. That is a fact of which you are well aware, so cease your waterworks. The question is, what shall we do about this latest little peccadillo, hmm?"

"Must we do anything?" Lady Palmerton asked, wafting a fan before her face. "He is still a most desirable *parti,* after all, and I am certain he will give up these flirtations once he is wed to Eunice. La, how could any man possibly sigh after another when he is in possession of our daughter's beauty?"

"Just so," the earl agreed. "His infatuation for his cousin cannot last. She is a taking little thing, to be sure, but no match for Eunice's classic looks. No, daughter, my advice is to stay the course. Offer yourself as a wholly proper contrast to his loose cousin and you shall soon have your declaration."

*"And* the wealth and power at your fingertips to see to it that he never dallies again," her mother added sweetly, glancing toward her husband. "Your father is right, dearest. Continue as you have been, conducting yourself with kindness and the utmost decorum, and, I vow, you shall be his countess before the end of the Season. Now, dry your tears; enough of this pother. Reginald," she said, setting down her cup and folding her serviette beside her plate, "you have promised to look over my plans for the new orchard this morning. Shall you do so now?"

"As always, my dear, I await your pleasure," Lord Palmerton replied, rounding the table to assist her from her chair. "But before we go, remember this, Eunice," he added, turning back slightly, "nothing has really changed. Stonegate knows the value of this marriage not only to him, but to his family. He will not wish to forsake his pursuit of you for an impoverished cousin. And take my word for it, my dear, his avowals of love to another woman before his marriage mean nothing. Why, once you and he are wed, one smile from you will have him eating from the palm of your hand." With a confident grin, Lord Palmerton winked at his daughter's tear-laved pout, then turned again to follow his wife from the room.

"Papa seems so certain of that," Eunice said into the quiet that settled over the room after her parents' departure.

"He has good reason to be," Stanley responded, smoothing jam upon a slice of toast. "Our father had three mistresses at the time of his marriage."

"Stanley!" Eunice gasped, her gaze locking with his. "How can you know such a thing?"

"Do not act so shocked, Eunice," her brother grinned. "Men say all sorts of things at their clubs. One only has to keep one's ears open."

"Stanley, really!"

Eunice dropped her gaze to study the scum forming on the surface of her cup of tea, her curiosity over Stanley's casual comment building to the point of temptation. Slowly, hesitantly, her focus slid again to center upon her brother.

"Has . . . Has anyone in your clubs, by any chance, mentioned Miss Baxter's name?" she asked delicately.

Stanley's grin widened. "Why, sister!" he exclaimed. "Could you actually be contemplating what it seems?"

"Stanley, do not mock me," Eunice pouted, sipping tea. "I am very concerned about her. You did not see the way he was embracing her on the terrace last evening."

Stanley took a bite of his toast and chewed, his grin slowly fading. "Eunice, there is really no need for concern," he finally said flatly. "Papa is right. Stonegate walks as straight as an arrow. Even his brother, Oliver, begrudged his rigid propriety. He will put the chit away from him as soon as he weds you, and he will not stray."

"I am not so certain of that," Eunice replied. "Some of the things that were said . . ."

"What things?" Stanley asked, his attention instantly centering upon his sister's face.

"It was as if there were something . . ." Eunice told him, "something that was keeping them apart. Miss Baxter said she had been counting upon him to save her but he had not . . . that he had come too late."

Stanley grinned wickedly. "Now what do you suppose our very proper earl was too late to save the lady from?"

"I have no idea," Eunice replied, sagging back against her chair.

Stanley took another bite of toast and stared at his plate thoughtfully. Suddenly he looked up. "You realize that if we found out, my dear," he said, fixing her with his gaze, "Miss Baxter might not be the only one whose reputation would suffer."

"Meaning?"

"Meaning that if there is something in her past . . . something scandalous . . . and if Stonegate knew about it, not only would Miss Baxter be shunned by the *ton,* but the earl himself might find himself beyond the pale. You have made no secret of your expectations concerning him among your acquaintances, Eunice. What would you do if the man everyone knew you were angling for suddenly found himself *de trop?*"

Eunice thought for a moment, pursing her lips as she inspected a fingernail, skimming the ecru foam from the rim of her teacup with her spoon. Long seconds passed, and then she shrugged. "I would have no choice, would l?" she replied matter-of-factly. "I would have to cut him dead."

"And you are willing to take the risk that that very thing might occur?" her brother questioned softly.

"It seems I have to," Eunice replied tersely. "I would never possess him anyway as long as that woman was a part of his life."

Stanley leaned back in his own chair, smugly satisfied. "Then keep your eyes open, my dear," he replied, his eyes gleaming. "The weapon we need to wield against Miss Baxter is out there somewhere. In time we shall discover it. One way or another, the chit's days in Town are numbered. You may depend upon it."

Bounding down the stairs for breakfast at Stonegate House the morning after the ball, Justin came to an abrupt halt as he entered the huge hall. The room was filled with lavish bouquets. Stunned, he stopped for a moment to touch a finger to one of the blooms and then read the attached card. Cartilage at the joining of his jaw rolled and bulged.

They were for Melanie. Every deuced one of them, he was certain. If he had entertained any thoughts about whether or not Society would find her acceptable, he now knew that he had been daft to doubt. His heart tripped possessively. A rose petal, perfect in its pink blush, broke free from its blossom and fell to the carpet near his foot. Justin eyed its delicate translucence momentarily, and then ground it beneath his boot. He had to face the fact, he knew. Somewhere, among all those dozens of bouquets, the one sent by her future husband undoubtedly reposed. The very concept constricted around his throat like a taut noose.

Several brisk steps took him the rest of the way across the hall to the dining room, where a wide-eyed footman grabbed for the doorknob and then sprang back out of the way of his master's stalking progress just as the earl swept by. Justin noted the man's startled expression and slowed, shooting the servant a half-smile of apology before continuing into the room. Self-absorbed, yet conscious that the object of his inner discontent was seated only a few feet away, he murmured a muted greeting to the room at large, strode quickly to the sideboard where he filled a plate, then seated himself at the head of the cloth-covered Chippendale table. A footman immediately filled his coffee cup.

"We were just discussing the plans for our dinner day after tomorrow, darling," Lady Stonegate informed him, setting down her cup to smile at her son. Dressed in a lavender and green plaid taffeta morning gown, and with her thick, graying hair combed smoothly over her ears and drawn into a cluster of curls at the back of her head, the countess was still a woman of commanding beauty.

Justin glanced at her with a soft grin.

"What dinner is that?" he asked, returning his gaze to his plate, spearing a morsel of ham.

"Our dinner for Lord Palmerton and his family, of course," his mother laughed. "Justin, never say that you have forgotten! It is for your benefit, you know."

Justin's gaze flickered involuntarily toward Melanie who was demonstrating a marked absorption in a slice of deviled kidney. "No . . . well, yes, I suppose I had forgotten temporarily. I remember now, however."

Lady Stonegate's dark gaze rested upon her son. "Darling, are you all right? You seem distracted this morning."

"Last night's ball, I misdoubt," Angela offered, her eyes twinkling. "Melanie seems quite put out of countenance as well. But then, with every eligible male of the *ton* fighting for a dance with her, how could a woman not be? Did you notice the hall, Mama? Our cousin was a great success."

"I did indeed, and the flowers are lovely," the countess replied, reaching over to stroke Melanie's blush-abraded cheek. "We are very proud of you, my dear," she said with warm sincerity.

"Thank you," Melanie responded, trying to recall the face of at least one of the young men who had danced with her. Guilt compounded her discomfiture. All she could remember of the evening was the earl's kiss.

"I am persuaded that you younger ones will want to attend the opera as well on the night," the countess continued. "Melanie must certainly enjoy it. I have asked Lord and Lady Palmerton and their family for six so that you might get away on time. They are presenting one of Donizetti's works, are they not? This morning's *Post* said as much."

"Mmm, yes," Angela responded, spreading a muffin with lemon curd. "Her Majesty's Theater is reviving *Lucrezia Borgia,* with the Grisis performing the principal roles."

"How delightful," the countess commented. "Melanie dear, you shall be enthralled by the music and the intrigue. And do not let the open stares of the men present keep you from enjoying the performance. Ignore them, one and all. Besides, they shall think you the most fascinating of women if you do. Have you a suitable gown yet to wear?"

"Oh, yes, ma'am," Melanie replied uneasily, struggling to keep her gaze from darting toward the head of the table. "Lord Stonegate has been most generous. Several new gowns were delivered from the modiste just yesterday."

"Excellent," her ladyship exclaimed. "Was the orange silk among them?"

"Yes, I am certain it was."

Then you must by all means wear it for our dinner party. The design we chose was the *dernier cri,* and it will look exquisite on you, my dear. Now tell me, what are your plans for the day?"

"I believe that I should like to pass a quiet day today, my lady," Melanie told her, hoping that her discomposure in Stonegate's presence did not also reveal how far she was stretching the truth. She did, in fact, intend to spend her day quietly . . . but in the company of Gran and Bess. "I am not yet accustomed to quite so much society."

The lady nodded. "Of course you are not, and you must certainly be tired. I shall instruct Rose to prepare your room for you after luncheon, shall l?"

"Yes, thank you, my lady." Happily settling upon her avenue of escape, at last Melanie smiled.

"And you, Simon dear?" Lady Stonegate asked.

Caught stuffing a fork full of fluffy egg into his mouth from his overladen plate, Simon choked, hastily swallowed, and blushed painfully. He still could not accustom himself to the plentiful abundance of food available in the earl's household. Each meal since his arrival had been an exercise in controlled gluttony. But now, to have drawn the notice of the countess! Bloody hell!

"I shall be out most of the day, ma'am," he answered, smiling sheepishly while avoiding Melanie's scowl.

"Indeed," the countess commented with a warm grin. "And what shall you be out doing, Lord Westbridge?"

Simon fidgeted only slightly before he sensed from the countess's amusement that his social gaffe had been understood and forgiven. He returned to her one of his irrepressible, and most charming, smiles.

"Morty Greenough and Freddie Pierce are taking me to Ackerman's Repository after breakfast. We are to 'see what we can see,' ma'am," he said, easily setting aside the rest of his embarrassment as the thought of another adventure elevated his increasing enthusiasm. "They said one could find anything there."

"I imagine one still can," the earl interjected as he sipped his coffee, "or at Fortnum and Mason."

"I thought that was a grocer's," Simon said with a frown.

"It is that, but still quite interesting," Justin informed him.

"Well, not that I doubt your word, cousin," Simon hedged, "but I do not think Morty and Freddie will find a grocer's as exciting as Boulton's Chop House. We are to go there after Ackerman's. Morty said that his father used to go there, too, with his bows, and they would order a rump and a dozen, and wash it down with a quartern of stingo."

"Simon!" Melanie scolded. "Cant?"

Justin's amused gaze flew toward hers for the first time that morning, caught it, held. Slowly, he elevated one gently arched brow. Melanie knew perfectly well what the earl was thinking, drat the man. He was recalling all too well Mel, the cabbie's, dialect. Her gaze struggled against his; she blushed furiously.

"I cannot like it that you seem to be running wild all over London, Simon," she insisted, tossing the earl a second's worth of glower before she tore her gaze away.

"But, Melanie—"

"Everything you do reflects upon your future in Society, Simon," she told him. "You must be careful."

Justin shifted in his chair, then cleared his throat in interruption. "You are right, of course, my dear. But there is a great deal of life Simon has had to miss because of his past. Do not begrudge him a taste of it, now that he finally has the means."

"But so much is at stake," Melanie argued with more heat. "Everything we have worked for."

"That part of Simon's life is over, Melanie. You have taught him well. Trust in his judgment. He will comport himself properly."

Melanie bristled at the earl's interference, wanted to remind him spitefully that he had not trusted his own brother to such a degree, but she could not sustain her pique. She knew that the earl was right. And, as he had become Simon's guardian, his opinion now held more weight than hers. Yet she could not think ill of it. She had worked eight years for this day. The earl had successfully taken her place, just as they had planned. It only remained now for her to begin the inevitable separation from Simon. She hoped she had the strength.

Slowly, she let her gaze settle upon the earl's. She nodded, her eyes softening, her smile signalling her yielding. She could not shake the warm, sudden daydream that she was wife to this man, arguing over one of their own children, deciding between the two of them what was best for him. She remembered the feel of his arms around her, the pressure of his body, the demand of his lips. He was a part of her, as intimate and familiar as an indrawn breath, and yet he was not . . . could never be. The daydream was impossible. Her gaze returned to her plate.

Lady Stonegate's intent gaze traveled repeatedly between her son and Melanie, slewing then to link with Angela's. She raised one finely sculpted, questioning brow imperceptibly. Angela, understanding her mother's request perfectly, answered in kind. With only the slightest of movements, she smiled at the countess and nodded. Lady Stonegate contemplated the subtle response for a moment, and then grinned.

The countess drew a deep breath. "I am satisfied that

Simon is well launched in his new life," she declared suddenly.

All eyes turned toward her.

"Oh, yes," Melanie responded into the brief silence. "Simon and I are most grateful for all you have done. But I am sensible of the risk our presence poses to you, my lady. I still cannot comprehend why you so willingly agreed to take us in when Lord Stonegate showed up at your drawing room door with us in tow."

"Stuff and nonsense, my dear," the lady replied warmly. "No matter what scandal broth my family managed to get up to, the *ton* knows it cannot harm me. Besides, when Justin informed me that you were dear Philip's children, not for the twentieth part of a moment did it occur to me to deny you your place in our family. You cannot know how much my husband loved your father, my dear, nor how pleased I am that you are now where you belong. It has given me the greatest of joys to set Simon in his rightful place, but I do not think we have done so well by you."

Justin's brow furrowed. "What are you thinking, Mama?"

"That Melanie must be launched as well," the countess replied with satisfaction.

"Of course!" exclaimed Angela, taking her mother's cue. "Mama, we must give our cousin a ball."

"Exactly so," proclaimed Lady Stonegate, glancing at each one present as she drew her cup of tea to her lips.

"Oh, ma'am," cried Melanie, "I cannot think it a good idea—"

"Fustian," the countess corrected. "You must be where the young men of the *ton* can get at you, my dear, and a ball is just the thing."

Justin's cup clattered into his saucer. His mother fought her smile.

"Can you possibly have forgotten, ma'am?" Melanie asked as her eyes flickered toward the startling noise and then back again. "I am a scandal waiting to happen. I cannot afford to place myself under the notice of others."

"Oh, Melanie, my dear," Angela laughed. "Have *you* forgotten the flowers in the hall? I very much fear that it is far too late."

Melanie bit her lower lip. Justin ground his teeth.

Simon's gaze grew tender. "Perhaps nothing would come of it, Melanie . . ." he said softly.

"How can I take that chance?" she cried, rounding on him. "You know what we planned, Simon, and why. None of the *ton* would suspect you of such a ruinous background . . . you were a street sweeper whose head was always tucked safely down. But I have been carrying these people in my hansom for years. Sooner or later, someone will recognize me. That is why we both knew that I could never join you in Society . . . why we planned to separate as soon as it happened. As long as I am with you, you are in jeopardy. You all are! I cannot allow—"

"Hush, Melanie." Justin's words were abrupt, commanding.

Melanie complied instantly, her argument dissipating as her gaze slewed toward the earl in astonishment.

"You shall have your ball," he told her quietly.

Melanie shook her head. "It is a great expense, and . . . and far too dangerous, my lord," she argued.

"It is necessary."

"Why?" she demanded, rising to her feet.

Justin rose with her, towering over her even from several yards away. "Because you deserve your chance, too," he asserted, hands fisting at his sides. "Because you must have a life of your own as well . . . a chance for happiness . . . a husband, children . . . and I cannot—" The earl bit back the rest of his words, his lips tightening against his emotions as his dark gaze sought the frescoed ceiling. In moments, he was again in control. "Because it is quite tedious to be around someone who is so damnably selfless. Deuce take it, Melanie, because I am the head of this family and I say so!"

Silence ensued.

The dining room door opened, then, and an elderly man entered. Somewhat startled, he spoke softly into the palpable tension. "I beg your pardon, my lord."

Justin turned away momentarily, sweeping a hand across his face. Almost giddy with tightly held restraint, he turned back toward the man.

"Yes, Weems, what is it?"

"Visitors, my lord," the butler replied. "Viscount Walmsley, Lord Tobias Rington, the Marquess of Chantry—"

"I barely know the men, Weems," Justin interrupted with a scowl. "What business do they have with me at this hour?"

"Oh, they did not come to see you, my lord," Weems replied with a tiny twitch of his mouth. "The gentlemen are here to see Miss Baxter."

"Me?" Melanie asked in disbelief as Justin's gaze grew thunderous. "Oh, but I do not think—"

". . . Oh, cousin, how exciting!" Angela exclaimed, enjoying her brother's ire. "You have only attended one function and already you have attracted a drawing room full of beaux!"

Justin shot his sister a scathing glance.

"Why, Melanie, this is delightful," Lady Stonegate said, intentionally stirring the storm in her son's eyes. "With this much eager attention, I am persuaded that you will have to give up any thoughts of rest today. In fact, you seem to be quite pleasantly launched. I cannot see that we shall need to give you a ball after all."

Melanie's eyes flashed between them, astounded. "Are none of you sensible of what I was saying?"

Justin clenched his teeth and steamed, caught between his desire to assure Melanie a life in which she might find fulfillment and happiness, and his even greater need to pulverize every lip that was now idly sipping tea in his drawing room. In the end, he rounded the table, seized Melanie's elbow in his shaking fist, and marched her toward the door, determined, even if it killed him, to do the right thing.

"I am sensible of this, my dear. You have guests awaiting you in the drawing room. You will go there immediately," he growled through his teeth.

Melanie's fists settled stubbornly upon her hips. "And what shall you demand of me then, my overbearing lord," she spat at him, her eyes sparkling sherry in the warm morning light.

"Why, then you shall entertain them, scamp," he answered through his teeth. "You will smile, you will accept their invitations to ride in the park with them, and, in a week or two, you will invite the bounders to your damnable ball!" Upon that note, he all but shoved her into the flower-bedecked hall.

Glances flew between Simon, Angela, and Lady Stonegate after the other two had left the room. The atmosphere shimmered with expectancy and tightly contained mirth. Only one of the three made comment into the fragile silence: Lady Stonegate. Looking toward the empty doorway, she angelically clasped her hands beneath her chin, rested her elbows upon the table, and murmured, "My, my."

* * *

"There, how does that feel, Gran?" Melanie asked, laying strips of cloth soaked in the warm oils of anise and eucalyptus across the woman's shriveled chest.

"Better, lass," Gran wheezed. "It be easin' me."

"Good," Melanie responded, rising to sprinkle more herbs into the pot simmering on the brazier. "Sanjay's wife . . . he was the head man of our village in India . . . treated chest problems in this manner. I was hoping the oils might bring you some relief."

"We be that surprised ye could come today," Con said, tenderly holding his mother's hand as he sat on his platform beside her pallet.

Melanie glanced up. "I almost could not," she told them with a smile.

"Did they try an' stop ye, then?" Bess asked from her more comfortable seat at the nearby table.

"No . . ." Melanie admitted. "In truth, only Simon knows about my visits to Portpool Lane."

"Ye be lyin' to 'em, girl?" Con interrupted.

"Not exactly," Melanie responded. "I have just not told them. You see, it is very risky for me to dress in my man's clothing and return here, Con. Not just for myself or Simon, but for his lordship and his family. If the *ton* ever finds out how Simon and I lived before we came to Stonegate House, all our reputations will be ruined."

"Then why 'ave ye risked it, child?" Gran breathed noisily.

"Oh, Gran, how could I not?" Melanie replied. "You are my family, too. Besides, I promised Bess to attend her lying-in. How could I go back on my word, especially when the time is so close?"

" 'Ow is ye gettin' away without no one seein' ye?" Con asked.

"It isn't easy!" Melanie laughed, pouring some of her

herbal concoction into a small cup. "Why, just today I had to make excuses to a room full of visitors and go over the garden wall!"

"Cor, Melanie, ye'll get caught fer sure," Bess moaned.

"I shall not," Melanie insisted, walking back to Gran's side. "And you are not to worry, Bess. When you need me, I promise I shall be here."

Bess nodded, her smile of trust banishing the fear in her eyes. "But, Melanie, seein' as it ain't safe, 'adn't ye best stay away until me lyin-in, when ye ain't got no choice but to come?"

"Bess is roight," Con agreed, reaching up to touch gnarled fingers to her arm. "It be best, lass. No sense in yer takin' chances. The rest o' us kin care fer Gran if ye tells us wot to do."

"Perhaps," Melanie responded, nodding slowly, carefully spooning her tonic into Gran's mouth. "No, I know you are right, Con. But I shall miss all of you. And how shall I know if you have found out anything about the footpads?"

"We'll send word to you," Con told her. "Ain't been much news anyway. Only found out one thing so far."

Melanie's attention riveted upon him. "What, Con?"

"Folks be pretty sure them two ain't from Saffron 'Ill. There be word that two mean pieces o' kennel garbage wot was from Spitalfields disappeared about the time them two footpads o' yers went to gaol. Oi'd wager me last farthing they be one an the same, Mel."

"The timing of their disappearance certainly fits," Melanie stated. "But was there no word of who might have hired them?"

"Not yet. But Bart an' Jack got their ears open," Con reassured her. "They'll 'ear somethin' sooner or later."

Melanie nodded, masking her disappointment. "Thank

you for your help in this, Con, and do, please, keep on trying. Thank Bart and Jack for me, too, will you?"

"Ye knows Oi will," Con replied with a rare smile.

"Well, then, I should go," she told them, crossing to lay a soft kiss upon Gran's forehead before lithely rising again to her feet. "I—I suppose I shan't see you again until it is your time, Bess," she said with restrained emotion, drawing forth a bundle of herbal packets from her pocket, "so I shall leave these with you. They are the herbs I use for Gran. I am sensible that you cannot read the labels, but you will recognize from their scent what they are. If you still need help, send Annie or Freddie with a message to the back door of Stonegate House. I shall come right away. And, of course, you must send for me when the baby is coming."

"Oi will, Melanie," Bess said drawing her into an awkward embrace over the top of her abdomen, "an' bless you, dearie."

Melanie returned a watery smile. "Well, then," she said, swallowing down a huge lump as her eyes scanned the familiar room, "I shall see you on the day. Take care, all of you . . . and . . . and good bye." After giving each of them a speaking glance, she turned quickly, gathered her cutaway about her slender frame, and fled into the cluttered hallway.

# Nine

Melanie's skin pebbled under a soft slither of orange silk.

"Oh, Rose, it is beautiful, is it not?" she breathed after her evening gown had slipped into place and the maid had fastened it snugly around her slender form.

Enthralled, she studied herself in the cheval glass, twisting from side to side as she noted with delight how the soft, draped folds of the gown's bodice accentuated her small breasts while the large, bouffant, off-the-shoulder sleeves minimized her boyish slenderness. A wide, satin ribbon hugged her tiny waist, and below it, three flounces of the same ribbon marched about the hem. She had never possessed anything so stunningly feminine in all her life.

" 'Tis that, indeed, my lady," Rose replied with a satisfied smile. "It suits you perfectly, if I may say so. I have never seen you look so lovely."

"Oh, I do hope you are right, Rose," Melanie stated, biting her lip against a tug of worry. "Miss Parkes always appears dressed to the nines. I would not wish to be an embarrassment to his lordship."

"You'll not be that, my lady," Rose told her confidently. "I'll be that surprised if his lordship, or any other gentleman, can keep his eyes in his head when he sees you. You shall outshine everyone in the drawing room, *and* at the theater."

"Shall I draw too much notice, do you think?" Melanie asked, her molten eyes growing large with concern. "Rose, you know of my past . . ."

The maid chuckled heartily. "Aye, they'll notice, my lady, but the last thing they'll be picturing you in when they see you in that gown is a pair of old pantaloons and a cutaway. Now, come sit at your dressing table and let me style your hair."

Melanie laughed softly. "What, this?" she queried, tunneling her fingers through her curls. "There is nothing to style. It is still too short, and unfashionably curly. No, you must go now to assist the countess or Lady D'Antry. I shall just brush it as I usually do."

"Very well, miss," Rose yielded with a smile. "But I left a length of ribbon on your dressing table that Lady D'Antry thought might match your gown. Try threading it through your curls and tying it at your crown in a simple bow."

"I shall indeed, Rose," Melanie replied, spotting the ribbon and smiling. "And do thank Lady D'Antry for me."

When Rose had gone, Melanie seated herself at the dressing table, pondering her image assessingly in the attached three-sided mirror before she blew out an exasperated sigh. Capturing one of the midnight curls that sprawled in disarray upon her forehead between her fingertips, she pulled it straight down, measuring its length as it tickled against the tip of her nose. Chagrinned, she released it to spring back into place on a puff of expelled air. There was no hope for it. It would be years before her hair was long enough to fashion into one of the current sleek styles featuring concealed ears and rows of sausage curls.

She picked up her brush then and began to wield it aggressively, wondering how it had come about that she was even concerned about such a thing. Eight years ago she had set her course determinedly. She would forsake her own place in Society in order to see Simon safely into his, and then leave him to make her own way. Yet suddenly, even the time of breaking her fast was no longer under her control. Nothing was. Because of a chance meeting with Stonegate. Now, because of him her every movement came under someone's scrutiny. Her days loomed ahead of her like a chain of restrictive shackles; her past hovering over her like an executioner's blade.

But no, it was worse than that. Soon she would have to watch while Stonegate took another woman to be his wife. She trembled violently at the thought, dropping her hairbrush to bounce and clatter upon the polished floor. Her face fell into the cup of her hands. How could she bear it? She loved him so . . . too much to stay and see it happen . . . too much to leave.

She took the ribbon into her hands, then, and began to thread it through her hair, gathering herself in the performance of familiar motions. Perhaps she could marry as well. There were several gentlemen who had seemed particularly interested in her. She had, in fact, spent the afternoon driving in the park with Lord Rington, and he had been most attentive. He was a mere baron, too. Perhaps his family would not care as much about her scandalous past as would the family of an earl. Yet even as the thought came to her, she rejected it. Marriage to another was not for her. Just the thought of another man taking her into his arms, kissing her in the manner that Stonegate had, possessing her . . . No. Oh, no. Never. Not ever.

And yet what was to become of her? Was she to ever after be in the position of a poor relation, a constant drain upon Stonegate's purse? The thought was intolerable.

Somehow, hopefully before his marriage ever took place, she must find an acceptable situation for herself, something in a place where she was certain of never having to encounter him again. She wished that the situation would make itself known to her soon. She knew that she did not have much time. Yet at the moment, she had no idea what that situation might be.

She nipped at her lips, then, as Angela had schooled her, and pinched her cheeks. Rising from the table, she drew in a deep, steadying breath. The way would open for her when the time came. She had to trust in that. Besides, there was nothing she could do about it tonight anyway. And she was going to need all her focused energies just to endure the evening ahead. Resolving that, if she did nothing else in the time she had remaining with him, she would make Stonegate proud of her, she put her concerns behind her, slipped on her long, orange gloves, and stepped determinedly toward the door.

Far down the long, wide gallery from which all of the bedrooms debouched, Justin stepped from his bedroom at exactly the same time. Their eyes met, copper colliding with crystaline coal. Simultaneously, the two stilled, their lips parting first at the unexpectedness of the meeting and then with an overwhelming urgency to close the gap between them. A sudden tension flared as the bond pulled, puckered, drawing them toward one another even as their conscious thoughts urged them to flee.

Inhaling deeply, Justin fought the fire building within him, searched for inner ice in which to contain it, but found nothing but the remembered warmth of Melanie's husky voice and smile. Slowly, helplessly, he yielded, starting forward, his gaze never varying from hers in its awestruck regard. In moments, the two stood face to face at the head of the stairs.

"You look lovely, Mel," he said gently, gritting his teeth against that Banbury tale. She was perfection, so beautiful to him that it hurt to look upon her; a slender pixie whose dark curls he was itching to crush in his hands.

"Thank you, my lord," Melanie murmured in response. "You look quite well also." Quite well? She bit back a nervous gasp. He was the most handsome man she had ever seen. Tall, commanding, impeccably clad in the crisp contrast of black and white, he presented the pattern card of highborn elegance. How she wished she could kiss the small cleft in his chin!

"I approve of your gown," he told her, thinking as his eyes roamed over her that he would very much like to tear it out of the way.

"Thank you. Your mother thought that you might find it acceptable," Melanie returned, reveling in the way his gaze covered every inch of her, remembering, centering her avid attention upon his mouth.

Justin's heart thundered as he saw where her copper gaze had settled, knowing what she was thinking; his fingers twitched against his muscled thighs. "Acceptable. What a useful word . . . and how utterly inadequate. But come, my dear. Our guests should be arriving soon. Allow me the honor of escorting you to the drawing room." Cursing decorous restraint, the earl reached out and took possession of Melanie's slim elbow, aware as he had never been before of the difference between them, male and female; feeling the fragility of her bones.

"Thank you, my lord," Melanie whispered, relishing the warmth of his hand, his closeness as he drew her near to the heat of his body; leaning into his offering. Staring into one another's eyes for yet another lingering moment, their hearts pounding in silent, antiphonal yearning, they turned together and began to descend the stairs.

* * *

Lord Palmerton's brougham arrived at the entry only a few moments after Justin and Melanie had joined the others in the drawing room, spilling its occupants into the hall below with a flurry of wrap-taking and last-minute, whispered advice. At the sound of footsteps on the stairs, Justin stood to his feet along with Simon, the young man resplendent in his new evening clothes and looking every inch the earl. The two waited politely as Weems ushered their guests up to the first floor and into the family's presence.

"Good evening, my lord," Lady Palmerton cried, accepting Justin's bow of greeting as she sailed forth into the elegant room dressed in a gown of rose and lavender stripes. Miss Parkes entered in her wake.

"Good evening, Lady Palmerton," Justin replied warmly, raising her gloved fingers to a spot just under his lips where he hovered for an appropriate length of time before returning them to their owner. "And Miss Parkes. I am honored to welcome you to my home." Again, with careful propriety, he repeated the courtly gesture.

"Thank you, sir," Miss Parkes breathed sweetly. "So kind in you to invite us."

"And Evelyn, dear," Lady Palmerton continued, pulling away from the earl to join Lady Stonegate upon the sofa. "I have not seen you this age! And, I vow, this room is just the same. La, dearest," she chided prettily, "I should have thought by this time you would have been able to persuade Stonegate to modernize and redecorate."

"Goodness, no!" laughed Lady Stonegate, sweeping open her fan. "Justin does not care for the current fashion of filling one's home with competing patterns and bric-a-brac. I cannot say that I disagree." Smiling, the countess looked about her fondly, each piece of carefully collected furniture holding a memory.

At Justin's insistence, and her ready compliance, the drawing room still retained the clean good taste of decades gone by, its walls painted in a soft, warm yellow, its wood-work and plaster scrolling a pristine white. An Axminster carpet woven in deep green and yellow with touches of red lay in pleasant counterpoint to the striped fabric of the several Sheraton sofas and chairs that stood conversationally. Tables inlaid with brass and burl were situated about the room for the occupants' convenience. It was a welcoming room and a calming one, a setting she knew Justin relished.

Weems entered then, as further greetings were made and Simon was introduced, carrying a silver tray containing glasses and a decanter of sherry. As he passed before the fire, the amber liquid was lit from behind by the flames. Justin briefly closed his eyes as sudden thoughts of Melanie filled his mind. The color of the fire-washed sherry echoed her copper-colored gaze.

"Thank you, Weems," he said in a voice that was suspiciously tight. "Ladies, gentlemen, may I offer you a glass?"

Melanie recognized his tone. She had heard it last just before Stonegate had kissed her. Trusting action to dissipate her sudden trembling, she moved to stand close to Simon's side.

"I should love some, darling," Justin's mother replied. "In fact, I am sure we shall all have some."

Justin nodded, then, turning his back on the group, breathing some control back over his desires as he deftly poured the drinks. Without conscious thought, he took a glass first to Lady Palmerton and his mother, then to Angela and Eunice. But when he raised the last glass toward Melanie, she politely declined.

"What?" inquired Stanley with studied casualness, per-

ceptively sensing her slight discomfiture. Allowing an in-
quisitive smile to settle upon his lips, he joined Justin beside the decanter, negligently pouring himself and his
father a glass. "Are you a follower of the temperance movement, Miss Baxter?"

"Oh, surely not," Lady Palmerton exclaimed, her attention drawn from describing her newly renovated drawing
room to Lady Stonegate. "One small glass cannot hurt anyone. It is, in fact, quite settling. I am persuaded that Miss
Baxter has simply never acquired a taste for the drink, dearest, coming as she has from somewhat straitened circumstances . . ."

Beside her, Melanie felt Simon stiffen. Quickly, she
placed calming fingers against his hand. "I did not take
the glass because I did not wish to, Lady Palmerton," she
said quietly.

"Oh, my dear Miss Baxter," breathed Miss Parkes with
great sympathy, "how very dreadful for you! Have you
developed a . . . a problem?"

"No, of course she has not!" said Simon with too much
heat.

Justin's gaze flicked between the four of them, wondering what the deuce was going on.

"No need to get defensive about it, my boy," Lord Palmerton soothed, taking a glass from his son. "I daresay there
isn't a family in the *ton* that hasn't its tippler."

Melanie's face flamed. "I do not have a problem, Lord
Palmerton," she insisted more warmly, her mind trying to
dispel images of her father.

"She most certainly does not," exclaimed Angela. "This
whole conversation has become distasteful in the extreme."

"I would agree," Justin concurred acidly.

"I do beg your pardon," Stanley smiled with a slight
bow in their direction. "No offense was intended, of course.

No doubt Mama is right and Miss Baxter merely lacks . . . experience."

"I do have a glass of wine with my dinner," Melanie inserted, feeling a need to justify herself, yet lost in an unfamiliar social sea, "but no more than that. I . . . I have seen what too much drink can do . . ."

"Indeed, Miss Baxter?" Stanley interrupted, his gaze keen as he fastened upon her words. "How remarkable. It seems to me that one would have to have experienced quite a devastating problem to become so cautious about imbibing."

Melanie's gaze flew to Justin's, seeking help. "I . . ."

Caught between his desire to avoid giving offense to his future relations and his need to inflict serious damage upon Nesbitt's sneering face, the earl hesitated a moment too long, his eyes flaring, his lips drawn and pale.

Into the uncertain atmosphere, the strange conversation continued.

"Did this experience occur in the country where you were brought up, Miss Baxter?" questioned Miss Parkes with great solicitude shining in her blue eyes. "Was it quite . . . horrible?"

"Oh, this is the outside of enough!" Angela exclaimed.

Justin, too, reacted, his fierce need to defend Melanie, to protect his own, finally overpowering every other consideration. "Really, Miss Parkes," he said, forcing what he hoped was a smile. "One would think from your questions that you relish the macabre."

Eunice subsided immediately, as wary of Stonegate's finding her interest improper as she was of his suspecting her motives. "La," she laughed descendingly, fluffing the Victoria sleeves of her soft blue brocade, "nothing of the sort, sir. I merely find the customs and proprieties of other countries quite the most interesting thing. Do you not as well, Lord Stonegate?"

"Most certainly," Justin answered, regaining a measure of control as he strolled over to stand before her and bowed over her hand. "And if you will grant me your company for a drive on the morrow, my dear, I believe I know just the means to satisfy your every curiosity."

"Indeed, sir," purred Miss Parkes on a delicate giggle. "How shall you do that?"

"Why, I shall take you to Mudie's, of course," Justin responded with a smile, taking her hand and drawing her to her feet. "One can find all the information one wants on foreign customs in the circulating library." And then his voice hardened slightly. "When we are finished, my dear, you shall never have cause to be curious about the country of Miss Baxter's childhood again.

"But come, Weems has just rung us to dinner. Lady Palmerton, if you will allow me to give escort to both you and my mother, and if Lord Palmerton will take up my sister, Lord Westbridge escort Miss Parkes, and Lord Nesbitt bring in Miss Baxter, I do believe we gentlemen shall be able to escort you ladies to the dining room with no offense either to our several ranks or my sense of propriety. Shall we go?"

It was a very neat maneuver, Melanie thought, hiding a smile as she took her place beside Lord Nesbitt. In one stroke, Stonegate had silenced a very awkward line of questioning and deflected the attention away from her. She was grateful. She had not known how to extricate herself from their avid inquiries. Had she not known better, she might have thought that the interrogation had taken place on purpose, that the brother and sister had been fishing for something with which to discredit her. But that could not be. She was no threat to them, certainly not to Miss Parkes.

Shrugging internally, she took the viscount's arm and followed him toward the stairs, letting her thoughts drift on to other things.

The crescendo swelled and flowed over Melanie as the second act of the opera came to a close. She sighed quietly, savoring the intricate melody, the settings upon the stage, the performances of the Grisi's, and, most of all, the dark closeness of Stonegate's box which allowed her to enjoy it all as if she were completely alone.

Thunderous applause suddenly broke her reverie. Startled, she cast an embarrassed glance toward the others as the house lights went up. Stonegate was studying her intently, his chin supported on a loose fist, a slight smile stretching one corner of his chiseled mouth.

"Well, I, for one, shall need to stretch my legs a bit before the final act," Viscount Nesbitt said from behind them, rising to his feet. "Lady D'Antry was fortunate to have had her son's sudden tooth ailment as an excuse for declining to accompany us. This evening's performance is as tedious as that aborted equestrian act at Vauxhall. Shall you join me, Eunice?"

Miss Parkes, reluctant to leave Stonegate alone with his cousin, hesitated. "My lord?" she queried him with a sweet smile. "Shall we all go? I should enjoy a stroll."

"Then by all means attend your brother, Miss Parkes," he responded, his gaze still upon Melanie. "I have not found the evening's entertainment the least bit tedious. Miss Baxter and I shall join you when the crush at the refreshment counter has subsided somewhat."

Stung, Miss Parkes murmured, "Very well." Taking up her reticule, she stood, giving the cousins a speaking look that passed unregarded. Biting the inside of her cheek, she spun around quickly and left the box with her brother.

A rustling silence engulfed Melanie and the earl when they were at last alone, a silence that shifted, hummed, abraded against Melanie's edginess. Muffled murmurs drifted in to them from the corridor, punctuated by trills of feminine laughter. Under a perverse compulsion, Melanie dragged her gaze away from her tightly entwined fingers and sought the earl's. He was sitting exactly as he had been before. Intently watching her.

"Have you been observing me through the entire performance?" she asked him softly, her lips parting slightly on a small tremble.

"Yes."

"Why?"

The earl's avid gaze softened. "Because you are the most beautiful woman I have ever seen."

Melanie blushed crimson as she dropped her gaze again. Quickly, she shook her head. "You must not say such things."

"I know."

"H-Have you enjoyed the performance so far?" she asked him, seeking for safer subjects.

Justin shrugged slightly, his grin fading into a soft smile. "I have not seen any of it."

Melanie's eyes flew to his. "Because you have been watching me?" she breathed.

"Yes."

Again she flushed and looked away, fidgeting. "I have never seen the opera before," she confessed, rearranging orange silk.

"I guessed as much," Justin said, still smiling, still resting his chin upon his hand. "I imagine you were the only one present who was actually watching it."

Her eyes became a coppery question. "What were the rest doing then?"

"Watching you."

Stunned, Melanie glanced about her. Several of the boxes had begun to fill again as their occupants returned from their rounds of other boxes, strolls along the corridor to see and be seen, and their partaking of oranges or wine. Wherever Melanie's gaze rested, to a man, the gentlemen were staring directly at her.

"Oh, my lord!" she whispered, her eyes growing round as she glanced about. "Have I done something to call attention to myself?"

"Absolutely," Justin replied softly.

"But what?" she hissed. "I have been sitting quite still for the better part of two hours! What could I possibly have done?"

Justin sat forward then, resting his forearms upon his thighs. Piercing her with his hungry, dark eyes, he told her, "You came."

Swiftly, the earl rose to his feet. "Come with me now, Melanie. We must join our guests. For both our sakes."

Melanie nodded, rising shakily to take the earl's arm, wary of leaving the cocoon of his box behind. Gripping him tightly, she stepped into the corridor, her pulse pounding against her throat, aware now of the *ton's* blatant interest, wishing to evaporate. She stiffened with apprehension as several gentlemen started toward them, confident that their acquaintance with Stonegate would gain them an introduction. Lord Rington caught the edge of her notice with an enthusiastic wave before Stonegate's broad shoulders blocked him from her view. And then a gun exploded in the tight passage with a deafening report, and suddenly Melanie was flat on her back upon the burgundy carpeting, her body blanketed completely, protectively, by the tall, muscular form of the earl.

"My God, Melanie, are you all right?" Justin questioned over the sounds of shouting and women's screams. His face was dusky with concern and outrage.

"Yes. Are you?" she cried worriedly, drawing both hands up from between them to bracket his cheeks and search his dark eyes.

"Yes. The bullet just missed me," he told her, threading his fingers through her curls.

"Come on, we've got to get out of here."

Instantly, Melanie felt the heaviness of the earl's body leave her and she was pulled effortlessly to her feet. His arm came around her then, drawing her protectively into the slight crouch of his body before he began to elbow his way through the crowd's panicked flight, guiding her unerringly toward the flight of stairs leading to the outside and safety.

Suddenly, a form appeared out of the pandemonium to stand beside her. "Miss Baxter, are you all right?" Lord Rington shouted, shouldering the flow of people aside as he struggled to remain near her.

"Y-Yes," she cried, still clinging to the earl, wincing as he crushed her face against his chest just in time to prevent her being battered by a wildly swinging elbow.

"My lord, how may I help?" Lord Rington shouted again over the cacophony.

"Have you seen Viscount Nesbitt and his sister?" Justin shouted in return, bracing his shoulder, too, against the surge of the crowd.

"Only once . . . a bit earlier," the baron answered, deflecting a swinging reticule. "They were in conversation on the stairs near the entrance. They looked to have just returned from a stroll outside."

Justin nodded, moving Melanie into a gap in the press of bodies. "Perhaps they are awaiting us outside then. Come, help me force a path through this stampede. I am concerned for Miss Baxter's safety."

The young man nodded and immediately turned to position himself ahead of Melanie. In only a short time, the two men had again wedged themselves into the press of people and had shouldered their way through the melee to the walkway outside the theater. Again Justin drew the three of them aside and against the granite facade of the building, into one of the human stream's calm eddies. Immediately, the earl's gaze began to scan the area intently, as did Melanie's.

"Look," she exclaimed, unclenching one fist from its tight grasp of the earl's waistcoat to point down the street. "There is the Palmerton brougham. But it is leaving."

"Yes, I have seen it," Justin responded, uncaring, his eyes still searching the shadows. "Nesbitt is undoubtedly seeing to his sister's safety. We should be grateful, I suppose, that at least this time he is not doing it by throwing her from a moving carriage."

"But he has left us behind!" huffed Melanie in her husky voice.

"No matter, Miss Baxter," Lord Rington said, taking her hand. "I have my cabriolet. It shall be a tight squeeze, but I should be honored to take you and Stonegate home."

The earl's lips pursed. "That is most generous in you, Rington," he replied, scowling slightly. He was well aware that Melanie would be seated in the middle of that proffered squeeze. Her hips might be deliciously pressed against his own during the length of the ride, but they would also be pressed just as tightly against the baron's. "Miss Baxter and I are in your debt. By the way, did you happened to have seen who fired that gun?"

The baron nodded. "A man. I had just picked up my glass of wine and had turned to look down the stairs to see if it had begun to rain when it happened. He shot from the shadows, however, so I could see nothing but the gun and his hand."

"Nothing of his clothing?" Justin asked quietly.

"No, nothing else. But the hand was most definitely masculine."

Justin nodded, his lips thinning as his resolute gaze sought Melanie's. She regarded him unmoving, silent. Her gown had been ripped in several places and a single orange ribbon had deserted the adorable disarray of her dark curls to dangle from one ear. She had every reason to be sobbing uncontrollably, yet she was not. Instead, her face shone in the gaslight with calm, with unvarying support.

Slowly, Justin lifted his hand and removed the errant ribbon, carefully tucking it into his pocket, taking strength from her trusting expression as he once again felt the bond between them thrum. They both understood the significance of what had just happened, he knew; understood it, and accepted it. There was no doubt in either of their minds for whom the bullet was intended. The threat had not evaporated with the death of the two footpads or the tampering with the Palmerton brougham.

Someone was still trying to kill him. Bloody hell.

# Ten

The message that Bess Hicks was about to give birth arrived a week later, just after dawn on the morning of Melanie's come-out ball.

"Wake up, Miss," Rose whispered to her, gently jiggling Melanie's shoulder as she drifted into awareness from the depths of a pleasant dream. "The lad's come . . . young Fred, he said his name was. It's Mrs. Hicks's time."

Melanie blinked slowly, focusing. "I must go to her right away," she finally stated in a husky, sleep-roughened voice, forcefully shaking herself into full wakefulness as Rose pulled back her curtains, flooding her bed with pale morning light. "I am glad that I managed to coax John Coachman into hiding my hansom in his lordship's mews several days ago. I had wanted to be able to reach the Rookery quickly when Bess's time came, but I had not thought to need my cab so soon. Has anyone else in the house awakened yet, Rose?"

"The countess," breathed the maid, readying Melanie's slippers, "and his lordship, I believe."

Melanie's lips twisted with exasperation. "Of all the mornings for them to awaken early, why did it have to be this one?"

"Why, indeed?" chuckled the maid. "Are you forgetting what day this is? The countess is at sixes and sevens wanting everything to be perfect for your ball tonight. Certainly she would not be able to sleep."

"Dear heaven, I did forget!" she admitted, looking appalled. "And of course the countess would be anxious. After all, it is not often a lady of the *haute monde* launches a London cabbie. Well, there is no help for it. I still must go to Bess, and I must avoid them if I can. I shall just have to sneak down the servants' stairs when I leave. What did Freddie say when he came?"

"Just that Mrs. Hicks was asking for you, miss," the maid responded in a worried whisper, "and that you're to come right away."

Melanie rubbed her eyes with her fingertips and yawned. "Very well," she nodded, folding back the covers and hanging her feet over the edge of the bed. "My cabbie's clothing is tucked in the back of the bottom drawer in my clothes press, Rose. Would you get them for me?"

Even as Rose obeyed, she voiced her objections. "But the ball, miss," she said, bending to shuffle through the drawer's contents before drawing forth the small bundle. "You can't think to leave the house today!"

"I made a promise, Rose," Melanie countered, pouring water into her washstand basin and rushing through her ablutions. "I have no choice."

"But you will be missed, my lady," Rose said, enfolding her in soft toweling and rubbing her briskly. After she had rendered her ruddy, she handed Melanie the rough linen shirt. "How shall I explain your absence? What shall I say?"

Melanie paused for a moment, thinking. "You can tell them I am determined to spend the day resting in my room," she finally said. "Tell them I do not wish to droop at my own ball. That should not inspire comment as the countess already knows I am not yet accustomed to the pace of Society. And Simon will help, too. Tell him where I have gone when he awakes, and ask him to mention to the others later in the afternoon that he has seen me and that I was reading quietly. That should eliminate any suspicions that might have arisen by that time."

"But what of the ball?" Rose questioned, helping Melanie to fasten her pantaloons and slip on her rudely fashioned shoes. "You cannot know how long Mrs. Hicks's lying-in will be. What if you do not return in time?"

Melanie tossed her a pert grin. "Then, I suppose, I shall just have to be fashionably late," she replied. "Try not to worry, Rose. Bess has been delivered of six other babes. I doubt I shall be gone long enough to miss nuncheon. Now come, see if the gallery is empty. If it is, I shall dash across it to the servants' stairs and be on my way."

"Did you have plans for the day, Justin?" Lady Stonegate asked him over breakfast.

The two had awakened well ahead of their usual hour, the lady because of the bevy of last-minute preparations for the ball that must be attended to, and the earl because, over the past several days, he had been deliberately avoiding Melanie, and as a result was blue-deviled, miserable, and sleepless. Mother and son were alone in the dining room.

"Yes," the earl replied, setting down his coffee cup with a smooth motion that barely creased the chocolate-colored redingote hugging his shoulders or his wide sapphire cravat. "I shall be taking Miss Parkes to view the zoological gardens in the park a bit later."

"It sounds like a lovely outing," his mother replied with a perceptive sparkle in her fine eyes, "and you have a fine day for it."

"Yes . . . I have not been as attentive toward the lady as I might in the past few days."

"And why is that?" his mother asked, purposely prodding.

"I have had much on my mind," Justin replied, spearing a soft fold of egg.

"I had noticed that," the countess told him gently. "Perhaps you should cry off your outing with Miss Parkes today and visit Clarisse instead."

Justin's shocked gaze sprang to his mother's. "What did you say?" he breathed.

"I merely suggested that Clarisse's ministrations might be of more benefit," she responded evenly.

The earl's breathing ceased. "What do you know of Clarisse?" he rasped.

"More than you thought, obviously," his mother chuckled. "Oh, Justin, really!" she said with a brighter laugh. "Can you honestly believe that I would not be aware of the woman to whom both my sons gave *carte blanche?*"

"Mama, this is hardly a fitting topic—"

"Of course not," she broke in. "But because we do not discuss it, does not mean that the reality does not exist. I have known of Clarisse since Oliver first gave her his protection. I also know that it has been quite a while since you have visited her. Not since Melanie—"

"Mama, please," Justin exclaimed beneath a deeply grooved frown.

"Your father had a mistress before we were married," his mother informed him, gazing fondly beyond his shoulder to her husband's portrait, ignoring her son's discomfiture. "He loved her to distraction. Did you know that?"

Justin's frown faded into surprise. "No . . . I did not."

"Well, he did," she told him softly, her gaze returning to him as she rose to her feet. "He was so very proper in your presence, Justin . . . so demanding that you be perfect in your comportment as well. I always told him it was a great mistake. You never saw that he was also very human, too." Rounding the table to place a tender kiss on her son's forehead, the countess quietly left the room.

"Oh, how lovely! The rose garden!" exclaimed Miss Parkes later that same morning as Justin pulled his rented cabriolet to a halt beside the curb of the inner circle in Regent's Park. The air above them was clear and warm, somnolent with the sound of insect drones, heavy with floral perfume.

Justin bounded lithely down from his seat and rounded the carriage, taking Miss Parkes's hand as he helped her down. "I am glad this area of the park is more to your liking," he told her, turning to guide her down the central walkway. "Again, I must apologize for not giving proper consideration to your sensibilities when I planned this outing. I had not realized that the zoological gardens would not be to your taste."

"Oh, but I do enjoy viewing the animals, sir," she responded quickly, hoping to soothe any offense. "It is just the odor . . ."

"Yes, of course," Justin broke in, duty bound to ease her embarrassment. "Please give it no further thought. We shall enjoy these gardens instead." Taking her arm through his elbow, he turned her onto a smaller path leading toward sweetly scented masses of floribundas.

Miss Parkes inhaled deeply as they strolled between each abundantly blooming display, reveling in the sweet fragrance that surrounded her. "This is so kind in you sir," she said after a period of silence that Justin found strangely uncomfortable, her blue eyes peeking shyly out at him from behind the brim of her capote-style bonnet. "I do love roses. I have a garden of my own at our principal seat in Berkshire."

"Do you?" Justin inquired politely.

"Oh, yes! Do you see that near-violet bloom over there?" she asked him, pointing with a slim, gloved finger.

"I do, indeed," the earl responded, following with his gaze.

"It is all the rage. It is the newest variety to the garden. I have been trying to wheedle a cutting out of the gardener here for ever so many weeks," she told him conspiratorially. "I should like it above all things."

Justin smiled indulgently. "My mother seems to have succeeded where you have failed, Miss Parkes," he commented as he turned her toward the path leading to a display of climbers. "Several weeks ago she grafted a cutting of that very plant onto a potted rose she has growing on the terrace. I believe she intends to plant it at her dower house when we remove from London in the autumn."

"Oh, sir!" cried Miss Parkes, displaying more animation than Justin had ever seen in her before. "Would she let me see it, do you think? I should like it above all things."

"I am sure she would be delighted to show it to you," he responded with a forced smile, mildly disgruntled that the *coup* of possessing a new rose variety was more exciting to her than an outing with him. "It is doing quite well. I am certain that we could persuade Mama into taking a cutting for you from her plant if you like."

"Oh, I should be *aux anges,* sir," Miss Parkes breathed, clasping her hands in front of her ample breasts.

"Then, since you wish it, my dear, we shall of course stop by Stonegate House on the way back to Green Street," Justin replied.

"Oh, I should like it—"

"Yes, I know," Justin murmured, ". . . above all things."

"Yes, my lord," Miss Parkes repeated, oblivious to his mood. Already, in her inner musings, she was rubbing her *coup* under the noses of her friends. "I should indeed like it above all things."

An uneasy silence fell between them. Justin twirled his silver-headed cane, searching for a conversational topic he could share with her, thrusting aside the knowledge that he was growing increasingly bored. As their slow stroll took them into a bank of old roses, he found himself wondering what the deuce he was doing there. He didn't have to be. No one was holding a gun to his temple. The choice of whether or not he continued to see the lady was his. So why was he?

Because she was his ideal. The pattern card he had been waiting his adult life for. He cast a sideways glance at the young woman beside him. She did not disappoint. She was dressed in a full skirt and a close-fitting jacket bodice of slate blue taffeta over a white satin waistcoat and a pleated, lacy chemisette. Every item of her wardrobe was the highest stare of fashion, and she looked lovely in it. Her behavior had been impeccable; she had exhibited only the most perfect of manners over the span of the afternoon. She had not varied even a whit from the ideal of his expectations. So why the devil did he wish to be any place else but in her company?

He knew the answer to that even before the question had left his thoughts. It was because of Melanie. He had tried, but she could not be banished from his mind. He loved her. It was as simple as that. And yet it was not simple at all. She was beyond his reach, beyond his ability to rectify what she had done. And that left Miss Parkes. She was the perfect choice for him, the one his father would have approved. He had to find a way to cut from his heart his foolish feelings for a London cabbie and offer for her. Somehow he had to force his mind to accept that necessity. Of a certainty, his heart never would.

"Would you care for a glass of lemonade, Miss Parkes?" Justin asked after they had entered a large, open park containing an outdoor theater and a refreshment pavilion.

"Yes, thank you, sir," she replied, tipping her parasol upward slightly so that she might see him better. "It has grown quite warm, has it not?"

"Yes indeed," Justin answered. "Take a seat on this bench, why don't you, Miss Parkes? The tree will shade you. I shall return in just one moment."

Eunice readily did as Justin suggested, then watched as he turned from her and his tall form receded, quickly disappearing into the crowd clustered near the pavilion. Her thoughts gave birth to an unwanted frown. He was slowly withdrawing from her. Each time they were together, she sensed his reluctance to advance their courtship more and more. Her parents had again assured her only this morning that she was comporting herself properly and that she must continue as she had been, but she was no longer so certain of success.

Why had he not declared for her? What could be holding him back? . . . except Miss Baxter, of course. And their illicit feelings for one another. Eunice's frown deepened. Somehow she must refocus his attentions upon her. Suddenly, a smile softened her features as she remembered something he had just said. Her mind considered the risks, and then rejected them. It could work, she reasoned inwardly, but it would require the most subtle of suggestions. . . .

Justin returned after a short time, seating himself beside her before handing her a chilled glass.

"Thank you, sir," she said, casting a shy glance in his direction.

"You are most welcome, my dear," he returned with a smile. "Take my advice and drink it quickly. I confess that I have already consumed one glass at the pavilion. It works wonders to cool one off."

"Oh, no, my lord," she replied, shaking the sausage curls that framed her face, "I cannot think it proper to do other than sip." She did so, then, using the motion to mask her trepidation while she gathered her nerve. At last, with her gaze fastened upon the moisture trickling down the side of her glass, she ventured, "Does your mother intend to take up residence in the dower house soon, by any chance?"

"I beg your pardon?" Justin queried, cursing the bonnet brim that hid her face from his assessing gaze; uncertain what part of her feminine mind the question had sprung from, and even more unsure as to why.

"You had mentioned that your mother wished to plant her new rose variety in her dower house garden," Miss Parkes reiterated softly, tentatively. "I thought perhaps there might be a particular reason for it."

Devil a bit! The chit was angling for his declaration! he realized. He drew on his glass of lemonade as he felt his face grow hot. And then he paused, swallowing. Did she not have the right? He had, after all, been courting her. Was she to be scorned because she wanted to know where his attentions were leading? Perhaps it was not such a bad thing that she had broached the subject with him. Perhaps it was finally the time to discuss their future together. It looked to be the perfect opening, the best of all his dismissed opportunities. He hadn't talked to Palmerton, of course, but these were modern times. There was no reason why he could not discuss the subject with his daughter first. All he had to do was gain her attention, take her hands, and, God help him, just say the words.

Justin tried. Taking a deep breath, he turned toward her,

set aside her lemonade, and locked her gaze within the intensity of his. Blue. Lovely, clear, fathomless blue. Perfect in every way. Except that they did not shine like bright, new copper coins.

"No reason that I know of," Justin said in a rush of words. And then he blinked. He hadn't asked her . . . and his body was almost trembling with relief.

"Oh," Miss Parkes replied, pulling her hands from his tight grasp, her tone heavy with disappointment. "It merely seemed a trifle odd."

"Yes, I suppose," Justin agreed. "But then, my mother does not always do the usual, Miss Parkes. I have learned to live with it, of course. Shall we start back now, my dear?" he asked, suddenly lighter than air and eager to be away. "It has been a most enjoyable afternoon, but I must be careful to return us both in time to prepare for my cousin's come-out ball. And, of course, we must not forget to stop by Stonegate House to procure your cutting, now, must we?"

Taking her arm once again, Justin helped her gain her feet. Then, squelching an urge to whistle, he led her back toward the petal-strewn paths . . . paths that soon reshaped themselves, to his chagrin, into dozens of entrapping, leg-shackling wedding aisles. He groaned silently. He may have escaped making his offer yet again, but the damnabale business would have to be faced sometime. He had done himself no favor this day . . . only prolonged the inevitable. His elevated mood deflated like a hot air balloon in mid-July.

"You may come in now, Bart," Melanie said from the connecting doorway, her low voice cutting through the thick tension in the room like a blacksmith's wedge through white-hot iron. In the mid-afternoon shadows behind her, Maeve and Maudie worked over a tiny infant, starting it breathing, cutting its cord. "Your wife would like to introduce you to your son."

The members of both families had removed to the Hicks's tiny room when Bess first went into labor, giving her more privacy while the three women tended to the birthing. Now, to a person, their expectant faces quickly transformed into broad grins before each of them broke out into loud cheering.

"Me . . ." the big costermonger stammered as tears spurted into his blue eyes and he was inundated with hugs and slaps upon his broad back, "Me son?" In spite of the pummeling he was receiving, still he stood immobile, stunned.

"Your son," Melanie confirmed, tears flowing from her eyes.

"And 'e be—"

"Can you not hear him?" Melanie laughed joyously. "He is well and healthy, Papa, and possessed of a costermonger's lungs!" As if to prove her point, from behind her, the young lad in question immediately set up a braying howl.

Bart gasped, laughed, and nearly crumpled against his companions in relief. Brushing aside a steady river of tears from his weathered face, he immediately began to make his way around the room, enveloping each one as he came to him in a boisterous hug, tossing Ben and Tom into the air to the sound of their delighted shrieks, and finally stooping to plant a wet kiss upon Gran's fevered face.

"Oi has me a son, Gran," he whispered near her ear, his tears bathing her cheeks.

"So ye does, lad," Gran rasped in return, her arm straining weakly upward to embrace him. "So ye does. Now stop all this blather an' go make yerself acquaint' wiv 'im."

Bart nodded against her withered neck and straightened, again whisking tears from his cheeks. Then, turning, he walked straight toward Melanie and enfolded her into his overpowering embrace. "Oi ain't got no way to thank ye, Mel," he told her softly. "Not loike ye needs to be thanked."

"Rubbish," Mel responded, hugging him back. "Go on in and take a good look at Bess's face. You shall understand why I say that I need no thanks."

Bart nodded, his emotions too close to the surface to speak his heart. Yet he did hesitate as he pulled away to go in to his wife and son, his eyes intent upon Melanie's. "Oi be namin' me son Melvin," he told her in a roughened voice, "so's 'e can be Mel . . . after you."

Melanie bit her lower lip to stop its trembling against her vibrant smile. "Melvin," she repeated, her heart overflowing. "I shall be very proud of that."

Bart nodded once again, his eyes speaking all that he was feeling, then he turned abruptly and, after six tragic losses, finally went in to meet his thriving son.

"Come sit down at table, dearie," Maudie commanded kindly, slipping with Maeve into the room to give the new parents some time alone. "Ye be wore out, an' all."

"Aye, lass," Maeve agreed, gently shoving her toward one of the chairs. "Oi'll fetch ye a bumper o' small beer. Ye could use it, Oi thinks."

"Thank you both," Melanie grinned, taking a seat and, pulling six-year-old Ben up to her lap, kissing him soundly. "I am tired, but far too elated to feel it."

"Ye will," Con told her as he rolled his platform over to the low bench nearby and accepted a brimming glass of beer from his wife. "Right abou' the time yer ball begins, Oi expects."

Suddenly, Melanie gasped, her eyes widening. "Oh, no!" she wailed. "How do I manage to keep forgetting about it!

I have to go . . . but, Con, I have not had a chance to tell you what has happened yet."

"Then say it quick-loike," offered Ben from her lap, helping himself to her glass of beer.

Tom, ever the copycat, immediately pulled the glass away from his brother and took a large swallow for himself, an affront which started Ben growling possessively and earned both the boys a solid tap of their father's hand upon their skulls in punishment.

Melanie's eyes danced above her constrained demeanor. "Very well, little monkey, I shall," she told him, kissing the top of his head again as he leaned back against her. "Con, another attempt was made on Stonegate's life. This time it was a gunshot in the lobby of Her Majesty's Theater."

Con's gaze intensified. "Was either o' ye 'urt?"

"No, nothing like that, Con, but it was close."

"Did ye see the bastard?"

"No, but a friend of ours saw the gunman's hand," she told him, aware that the room had grown quiet and now everyone was raptly listening to their conversation. "He said it was a man's hand."

"Did 'e shoot from outside?"

"No, from the lobby. Why do you ask?" she inquired.

" 'Cause if the man be outside when 'e fired, 'e coulda been anyone, Mel," Con responded. "But if 'e be inside, 'e'd have to be dressed in them evening clothes, wouldn't 'e? Otherwise, them majordomo's wouldn't let th' bloke in the door."

"Con," Melanie breathed as the implications of what her friend had said sank in, "I never considered that. But that would mean that the killer was someone in Society!"

"We can't know that fer sure, Mel," Con said levelly, "but Oi doesn't think ye should ignore the possibility."

"Dear God, Con," Melanie sighed, heartsick by his revelation. "His lordship has so much in his dish. Not only have there been three attempts upon his life, but he has only just recently recovered from his feelings of guilt over his brother's death two years ago. Now this."

"Close was they?" Con questioned.

"I think so, yes," Melanie told him, "though from what I gather, they were quite unalike."

"Why'd 'e feel guilty?" Maudie asked from in front of the brazier, not caring if her question might be considered prying.

"Until recently, he thought it was his fault," Melanie responded.

"Don't make no sense," the woman muttered, turning again toward the preparation of the meal.

Melanie laughed softly. "It does if you know Stonegate," she replied. "His lordship felt strongly protective of his rather scapegrace brother. Too much so, perhaps. He told me about the night it happened . . . about the argument that led to their separation so that he was at home when his brother's accident occurred and he was killed . . . about how he had been beset with trying to keep his brother out of trouble when all his brother could think about was his new green waistcoat."

"Green waistcoat?" Ben questioned from her lap.

"Yes," she smiled down at him. "Evidently, he was very proud of it. Tragically, it was all that remained with which to identify his brother after his fall into the Thames."

"Aw, that bloke wiv the green waistcoat didn't fall, Mel," Ben commented quietly, picking at a scab on his elbow. " 'E were pushed."

The room fell silent.

"What?" Melanie queried, astounded.

" 'E were pushed," Ben reiterated, twisting his head

against her shoulder to look at her. "Oi seed it 'appen. Oi remembers tha' green waistcoat."

"Ben Pollard, that were long afore dawn when it 'appened!" his father growled. "Wot was ye doin' down at the mud flats then?"

"It were after tha' big storm, Da," the boy told him, "the one wot comed close on to me birfday. Oi was tryin' to best Bob Thompson an' them older boys wot'd been teasin' me, an' all. Oi made up me mind to 'ave first pickin's."

"So ye left the 'ouse in the middle of the night," Con rasped. "Bugger me! Ye coulda been stole away!"

"Con," Gran wheezed, "it were two years ago. Let th' lad explain."

"Yes, please, Ben," Melanie said, casting an apologetic glance toward the bristling Con for her interruption of his parental prerogative. "Tell us exactly what you saw."

"Well, Oi was workin' Westminster," he began. "From the light, Oi could tell it were on about an hour from dawn. Oi seed this carriage lose a wheel as it were comin' toward me spot out on th' flats, an' then the driver, the lord wiv the green waistcoat, 'e climbed down and started swearin' something awful. Then 'e kicked th' door."

"Then what happened?" Melanie questioned softly.

"Then these two blokes comed up be'ind the lord on foot . . . quiet loike. One o' the blokes hit the lord on his 'ead, an' the other pushed him roight in."

Melanie stroked Ben's hair as her eyes flew to Con's.

"It moight not 'ave been the same man, Mel," he said reasonably, reading her thoughts.

"No," she agreed. "But it is a rather large coincidence, wouldn't you say? Oh, Con, it had to have been Stonegate's brother Ben saw. And if that is the case," she told him as her eyes grew cold and dark, "then I cannot escape the conclusion that whoever succeeded in murdering Stonegate's brother, and whoever wishes to see Stonegate dead, most likely are one and the same man."

Melanie pondered Ben's shocking revelation all the way back to Stonegate House from Portpool Lane. Yet the more she considered it, the less it made sense. Who could want both brothers dead? She had existed in the upper stratum of Society long enough to know that the earl had no overt enemies . . . no covert ones either, if she were to guess. Yet someone had tried to kill him, and had succeeded in doing so to Oliver. In some way, a way she was not yet aware of, there was a link between the two attempts . . . a common thread.

She turned her hansom into South Street, then, still lost in thought, but not so deeply that she was unaware of her surroundings. So close to the earl's home, anyone might recognize her. She must now take special care. Cautiously, therefore, she pulled her wide-brimmed hat down far enough to conceal her face, surreptitiously casting her glance about her as she threaded her way through the traffic toward the entrance to the South Street mews. A rented cabriolet stood in front of Stonegate House, but only a footman was in the vicinity; disinterestedly holding the horses. The carriage itself was empty. She breathed a shallow sigh, grateful for her luck. She had entered the street from a direction which would not take her past the earl's home, and it was only a short distance to the mews. She smiled slightly and relaxed. In moments, she would be safely out of sight. Spotting an opening between a brougham and a laden dray, she clicked to her hack to hurry his pace.

Suddenly, the heavy mahogany door opened at the entrance to Stonegate House. Startled, Melanie involuntarily looked up just as the earl and Miss Parkes stepped outside and started toward the awaiting carriage. He did not see her, concentrating as he was on helping the lady negotiate the flagstone walkway passing beneath her voluminous skirts, but Melanie's copper gaze connected solidly with the deep blue of Miss Parkes's.

Her heart thumped wildly within her even as she instantaneously ducked her head. And yet she knew that her action to conceal herself had come too late. She had seen the exact moment when the lady's eyes had widened and recognition had dawned, and Miss Parkes had realized of a certainty that Lady Melanie Baxter was also Mel, the cabbie.

# Eleven

A little before the hour of eight that evening, Melanie descended the stairs on Simon's arm dressed in an off-the-shoulder gown of white peeking through an overskirt constructed out of wide, scalloped tiers of pale yellow lace, her heart thumping tellingly against the cords of her neck. Dainty yellow rosebuds crowned her midnight hair.

She glanced about her hesitantly, her gaze snagging briefly on the smiles of the others of the family who had gathered in the hall earlier, awaiting the time when they must form the reception line. She fought panic. Stonegate was not among them.

Her gaze quickly swept the hall, then, barely appreciating the beauty of the space in her apprehension. The countess's tasteful decorations for the ball had been carried out to perfection. Interiors gleamed a soft amber from the play of candlelight on freshly scrubbed walls and newly polished wood and brass. Bouquets of captivating flowers scented the air, while tables regally reposed in expectation of their burdens, garbed in crisp white damask and silver. Even now the orchestra, a collection of piano, cornet, violin, and cello, tuned to each other in a distant room.

"Melanie, dear, how lovely you look," the countess said, stepping gracefully toward her in a gown of striped claret satin piped with cords of rose and ecru. Twists of the same fabrics formed a becoming turban stylishly capping the back of her head.

"Thank you, ma'am," Melanie breathed, reassured by the lady's smile. "And your preparations are beautiful. I am overwhelmed."

"Not another word, my dear. It has been my pleasure. But you, young man," she grinned, tapping Simon upon his sleeve as she scanned his immaculately cut black tails. "I vow, the young ladies shall have to double their chaperones when you come of age."

*"Au contraire,* Mama," Angela countered, sweeping up to them with welcoming hugs. "When our cousin comes of age, he shall need bodyguards to keep the ladies from *him."*

As Simon's face scorched, Melanie slid her arm about his slim waist and, with a tension-releasing laugh, pecked him on the cheek.

"What is this? A new parlor game?" Justin's voice rang out suddenly as he stepped into the hall from his study and eyed the group carefully.

Melanie stilled, clutching Simon closer.

"Ah, punishment by kisses, is it? No, do not tell me," he continued, holding up his hands. "The one who is blushing the most must pay the penalty. I can see that quite clearly from Simon's face. Well, as head of the family, I insist upon taking my turn next. Who then shall receive my odious penalty?" His dark eyes sparkling, he strode into the midst of them and intently scrutinized each face.

"Shall it be you, Mama?" he teased, taking her face between his palms. "No, you never embarrass, do you? But I shall kiss you anyway." And he noisily smacked her upon her powdered cheek.

"Angela, what about you?" he said, capturing her face next with one hand while squeezing her cheeks into a comical grin. "No, the only way to make you blush is to remind you what you called Henry when you were in labor with Fanny." Laughing at the sudden rush of splendid color that washed over her, he loudly smacked her, too, upon the cheek.

"Simon?" he said next, and then he burst out laughing as the young man released Melanie, stepped backward, and a horrified look swept over his face. "Rest easy, cousin," he told him over the remnants of his chuckles. "I have never in my life kissed another man's cheek. I have, however, kissed the top of Edward's head." Before Simon could react, Justin dragged his head down and bussed his dark curls soundly.

Instantly Simon's head bobbed up and he stumbled back upon the stairs. Gales of laughter erupted at the antic and soon he was joining in, his look of vexation melting into a wide, embarrassed grin as he drew himself erect again, brushing perfection back into his clothes.

The countess's eyes puddled with tears as she glimpsed a side of Justin she had never before seen. She reached for Angela, squeezing her hand tightly. And then Justin stepped before Melanie.

"And you, scamp?" he asked softly, taking her face between his warm hands. "Have you no blushes for me?"

Stonegate's sudden nearness overwhelmed her. Melanie could not speak.

"Ah, I see that you do," he murmured, close enough that his breath caressed her moistly. "What a shame," he whispered on a deep sigh. "You shall have to pay the penalty." And then his lips were softly skating across hers.

He had only meant to tease, to lighten her all-too-apparent anxiety, but at the first touch, he was lost. Undone by his need, heedless of the others around him, he drew her against his hard warmth, brushing his lips again and again over her eyelids, temples, the mounds of her cheeks. Playfully, his tongue rode the bridge of her narrow nose; his teeth teased its tip. And then his mouth found hers once more, drawing it within his own wet warmth, submerging her entirely within himself.

Melanie ceased to exist apart from him. Her heart's rhythm stumbled, thrummed wildly, then began to echo his. Her thoughts escaped her control, centered only on Stonegate; her senses fused with his, magnifying at the places where she was pressed against his body. The bond between them swelled with each racing heartbeat. She was lost, but it no longer frightened her. She never wished to be found.

"Justin, have your wits gone begging?" the countess cried, her astonished tone abruptly reminding them of the others' presence.

Stonegate slowly released Melanie, his fingers lingering against the soft skin of her neck. "There is no question of it," he murmured with a slow smile meant only for Melanie; and then, much louder, he told the others, "Have I misunderstood the rules, then, Mama? Ah, well, expect I need practice. I have never been one for games. Shall we all step nearer to the door? It is undoubtedly time to form our reception line."

Melanie barely felt her feet touch the floor as she floated on Stonegate's arm to her position in the line beside him. Behind her serene countenance, she swallowed thickly, still trembling slightly from the aftermath of the earl's kiss, but even more so from a returning trepidation. What would Miss Parkes do with her discovery? Perhaps nothing, but that did not seem likely. She recalled all too well the probing conversations that had taken place at the dinner Stonegate had given for them. In hindsight, the subtlety of the interrogation had screamed the obvious. And yet Miss Parkes had always seemed to be kind. Could she really mean to destroy her socially, knowing that Stonegate would be vulnerable as well? What was the point? She inhaled to steady herself, very much fearing that she would learn the answer tonight.

Across from them, the hall clock tolled the hour. As they watched it, Justin reached over and gently touched her hand, a spot of reassurance that eased her trembling. She smiled gratefully. Not unusually, as the *ton* were notorious late-comers, the door knocker remained silent.

Presently, the minute hand advanced past the hour. A sense of restlessness pervaded the room, each slow tick planting seeds of mystification as, still, no one arrived. They glanced at one another, murmuring comments of confusion until the quarter hour loomed, and it, too, passed. Still they waited, now with flickers of anger increasing their pulse beats. And still no one came.

By half past the hour of eight that evening, silence had settled over Stonegate House like a foul mood. Loathe to voice the obvious even amongst themselves, without speaking, they left their stations one by one to drift into the nearby morning room.

Melanie's gaze flickered over each of them as she seated herself beside Simon and took his hand, hesitating over Stonegate's broad frame for only a moment, too heartsick to remain. Of all of them, she alone knew the cause of what was happening. Even Simon did not yet know what Miss Parkes had seen, much less what she surely must have done to them.

She glanced at the countess, then, taking up her embroidery upon her lap, seemingly so calm and content. How would the lady ever be able to forgive her for what was about to happen to her family, especially considering the countess's unflagging generosity toward her? Melanie cringed.

"You are certain the invitations said eight o'clock?" Justin finally questioned tightly, peering out one of the windows, holding his body in rigid tenseness. His face was mottled with his effort to contain his humiliation and anger.

"I am positive, Justin," Angela answered pettishly, not pausing in her restless pacing before the fire, her turquoise and pearl ball gown sweeping perilously close to the flames. "There has been no mistake."

"Then what the deuce has happened?" he muttered through his teeth, leaning one hand upon the window frame. "It is already half past the hour, and no one has as yet arrived."

Melanie's desperate eyes flew to the small sliver of his visible face. Shifting unobtrusively, she clung more tightly to Simon's hand, trying to lend support in his confusion even as she sought to draw strength from him.

"They have found us out, of course," the countess said calmly, taking a stitch in her embroidery. "My dears, we are being given the cut direct."

Justin spun around, his eyes piercing into his mother's, his jaw straining against the resistance of his teeth.

"Mama, are you sure?" Angela questioned, shocked.

"Oh, yes, dear, I am quite certain of it."

"But . . . how? Oh, Mama, what shall we do?"

"Dismiss the orchestra, I believe," the countess responded. "Simon, dear, do ring for Weems, will you?"

Releasing Melanie's hand, Simon rose immediately and walked to the bellpull.

"Oh, do not look so Friday-faced," the countess chided them all with a smile. "No doubt we still have a few friends. We did receive Lady Palmerton's note of regret this afternoon, after all."

"Mama, how is that significant?" Angela queried with

exasperation. "All that tells me is that they have cut us with a bit more propriety."

"Nonsense," her mother replied. "The note said that the entire family had been indisposed after eating tainted meat. They must all be most wretchedly ill. How could any of them have been in Town where they might hear anything?"

A soft knock sounded at the door, then, and the butler entered.

"You wished for me, madam?" he inquired stiffly.

"Yes, Weems," Lady Stonegate told him. "The ball has been cancelled. Please dismiss the orchestra and set the servants to righting the rooms."

"Very good, madam," he replied, his brows elevating only slightly, "but one of the guests has just arrived. Lord Rington. Shall I show him in?"

The countess shook her head. "I cannot think . . ."

"The countess is incorrect," Justin suddenly interrupted. "We should indeed like to see him."

"Very good, sir," Weems replied, bowing as he backed away, closing the door behind him.

Lady Stonegate's eyes were questioning. "Did you think to learn something from him, Justin?" she asked.

"Yes," he responded tersely, turning back toward the window, again losing himself in thought. "He will tell us the truth." In moments the door had again opened and Lord Rington, resplendent in black evening garb, stepped cautiously into the room. "Good evening," he said quietly, making his leg, his eyes touching each of them, lingering upon Melanie.

Justin turned and gestured toward the sofa nearest the fire. "Good evening, Rington," he said flatly. "Please be seated. Brandy?"

"No, no thank you," the baron replied, a bit nervously. "I shan't stay long. But I-I felt you should know why no one—" Again his gaze flickered to Melanie. "You should know, sir, that things are being said."

"Indeed," Justin responded, his tone unchanged. "Please. Do enlighten us."

Rington's gaze skittered another time toward Melanie and returned. He swallowed. "Word swept the *ton* this afternoon that Miss Baxter—"

"Go on," Justin urged quietly.

"That Miss Baxter until recently earned her living driving a hansom cab." His tormented gaze flew toward Melanie, then, and locked. "Forgive me, Miss Baxter," he pleaded. "I did not wish to say such things to you, but several gentlemen are now saying that they remember you and that they suspected your . . . avocation . . . all along. I beg your pardon, dear lady, but I could not allow you to remain ignorant of what was being said."

"What rubbish!" Lady Stonegate defended, stepping into the breach. One swift glance at her son had persuaded her instantly that he was incapable at that moment of opening his jaw wide enough for civil speech. "It is most assuredly kind in you to tell us what is being bruited about, sir, but what is your opinion of these tales? Can you look at my cousin and believe her to have been a London cabbie?"

Lord Rington's gaze centered again on Melanie, swept over her, softened. He swallowed again, ensnared by long lashes and one wayward curl.

"Dear God, no," he whispered, unable to keep the huskiness from his voice.

His view was suddenly blocked by Justin's broad shoulders. "You have our thanks for your information and concern, Rington," the earl stated evenly. "Rest assured that I shall take steps to deal with the situation."

The baron blinked twice, and then nodded. "I was sure

of it," he replied. "And, of course, you may count on my denials on Miss Baxter's behalf."

"We would be most grateful," Justin said, still solidly blocking the baron's view. "Now, if there nothing else . . . ?"

"No," the baron replied quickly, "I have told you all that was being rumored."

"Very well, then," the earl responded, taking the baron's arm and turning him toward the door, "I am certain that you understand my family's need to consider our situation now. You have been most helpful, Rington. Again, you have my thanks." Almost before the baron could bid the others good night, Justin had escorted him into the hall.

"Really, Justin, that was quite rude," his mother scolded, once more taking up her embroidery at his return.

"But necessary," he replied, again closing the door. At once, he turned his full gaze, for the first time since they had left the reception line, upon Melanie.

She cringed. Stonegate's gaze was as it had appeared when she had first met him . . . empty, devoid of any warmth.

"You have had a difficult day," he told her without emotion. "I am sure you and Simon wish to retire for the night."

A swift shaft of anger stabbed at Melanie, forcing aside her despair, thrusting her to the end of her emotional tether. "My lord Stonegate, am I being dismissed?" she inquired archly, rising gloriously to her feet.

Justin's left eyebrow lifted slightly. "Yes," he told her solidly, his eyes suddenly gleaming.

"You shall be discussing me, shall you not?" she challenged, her eyes vibrant with metallic sparks.

Justin nodded. "Yes," he repeated.

Gathering herself, Melanie stood as tall as she could. "I am not a child, my lord, nor is Simon," she stated tersely. "We shall stay."

A glint of admiration flickered in the earl's eyes. How he loved it when she grew angry, when her eyes grew brittle with shards of copper fire! He could never imagine Miss Parkes opposing him so . . . and then his eyes closed briefly on an inhaled sigh. When he opened them again, his gaze was once more hollow, crystalized.

"You shall go willingly to your room, Melanie, or I shall have two of my burliest footmen carry you there."

Melanie stiffened, telling the earl exactly what she thought of his high-handedness with her speaking eyes. "Very well," she said hotly, *"but,* my condescending lord, remember this. Just because you think to plan the road of my life does not mean that I shall drive my hansom over it! Come along, Simon."

Grabbing her brother's hand by the large, bony knuckle of his index finger, she all but dragged him from the room.

"I think I shall strangle him," Melanie muttered as she preceded Simon up the stairs to the first floor. "How dare he think to make decisions about my life without my even being present!"

"Mel, what the deuce is going on?" Simon exclaimed in a loud whisper, snagging her elbow to stop her progress.

Just as suddenly as she had grown angry, Melanie relaxed. "Oh, Simon, I am sorry," she said with an apologetic smile. "A great deal is going on, I am afraid, and I have had no chance to tell you any of it."

"All I know is that you left this morning to deliver Bess's baby," he said with a confused grin. "Did everything go well for her this time?"

"Oh, yes, Simon," Melanie breathed. "It was a beautiful boy . . . and they named him Melvin, after me."

Simon laughed. "Melvin," he repeated, still chuckling. "I have never cared for that name."

"Well, they could hardly name him Melanie, now could they?" she scolded, not quite containing her grin. "But, listen to this, Simon," she continued more soberly. "After the birth, when we were all sitting around for a moment talking together, I learned from little Ben that Oliver's death was not an accident. Ben witnessed it, Simon! He was quite certain that Oliver was pushed."

"Bloody hell!" Simon cursed. "But how could Ben be sure he saw Oliver?"

"The green waistcoat," Melanie answered. "I just happened to mention it, and Ben remembered."

"Deuce take it, Melanie, that means . . ."

"Yes. Someone wants both brothers dead. I think it must be the same man. But there is more, Simon. On my way home, just as I was turning into the mews, Stonegate exited the house with Miss Parkes. He did not see me . . . but she did."

"My God, did she recognize you?" Simon breathed. "Of course, she did! The rumors . . . She is the one who . . ."

"Yes, she has to have been," Melanie agreed.

"Will you tell Justin?" her brother asked.

"No."

"But why?"

"Oh, Simon," Melanie sighed, leaning against the banister. "Stonegate told me on the first day I met him that he wanted her . . . that she was perfect for him. Now, after all that he is facing because of me, how can I in good conscience create doubts in his mind about his future wife as well."

"Perhaps it would be the kinder thing," Simon said softly. "Does it not strike you as odd that not an hour after the daughter learns of your past, the mother begs off an engagement pleading illness involving the entire family?"

"Yes, that had occurred to me, too, Simon. I have no doubt that the Parkes are cutting the Mayhews as well . . . merely a bit more tactfully. And that small kindness is most probably due only to Justin's attachment to their daughter."

"And, of course, neither the countess nor Stonegate would be suspicious of their true motive," Simon continued, "since Miss Parkes's involvement in this whole havy-cavy business is yet unknown to them . . . and will remain so, if you have your way."

"Which I shall," Melanie said firmly.

"I still do not understand why," Simon muttered.

"Because she is what he needs. Besides, I do not think her malicious, Simon. Thoughtless, of a certainty, but not evil. Once she is sure of him, I believe she *will* be the perfect wife for Stonegate. But I cannot think of that now. I am more concerned with what is being said at the moment in the morning room. It is my life they are discussing down there, and I shall be switched if I shall let them make decisions about me without my at least knowing what they are planning."

"We have been ordered to our rooms, Melanie. What the deuce are you thinking to do?" Simon asked in a strained whisper.

"Why, what I always did when you and Jack Pollard got off by yourselves to talk about girls," she told him with a grin. "I shall listen at the door."

Simon's jaw dropped. "Melanie!" he hissed with embarrassment, but she did not hear him. Even before his indignation had risen above his collar, she had already scooted furtively back down the stairs.

\* \* \*

". . . No need for you to do this!" Melanie heard the countess vow just as her ear flattened against the morning room door.

"Indeed there is not!" Angela agreed. "Justin, you are putting yourself on the level of some sort of human sacrifice!"

"Hardly," he returned coldly. "Marriage to Miss Parkes is no more than I had planned to do all along. I shall just have to act more precipitately. Beyond that, my ends are the same."

"You cannot tell me it is what you really wish, Justin," his mother said with emotion roughening her mellow voice. "If it were, you would have offered for Eunice weeks ago."

"Of course I wish it," he returned brusquely. "Miss Parkes will be perfect for me. I am surprised at your resistance, Mama. I have spoken of my intentions often enough."

"With your voice, yes," the countess replied, "but not with your eyes, nor your heart."

Justin made a small noise of irritation. "That does not signify. What is important now is that the reputation Papa worked to build all his life has been destroyed. For his sake . . . for all of ours . . . I must do what I can to reverse the damage, and I must do it quickly."

"Little of lasting value comes from actions performed in haste, Justin," the countess argued.

"Yet only haste may save us," he countered harshly. And then his voice softened. "Mama, what you said earlier is sensible. If there has been illness in the family, I am certain that neither Miss Parkes nor her family can have heard what has happened yet. I must go to them as soon as possible after I see Clarisse in the morning, explain what has happened, and make my offer for her."

"You are also to see Clarisse?"

"Yes," Justin responded flatly. "I must give her her *congé* before I make my declaration. I shall have enough in the way of uncomfortable explanations to give when I call upon Palmerton and his family."

"But, Justin, why do you think a precipitate engagement will help?" Angela questioned angrily.

"Because of Palmerton's standing in the *ton*," Justin returned quickly. "His support and continued acceptance of us, as well as Miss Parkes's acceptance of me, will do much to restore our name."

"Oh, Justin, how cold-blooded it all sounds!" Angela cried, dissolving into tears.

"What would you have me do in the face of this disgrace?" he asked her quietly. "The only other choice we have is to pack our bags and emigrate."

"Justin, really," his mother scolded softly. "You make too much of this. It will all blow over if we just give it a little time." The countess made an impatient noise, then. "You are so like your father sometimes, dearest. If you will just listen to me—"

"No, Mama, you must face reality," he said tenderly. "What has occurred has put us all beyond the pale. And, make no mistake, I am sensible that none of it would have happened if not for me. I was the one who brought Melanie into our midst, knowing what could happen, and yet not caring. She did not want to come, did you know that? She wanted to remain in the Rookery. God help me, perhaps I should have . . . But I would not allow it. I could not stand the thought—" His voice grew more controlled then. "Because she is my cousin, of course . . . a part of my family."

"Of course, dear, and you were right," the countess agreed softly. "But there were other options, Justin. Why did you not send her to one of our homes in the country?"

"Because . . ."

A long silence ensued. Melanie's eyes leaked tears, forming a wet tracery in and around the door's intricate carvings.

"What will you do with her now?" the countess almost whispered.

"She cannot be a part of my household after I am married," Justin replied dully. "She will be a constant reminder to . . . to the *ton*. I have no choice. I must send her away."

Melanie's fingers became claws upon the door's hard, polished mahogany.

The decision was made as Melanie was slowly ascending the stairs toward Simon's room, and along with it came peace. Her eyes closed briefly in relief as she reached the second floor and crossed the gallery. She had taken control of her life once again and the knowledge calmed her; she now knew what she must do.

"Simon?" she called softly, knocking twice.

The door to his room sprang open immediately and the young man pulled her inside, checking the gallery quickly before shutting it behind her. He had taken off his swallow-tailed coat and satin waistcoat, and unbuttoned several buttons of his shirt. The long ribbon of his cravat hung loosely around his neck. Melanie swallowed thickly, memorizing the look of him. He was becoming a very handsome man.

"What did you learn?" he murmured without preamble, scraping his fingers through his black, curling hair.

"Sit down, Simon," she returned quietly, leading him to a pair of chairs reposing before a sluggish fire. When they were seated, she reached across and took hold of both his hands. "It is time, little brother," she said brightly, in spite of eyes that were pooling with tears.

"What do you mean?" he replied, squeezing her hands anxiously.

"I mean that I must leave," she told him in a whisper.

Simon bounded to his feet. "Why?" he rasped angrily. "What did you overhear?"

"Stonegate is to offer for Miss Parkes tomorrow morning," she told him haltingly. "I am to be sent away."

"No, by God!" he cried. "I shall not allow it! I am Westbridge!"

Melanie chuckled softly. "So much arrogance, my lord earl, and hardly two coins to rub together."

"Aw, Melanie . . ."

"Simon, we always knew this day would come."

"But would it be so bad to live on one of Justin's estates?" he reasoned. "At least until I can restore the Manor?"

A soft smile touched her lips. "I have always been used to leading my own life, Simon. You know that. For all its comfort and beauty, the estate would still be my prison, and I would still be in exile, even should you restore the Manor and send for me."

"That's not true," he insisted. "Westbridge Manor will always be your home."

"And I shall always bear my taint," she reminded him honestly. "That is why we have always known that we must separate. I shall bring the *ton's* repugnance down upon anyone who houses me, Simon. Even you."

"Do you think I care?" he asked angrily.

"If you do not, you should," she said evenly. "Think, Simon. You will want to marry some day. Even if you find someone willing at the time to go against her family, accept my past, and let me live with you, how long do you think a woman used to Society will remain content as an outcast among her former friends?"

Simon's face fell. Slowly he seated himself beside her

again, dropping his face into his hands. "What will you do?"

"First, I must assure that Miss Parkes accepts Stonegate's offer tomorrow," she told him firmly. "I wonder that she did not consider the consequences of her foolish actions. She has thrust Stonegate beyond the pale as thoroughly as I. I am quite certain she will reject him now unless I convince her otherwise."

"You are actually going to the Palmerton mansion?" Simon breathed in astonishment.

"Yes, I am," she told him firmly, "while Stonegate is giving his mistress her *congé.*"

"But we know Miss Parkes was behind this whole bumblebroth!" he exclaimed. "Why would you wish to legshackle Justin to the likes of her?"

"Because, as he himself explained it to Angela earlier," she informed him patiently, "being linked in marriage to Palmerton will help to restore his family's name as nothing else could. Lord Palmerton wields immense influence in Society, Simon. With Eunice by his side, and Palmerton seen to be supporting him, he will undoubtedly be able to convince the majority of the *ton* of his innocence in all of this and come out of it unscathed. You, too, will remain acceptable because of him.

"And, too, as I said before, Simon, I do not think Miss Parkes to be an evil young woman . . . merely self-absorbed. Stonegate once told me that she is just the sort of female his father would have wanted for him. He needs her, not only to restore his family's honor, but to be his countess . . . a wife who will understand how to entertain his friends and keep his homes in perfect style. She will never go against his wishes or rip up his peace as I continually do. She will obey his every command with respect and the utmost decorum. And, Simon, Stonegate will never suffer humiliation because of her."

Simon winced exaggeratedly. "And by leg-shackling him to a marionette you think to do him a favor?"

"She is what he wants, Simon," Melanie scolded softly.

"I do not believe that," he stated firmly. "I believe he wants you."

"But I cannot bring him an untainted past, Simon," Melanie countered gently. "She can."

Silence stood between them.

Simon sighed. "All right, then, what do you plan?" he finally asked her, resting his forearms upon his thighs in defeat.

"I shall wait until Stonegate has left for his mistress's house in the morning, take care of my business with Palmerton, and then I shall leave," she answered quietly. "But, Simon, I shall need you to hide my absence for as long as you can. I want to be well away before my plans are discovered."

Simon nodded sadly, swallowing again and again. "Where will you go?" he asked, his voice becoming husky.

"I shall not tell you, dear," she responded in a whisper. "I do not wish to be found. I wish only to disappear so that people will forget all the more quickly that you have a cabbie for a sister, just as we always planned."

"But old plans are not the present reality, Melanie," Simon husked, his eyes flooding. "How can I let you go?"

"By holding me very tightly," she told him, her tears coursing down her cheeks, "and for a very long time. And then, by closing your eyes. I love you, Simon," she told him, rising to step into his embrace. "I will always love you. Never forget that."

"Oh, God, I love you, too, Melanie," he answered, crushing her against him, closing his eyes against the pain.

When he opened them again a long while later, he was alone.

# Twelve

Melanie left Stonegate House the next morning dressed in her cabbie's clothing, leaving everything behind but the items she had brought from the Rookery several weeks earlier. The only exceptions were the two miniatures she had saved from the sale of Westbridge Manor's furnishings; pictures of her mother and father. Those she left for Simon so that he might have in his possession that which she, being older, could remember.

She threaded her way between a dairy maid's swinging buckets and a seller of strawberries as she left the mews, driving her hansom some distance down the street where she brought it to a halt, thinking it best not to begin her own mission to Green Street until Stonegate also brought his rented cabriolet up from the stables and turned it toward his Bloomsbury retreat.

It came to her as she waited that the first time she had seen Stonegate, he had just left Clarisse. Shaking her head at a disgruntled gentleman who wished to hire her, she smiled slightly at the irony. She wondered if his dismissal of the woman would be brief. She hoped not. She had a great deal to say to the Parkes family and she would need a bit of time. And then her eyes widened in alarm. What could she be thinking? If Stonegate was not brief in his visit to his mistress, that would mean that he had chosen a far more lengthy, and most assuredly more intimate, form of goodbye. She scowled, then, her temper gaining the whip hand of her purer motives, her glower easily fending off another hopeful fare.

Suddenly he appeared, emerging from the mews and turning into South Street, feathering his cabriolet to the east toward South Audley Street, toward Bloomsbury and Clarisse. Melanie ducked her head immediately, not because she feared discovery . . . she knew he could not see her . . . but because she did not wish to look upon him any longer than was necessary to identify him, to prolong her pain. She had said her goodbyes to him after she had left Simon . . . within her own heart, of course, as she could not face him directly. All that remained for her now was to learn to forcibly place all thoughts of him behind her. It was the only way she knew she would be able, not to forget . . . no, she knew she could never do that . . . but to survive, day by empty day.

It helped to think of Clarisse, most likely the only woman Stonegate had undoubtedly touched and kissed even more passionately than he had her. He would soon be with her, Melanie thought, welcoming her eager twinge of pique. The thought chafed, and yet, as she clicked to her hack and started her hansom rolling smartly away from the earl's fast disappearing cabriolet, she began to smile quite smugly. Clarisse may have experienced with Stonegate what Melanie would never know, but, by his lordship's own admission, the Cyprian had always preferred Oliver. *He* had had to be content as a mere second place.

It took only a short time for the hansom to reach the Palmerton mansion in Green Street. It was as yet early, the hour when a good portion of London Society was just sitting down to break its fast. Melanie brought her cab to a quick halt in the street outside the black wrought-iron gate and dismounted briskly, knowing that if she stopped to consider what she was doing she would be appalled by her own audacity. Yet she knew she was doing just as she must, and one more blot in her copybook would not matter anyway. Shoving aside her reservations, she tied her horse by his lead to a nearby post and strode purposefully up the short walkway. Then, gathering all her courage into her small fist, she pounded upon the door.

It swung open on meticulously oiled hinges almost instantly. A mist of perspiration formed a sheen across Melanie's upper lip.

"Yes?" a tall, uniformed footman responded, seeing a rather undersized and rudely garbed cabbie standing before him.

"I wish to see Miss Parkes," Melanie told him firmly.

"You may give me the message," the footman informed her, stretching out his hand.

Melanie experienced a prick of anger. Apparently it was quite the norm for the man to only half-listen to what a visitor said.

"You misunderstand," she said more tartly, and with slow, perfect enunciation. "I am here to see Miss Parkes, not to deliver a message."

Starting somewhat, the footman's nose descended, then, and he gave her greater scrutiny, starting at the brim of her wide leather hat and slowly sinking all the way to her worn, dusty shoes.

"Impossible," he finally said.

"Unacceptable," Melanie rebounded instantly. "Think again."

"Incredible!" the man huffed. "See here now. If you have business with someone in the family, use the serving entrance. This entrance is reserved for guests."

"I fail to see what difference it makes," Melanie told

him in a tone she was sure was reasonable. "I shall end up in the same place. Now, stand aside, sir, and let me in."

"Impossible!" the footman vowed fiercely.

Melanie sighed. "Sir, we have just arrived back at the beginning. Am I to take it that you are determined to deny me entrance at my polite request?"

"I am," he stated, his eyes hardening with resolve.

"Very well," Melanie told him, stepping back a few paces and looking up at the rows of mansion windows stacked within each story, glinting in the morning sun. "But remember, please, that I did ask you nicely and with all decorum."

The footman's determination wavered into wariness. "Look here, now," he said, his voice reflecting his uncertainty. "What do you mean by that, you young bounder? What are you up to?"

"Well," Melanie replied with her gaze still roaming over the building's facade, "in this pocket," she said, patting a bulge in the vicinity of her hip, "I have some lovely pebbles . . . the smooth, round ones you find near the banks of the Thames."

"So?" the footman responded haughtily. "In my pocket I have ten bob. It don't signify."

"Ah, but it does," Melanie replied with a regretful smile, still scanning the sparkling panes. "Because in this pocket," she continued, at last lowering her gaze to pinion him as she reached deep into her coat and drew forth a dangling scrap of leather, "I have a sling."

The footman's eyes took on the aspect of a frog run over by a loaded dray.

"The family is gathered at the moment in the dining room, sir," he squeaked, gesturing her into the large hall as he stepped back out of the way. "Kindly follow me."

Melanie smiled sweetly and nodded . . . probably more condescendingly than the Queen.

"I wonder if anyone in the whole of London attended the Stonegate ball?" Viscount Nesbitt commented, his lips curling into a smirk.

"Oh, I think not!" his mother exclaimed, slicing off a piece of sausage. "Who would be so foolish?"

"Well, I, for one, think it all quite oversetting," Eunice commented, sipping tea. "I had truly hoped that the scandal would not also touch Stonegate. I believe I had begun to form a *tendre* for him."

"Did you, darling?" Lady Palmerton purred, shaking her head in regret. "Well, you have a lot of bottom, my dear. You shall soon shake off your megrims and turn your affections toward another gentleman."

"But he was so very handsome," Eunice sighed, stirring at a puddle of semi-dissolved sugar that had settled into the bottom of her cup.

"Hmph!" Lord Palmerton grumped from the head of the table. "Merely mutton got up as lamb, my gel," he told her, glowering. "You mark my word on it. The man was mutton got up as lamb."

Suddenly a husky voice intruded from the doorway.

"Coming it much too brown, don't you think?" Melanie interrupted tersely. "You have known Stonegate since he was in leading strings, my lord, and his father before him. You know as well as I that there is no more honorable man in Town."

"Good . . . God!" the earl gasped as his gaze swung toward the compelling sound, his jowls jiggling beneath his handlebar moustache.

Lady Palmerton's lips formed a perfect circle, matching

her eyes. "You! How dare you come here, you jade!" she sputtered. "Reginald, do something! Oh, this is the outside of enough!"

"Do not overset yourself, Mama, I shall take care of it," Stanley inserted hotly, rising to his feet and striding swiftly to grip Melanie's delicate arm.

Melanie winced, already feeling the bruises begin to form.

"Billings!" the viscount shouted, beginning to manhandle her toward the door. "I need a footman immediately!"

Gathering her dignity, Melanie dug in her heels. "Not a very intelligent move, Nesbitt," she said quietly, twisting her arm back and forth to loosen his crushing grasp. "If you toss me out in the street, I shall simply take my evidence straight to Scotland Yard."

Stanley paused, eyeing her suspiciously, then began again to shove her toward the door.

"What does she mean, Stanley?" his mother demanded worriedly.

"She can mean nothing," he ground out angrily. "None of us has done anything to warrant attention by the police. Obviously the tart thinks to aid the Mayhews by making idle threats."

"Nothing, Nesbitt?" Melanie asked serenely. "Not even murder?"

"Murder!" the earl roared, bounding to his feet. "Stanley, bring that female back in here!"

"Surely you are not giving credence to what the baggage says, Papa!" Stanley hissed, dismissing Billings and the arriving footman even as he dragged Melanie back toward the table.

"You should," Melanie informed them. "I am persuaded I have quite a good case."

"Papa, what is she talking about?" Eunice asked plaintively, her eyes searching Melanie's face.

"Reginald, do something!" the countess cried.

"Silence, all of you!" Palmerton bellowed, swinging his gaze around the room before bringing the full force of his glower upon Melanie. "Stanley, release her arm."

"But, Papa—"

"Do it, Stanley," came the low command.

Angrily, the viscount complied.

"Now, youn'g woman," the earl said, "before I have you charged with trespassing and brought up before the beak, I will have an explanation if you please."

"Of course," Melanie replied politely, still standing as she had not been invited to take a seat. "I have been thinking a great deal about it over the past few weeks, my lord, and I have come to the conclusion that Viscount Nesbitt, and quite possibly Miss Parkes as well, must be charged with the attempted murder of Stonegate."

"What?" Stanley cried, again gripping her arm and, this time, twirling her around to face him. "You must be daft!"

"Not at all," Melanie smiled. "Actually, I have quite a bit of circumstantial evidence."

"Oh, Papa . . ." Eunice breathed.

"Reginald, do something!"

"Quiet, if you please!" the earl ordered with a slash of his hand. Turning again toward Melanie, he smiled coldly. "You said your evidence was circumstantial. One cannot be convicted on only that."

"I am aware of that," Melanie responded with a nod, "but I believe that what I do know will certainly intrigue the police. Considering the interest Sergeant Hillman has taken in the earl's case, I believe he will want to begin looking quite closely into Nasbitt's past activities."

"This is outrageous!" Stanley cried, dropping her arm

to tunnel his fingers through his well-combed hair. "I have attempted no one's murder!"

"Perhaps," Melanie allowed kindly, "but, then again, perhaps not. That will be up to Scotland Yard to determine, will it not?"

"Dear God, Reginald—"

Lady Palmerton's plea was cut off by another slash of the earl's hand. Slowly, he lowered himself into his chair and relaxed against the back. "Very well," he said icily, glaring at Melanie from under wiry brows, "what is this evidence of yours, or are we not allowed to know it?"

"I shall tell you gladly," Melanie replied brightly. "It suits my purposes to do so, you see."

"Young woman, I see nothing at this point," the earl growled, "but I have no doubt that soon you will attend to that minor point."

"Yes, indeed," Melanie told him, smiling. "To begin with, I should tell you that as of this day there have been three attempts upon Stonegate's life."

"Oh, dear, Papa!" Eunice cried, pressing a sustaining fist to her ample breasts.

"Stonegate's recent stabbing was the first, of course," Palmerton commented, ignoring his daughter and concentrating upon Melanie.

"Yes."

"And you are actually accusing Stanley?"

"Of that attempt, no," Melanie replied. "I was acquainted with none of you then, if you recall, nor did I have any knowledge of your activities, so I cannot in all honesty lay blame . . . But it might prove interesting should Scotland Yard begin probing into where the viscount was that night."

"This is beyond anything!" Stanley cried, spinning away. With long strides, he stalked to the sideboard where he poured himself another cup of coffee before throwing himself into his chair in disgust.

"Murder is beyond anything, my lord," Melanie told him harshly, staring him down.

"Do continue, if you please," the earl demanded. "The hour grows late."

Melanie's gaze swung to his and she nodded sedately. "The second attempt took place on the night the viscount, Miss Parkes, Lady D'Antry, and Stonegate went to Vauxhall. I had a small part in his lordship's rescue, if you recall. It was also I who found that the harness traces had been cut."

"Cut?" breathed Eunice as her eyes sought her brother's. "We all could have been killed. Oh, Stanley—"

"Eunice, for the love of God!" he cried. "I did not do it!"

"Oh, Stanley, of course not!" she whimpered. "I did not mean that . . ."

"Then kindly keep your comments to yourself," he rasped. "You condemn me by innuendo."

Melanie slid her gaze toward his and, with a slow smile, delicately elevated one brow.

"The third attempt came when the four of us attended the opera," she continued, concentrating only upon the earl. "You would have heard of it, too, of course. But what you might not have heard was that the shot was aimed at Stonegate, and was almost certainly fired by someone in the *ton*."

The earl's scrutiny remained constant, determined to intimidate. Melanie swallowed as unobtrusively as she could, and held firm.

"How do you know this?" he asked in a low rumble.

"Because the shot was fired from inside the building," she responded readily, "a spot, by the way, where a witness said Nesbitt and Miss Parkes had been standing just prior to the explosion. I conclude that the assailant was a gentleman because, in that location, it is quite difficult to imagine that the staff of the theater would have allowed someone in anything other than evening attire to linger."

"Given that what you say is true," he finally asked, enunciating each word carefully, "what does any of this have to do with my son?"

"Upon each occasion during which I have had the opportunity to observe the viscount," Melanie responded, "he spent a long period away from Stonegate. There was ample opportunity, for instance, for him to tamper with the traces when he left the party to return to the brougham at Vauxhall, and both he and Miss Parkes left us just before the shot was fired at the opera and were seen in the exact vicinity."

"Papa, she *is* accusing me!" Eunice gasped, digging her fist deeper into her chest.

"Why should I not?" Melanie said calmly. "You have proven yourself an accomplished assassin already. Just look what you have done to me."

"Papa!"

"My God, that is enough!" the earl cried, again surging to his feet. "These accusations have no foundation. You have no proof!"

"I do not need proof, my lord," Melanie lashed back at him. "All I need do is plant the seeds. Scotland Yard will investigate your son *and* your daughter for months, digging into every aspect of their lives. Suspicions among their friends will be aroused. Society will begin to wonder just what sort of nest of snakes must live in the mansion on Green Street. In short, Lord Palmerton, your family will soon find itself exactly where Stonegate's now is."

Palmerton collapsed back into his chair. His nostrils billowed with each exhaled breath. Pinpoints of light spangled his eyes like darts of animosity as his gaze stabbed into Melanie, until, finally, his jaw sagged in defeat.

"What is it you want from us?" he asked wretchedly.

"Your support for Stonegate and his family, who are innocent of any of this, and your daughter's promise that when Stonegate comes here later this morning to offer explanations, and his hand, she will accept him."

"You would see us all ruined," Stanley bit out viciously.

"No," Melanie countered, still gazing at the earl. "Your father knows quite well that he has the power to restore Stonegate, and that none of you will suffer."

"Papa, is it true?" Eunice whispered, her clasped hands sliding up to rest beneath her chin. "Could he still be mine?"

The earl's gaze did not waver from Melanie's as he nodded. It was the truth. He had that much power.

"My daughter is aware that Stonegate . . . cares for you," he said bluntly. "No woman wishes to tie herself to a man whose heart belongs to someone else."

Melanie only just controlled her surprise. They knew! But how had they discovered it? Holding her features in rigid serenity, she calmed her thudding heart with several slow, deeply drawn breaths.

That will not be a problem," she told Palmerton honestly. "I shall be leaving London today, and I shall not return. In time, whatever Stonegate might feel for me will fade. However, my lord, in case you think to renege on any bargain we may strike because of my absence, I should tell you that my brother, Simon, knows everything. Should it become necessary, he will go to the police in my stead. He is to remain in Town with Stonegate."

Nodding his understanding of Melanie's terms, the earl asked, "That is it, then? The paltry extent of your blackmail?"

"That is all, my lord," Melanie responded softly. "The loan of your stature, and the hand that your daughter would have given to Stonegate anyway."

"Nothing for yourself? No money?"

"Only one thing for myself," answered Melanie, gazing at him steadily. "Your word."

The soft ticking of a Vulliamy clock above the Adams fireplace measured the next moments of tension, of resignation, with a relentless rhythm until, at last, the earl's shoulders rolled and relaxed.

"You have it," he declared softly.

"You will help him?" Melanie confirmed.

"I will."

"And Miss Parkes?"

"She will marry him."

Melanie nodded. "Then I have accomplished what I came for. I apologize for my untimely interruption," she said, backing toward the door. "As I shall not see you again, I wish all of you well. Truly."

Gracefully, serenely, she curtsyed, straightened her waistcoat, and stepped from the room.


First it was saying goodbye to Simon, then it was exiting the doors of Stonegate House for the very last time. Now she had just assured her own betrothed's future happiness with another woman. It was really getting to be the outside of enough! Melanie dashed away another trickle of tears that refused to abate, struggling to shove the jumble of unwanted emotions behind her as she feathered her hansom into Oxford Street on her way to Portpool Lane for another painful goodbye. Each step she took seemed to sever something inside her. It felt as if, one by one, she were tying off her veins.

And she had not been able to give Stonegate his wedding gift. That distressed her most of all. And then she smiled ruefully. Perhaps, after all, she had served him better. She had thought she would be giving him the name of his assailant as his gift. Instead she had given him his bride. Still, she did not care to leave knowing that he remained in danger. Someone, possibly someone he knew well, still wished to end his life.

She knew that the killer was not Stanley. She had known that even before she had barged through Palmerton's dining room door. Her accusations concerning the brother and sister had, of course, been nothing more than a bluff. She thought of the strangled look on Nesbitt's face when she had stated her evidence, and could not help but smile. No, he was not the one. As caustic as his words always were, there was genuine love in his eyes for his sister. He could not cut the traces on a carriage knowing she was soon to be traveling inside.

He was, however, undeniably hostile toward Stonegate. Melanie could only venture a guess as to why. Judging by the differences in the two men, it seemed most likely a simple case of jealousy.

Quite naturally, and despite her avowed wish, her thoughts wandered then to Stonegate . . . and then, of course, they stumbled quite perversely over to Clarisse. She wondered if he had left the irksome woman yet and made his way to Green Street. Or was he even now reveling in her octopod arms while she remembered nothing but Oliver's warm embrace. Melanie's mouth took on a disgruntled droop. He was a man, drat it all! Of course he had stayed with her. She imagined that Oliver's possession of Clarisse's thoughts meant nothing to him as long as her body was his to possess. Deuce take it, she doubted it concerned him a whit!

And then, gasping, she stiffened, yanking her hack to a complete standstill right in the middle of busy Oxford Street. Curses flew about her like swarming bees as carriages, carts, and drays were forced to swerve wildly, flowing around her angrily as water around an impediment in a tumbling stream. Melanie was aware of none of it. Her jaw had dropped open, her eyes had grown suddenly vacant and horrified. The common thread had been there before her since the beginning, yet she had not seen it . . . and neither, she knew, had Stonegate. The link between the two brothers was Clarisse.

Coming quickly to her senses, Melanie's hands tightened on the reins. Then, with a shout that started several of the horses in the vicinity curvetting and bolting away in fright, she brought her whip down against her hack's leathery flank, launching her hansom like one of Mr. Whinyate's rockets toward Bloomsbury Way.

# Thirteen

Stonegate was not accustomed to knocking in order to gain entrance into his own *pied-à-terre*. As soon as he had brought his cabriolet to a halt, therefore, he jumped down to the cobblestones in front of the building and entered immediately into the narrow hall, pausing only long enough to toss his sable-toned silk top hat, cane, and matching gloves on a convenient table before striding into the house's small parlor.

"Good morning, Mrs. Belmont," he said, as he neared the cold fireplace, spotting the housekeeper on her knees between two Chippendale love seats, polishing an ornate brass andiron.

"Oh, sir!" the woman cried, struggling to her feet while tugging some order into her tiny, beribboned cap. "We did not expect you this morning."

"I realize that, Mrs. Belmont, and I apologize for the inconvenient hour," Justin replied, "but I must speak with your mistress. Will you announce me, please?"

"I believe she is still abed, sir," Mrs. Belmont replied, self-consciously smoothing her white apron.

"Wake her then," Justin commanded kindly.

"Yes, sir," the housekeeper responded with a hastily dipped curtsey, and then, ducking her head, she quickly scurried to do the earl's bidding.

When he was alone, the earl separated the tails of his buff redingote and lowered himself into one of the matched pair of sofas he had ordered covered in a soft aquamarine brocade. The comfortable pair were placed so that they bracketed the fireplace upon a thick swell of Aubusson carpeting colored a cool sea green, and were accompanied in their repose by immaculately polished tables carved in clean, graceful lines. Tension twisted the muscles of his broad shoulders, a physical acknowledgment that this was indeed the most miserable morning of his entire life. He rolled them into his skin's resistance, pushing against the ache as he stretched out his legs and crossed them at the ankle. As always, his thoughts belonged to Melanie.

It had taken all his willpower not to go to her room before he had left the house earlier. After the disastrous ball, he had wanted so badly to see how she had fared. But it had not seemed right to him, going to her when he was on his way to offer another woman his hand. Of course, she would not have known that, but he would have, deuce take it.

Reaching up, he scrubbed his face with his hands. He had treated her shabbily. Stunned by the sudden knowledge of his own ruination, he had acted toward her like an over-bearing, pompous martinet. No matter what kind of rag-mannered scapegrace he felt himself, he knew he must go to her as soon as he had secured Miss Parkes's hand and apologize. And then he would have to explain. Bloody hell, was he going to have to explain!

"Justin, darling, what a lovely surprise," cried Clarisse, shattering his reverie, flowing into the parlor in a lacy pink peignoir, drifting toward him redolent with jasmine.

Justin's shoulders drooped, but he dragged himself to his feet politely. "Clarisse," he responded taking both her out-stretched hands as he kissed her warmly. "Has my abomi-nably early appearance overset you completely?"

"Justin, what rubbish! If I were to be provoked with you it would be because you have not visited me for weeks," she laughed lightly. "Besides, you have awakened at my side often enough to know that mornings find me at my most creative. Shall we go upstairs?"

Justin's grip on her hands tightened. "Not this time, Clarisse," he told her softly.

Clarisse stilled, her smile fading, her eyes narrowing under his. And then she brightened almost immediately. "Ah, I see now. Really, Justin, how naughty!" she laughed, pulling away and walking toward the door. "Mrs. Belmont!" she called, standing in the entrance.

"Yes, madam?" the housekeeper said, quickly appearing from the depths of the hall.

"I have a taste for those cream cakes we buy at the corner bakery. Please go and get some for me."

"Very good, madam," the woman replied, immediately crossing the small entry hall to take her short black cloak from the cupboard nearby.

"Oh, and Mrs. Belmont?" Clarisse called again as the woman moved to the door and stepped outside.

"Yes, madam?"

Clarisse smiled at her brightly. "Do take your time."

The housekeeper nodded in understanding.

Justin watched with concern as Clarisse closed the door and turned back toward him, the silk of her peignoir molding to her every curve as she swept back into the room. Her behavior had shifted oddly when he had refused her invitation to accompany her to the bedroom. Discomfited, he realized that giving her her *congé* was not going to be as easy as he had thought. He studied her as she approached him, his concern blossoming. He could not account for the strange wildness in her eyes.

"Clarisse . . ."

"What shall it be, then, my scandalous lord?" she questioned flirtatiously, trailing lace-covered fingertips against his cheek as she drifted by. "You have never before been so bold, Justin. I believe I rather like the idea of being naked with you in the parlor. Shall you want me here . . . before the fire?" she asked, gesturing with a sensual laugh.

Her demeanor changed again quite suddenly as she glanced toward the sofas. "Oh, damme!" she spit out, twisting her fingers together in agitation, tossing her auburn curls. "There is no fire! Bloody, bloody hell. And the carpet is strewn with dirty rags and polish! Where is that woman? I shall beat her!"

"Clarisse!" Justin asserted with alarm, seizing her shoulders, staring into her eyes. And then he calmed his tone. "You sent her to the bakery."

Clarisse's eyes focused then. "Of course I did," she laughed apologetically. "You must think me hen-witted."

"No, Clarisse," Justin soothed, "but just sit for a moment now, my dear. I must talk to you abo—"

"La, Justin," she interrupted quickly on a high, sudden laugh. "I vow we cannot make love upon the sofas either. You are far too big. We should both end up falling off and polishing the andirons with our posteriors!" She burst into wild laughter, then, deciding that what she had said was inordinately funny.

"Clarisse, stop this," Justin asked her calmly.

"Did you not think it a wonderful jest, Justin?" she managed to say in the midst of her mirth. "Oh, no, I suppose not. You are such a humorless prig, you know. Not at all like Oliver."

Suddenly she pushed him down to the sofa. Caught off balance, Justin fell hard. Almost instantly, she was in his lap, curling against him like a sleeping cat.

"I know," she breathed, running her warm tongue along

the line of his jaw, "I shall take you in my mouth. You like that, do you not?" Flattening her breasts against him, she played a trickle of hot breath over the surface of his ear.

"Clarisse, you must listen to me," Justin commanded softly, seizing her hands and forcing her away from him.

"No!" she shouted, leaping from his lap to stand before him, radiating anger.

Justin held himself in calm stillness. Inside, he churned with alarm, astounded at the rapid changes in behavior he was witnessing.

"Clarisse . . ." he murmured gently.

"I know why you are here!" she shrieked, striding quickly toward a small writing desk and fumbling with something inside the narrow drawer. She spun around, then, and again faced him, her countenance mottled with fury. "You have come to cast me away!"

Justin forced his breathing to slow. "Clarisse, we talked about this weeks ago," he reasoned softly. "You knew that this day was coming . . . that I would soon marry."

As Justin watched, slowly Clarisse's eyes glazed, her focus growing distant, her skin whitening as she sank into the grip of memory.

"You have all done it," she whispered as if she were alone in the room. "My parents first, of course, but I could not punish them. They were already dead."

Justin remained silent, his features reflecting his growing astonishment.

"They had given me into the almshouse, knowing that they were both dying of typhoid," Clarisse continued, lost in the past. "I was three years old. Do you know what I had to do in that place? I had to pick apart old rope for its oakum, even though ships no longer even used it. My fingers bled every single day."

"Clarisse," Justin whispered in sympathy.

"When I grew older, the overseer took me to his bed and taught me how to pleasure him," she went on, ignoring him completely. "I did not mind so much . . . it felt good, and he gave me better food. But he stank and had no teeth in his mouth. I finally refused. The overseer beat me and cast me out that very day. He was the first one I punished."

"What do you mean?" Justin asked quietly.

She looked at him then, and smiled. The smile did not reach her eyes. "I crept back inside the next night," she chuckled, covering her mouth with her hand. "I took the very whip he had used upon me and wrapped it around his neck."

"And then?" Justin uttered, hardly daring to breath.

Clarisse's smile grew mischievous. "Then I pulled it tight."

"My God!" Stonegate breathed as, suddenly, everything became clear to him. "You are the one who has been trying to kill me . . . because you see me as casting you away."

Immediately the earl surged to his feet, reaching for Clarisse.

"Stop where you are!" she cried, withdrawing a pistol from the folds of her peignoir and leveling it at him.

Justin froze instantly. "Give me the gun, Clarisse," he snarled.

"Sit back down," she commanded equally as harshly, stepping back to a position of greater safety. When Justin remained as he was, she raised the barrel slightly and cocked the hammer. Slowly, the earl obeyed. "That was very rude, Justin," she scolded haughtily. "I have not finished yet."

"My apologies. By all means," Justin said with arrogant iciness, "do continue."

"I joined Long Jake's stable then," she complied, the gun sinking slightly. "You wondered why the other women were attacking me when Oliver happened by. I am afraid it was not jealousy, darling. It was because I had punished him, too, after he had threatened to have me killed if I did not leave London." She huffed a short, mirthless laugh then. "I was surprised at the reaction of his other whores, I can tell you," she told him, shaking her head. "They actually cared for him, the sluts!"

"Why did he threaten you?" Justin asked, wanting to keep her talking.

"He said I was cheating him, that I was keeping more than my share of the money I earned," she said frankly.

"Were you?"

"Of course! How was I to get off the streets else?" Clarisse answered, chiding his ignorance.

"What was your punishment this time?" Justin asked softly, wondering if he had time to make it to the door before she could fire.

"I made him eat my money," she laughed. "Was that not appropriate? He was dead within a week."

Justin's jaw clenched.

"And then Oliver took me away from all of that," she said, a sweet smile curving her well-shaped lips. "He was such fun, Justin, and so kind to me. Whatever I wanted he would buy for me, did you know that? He was so sweet. And he taught me things as well . . . how to dress properly, and eat politely . . . and how to talk like a real lady."

"I know you were devastated when he died, Clarisse," Justin said evenly, trying to gauge whether or not if he dived to the floor and rolled . . .

"Not really," she gurgled merrily. "How could I be devastated when I was the one who had had him killed?"

Justin's gaze slewed to hers instantaneously.

"What?" he asked in disbelief.

"Justin, really, must I repeat myself?" she said with irritation. "You heard me correctly."

For long moments, Justin could do nothing but stare at her, unsure that he could even speak. Then, raspingly, he grated out, "But why?"

All emotion leached from Clarisse's face. "He said he had grown tired of me," she said dully. "He gave me my *congé.*"

"How did you do it?" Justin breathed, his hands tight fists against his thighs.

"I hired two men to follow him and do the job when they saw fit," she said casually. "As I had finally climbed into a higher strata of Society, I am certain you can see that it would not have been the thing to actually do the punishing myself."

Justin knew at that moment that he, himself, could also have killed quite easily. "What are your intentions now?" he forced himself to ask.

Clarisse smiled indulgently. "Don't be such a slowtop, Justin," she chided, shaking her head. "Of course, you must be punished, too."

"You have tried before," he told her bluntly.

Her eyes hardened slightly. "Yes, and I admit, with little success. The two who responded to my signal when you last visited, for instance—"

"Signal?" Justin questioned.

"Yes. I had arranged with them ahead of time that if I opened and closed my draperies after you left, they were to attack you, but they proved incompetent as you know. I had certainly not expected that. Gracious, Justin, they had worked for me before. They were the ones who pushed Oliver off Westminster Bridge, don't you know."

Justin's mind shrieked.

"Who poisoned them?" he finally asked.

"I did," she readily confessed. "Do you know, it is quite easy for a woman to get into the men's cells."

"And the harness on the Palmerton brougham?"

"The work of another footpad," she confessed. "The same one, by the way, who followed you to the opera and took a shot at you from the entry." Clarisse laughed then, a sudden burst that filled the room with the sound of insanity. "It was such lovely irony," she giggled gaily. "The suit of evening clothes I gave him to help him gain entry into the theater was an old one that had been left here by you."

"Clarisse," Justin said quietly, trying to distract her, "you cannot keep shooting men who separate from you. As a courtesan, it is a part of your life that it will happen again and again. Such a response on your part is not sane."

Clarisse sobered instantly, her eyes again growing wild. "Not sane?" she whispered without emotion. "Is that what you think?"

"I think you need help, Clarisse," Justin said, rising slowly, positioning himself for his break for safety. "What you have done is not right."

"Oh, but for me it is, Justin," she told him softly, sadly. "It is just not right for you."

At the same time that the gun fired, Melanie burst through the door. Within a particle of a moment, she had taken in the scene, slipped her sling from her pocket, loaded it with a smooth, round pebble and launched the missile toward Clarisse. It slammed against Clarisse's temple just as Stonegate crashed back against aquamarine brocade, the blood flowing from his wound soaking into his sable silk neckcloth in a widening oval of red. Within moments, Melanie had dashed across the room and was cradling Justin's limp body in her arms.

"Oh, Justin," she sobbed, her tears dropping in a measured cadence upon his closed eyes.

"Mel?" came the earl's softly breathed whisper.

"Oh, Justin, yes?" she cried softly, her hands fluttering across his brow and cheeks.

"My eyes feel wet. Are you crying, or am I?" he asked, his eyes remaining closed, his lips curving slightly.

"Oh, what kind of question is that?" Melanie scolded, running her hands next over his body.

"A good one, scamp," he answered haltingly. "Considering that I have a hole in my chest, it is quite pleasant to still be able to . . . feel anything at all."

"Oh, Justin," she whispered, now a complete watering pot.

"I like that," he told her softly.

"What?" she asked, her husky voice a watery waver.

"You are calling me by my name without my even asking."

"Oh, Justin . . ."

"Well, now I know what it takes," he said, panting slightly. "You will call me Justin if I am dying."

Melanie's mouth hardened. "What poppycock!" she exclaimed officiously. "Do you think I shall allow such a thing? Have I not already saved your wretched skin twice? Am I one to waste such efforts? You are not to worry, Stonegate, do you hear me? I shall get you home safely."

"I know," Justin told her with the last of his strength. His eyes opened, then, her tears flowing into his own. With a gentle gaze, he smiled. "I love you, Melanie."

His lids fluttered; closed.

Melanie tenderly touched her lips to the cleft in his chin.

"I love you, too," she told him.

It took all of her strength for Melanie to muscle Stonegate up over her shoulder and carry him, bleeding and un-

conscious, out of the house and up into her cab, but she
did it, growling away the clustered crowd which had gathered outside at the sound of the gun's report, and even the
police, letting no one come near enough to help her, or to
touch him. With fear for him spurring her on, she struggled
up the difficult steps past the hansom wheel to the passenger compartment and lowered the earl to the squabs,
quickly stuffing all of her clean rags against his wound.
When that was done to her satisfaction, she covered him
with a blanket and secured it beneath his limp weight, then
clambered up to her own seat behind the earl and, taking
the ribbons in her gloved hands, slapped impatiently at her
hack's rump, urging him forward at a harrowing pace.

Melanie raced through London, calling upon her years
of experience as a cabbie to mentally chart the swiftest,
most direct path to Stonegate House, and one with the most
uncongested streets. She felt her hack tire in his headlong
gallop, saw him gasp, grow flecked with foam. Yet still she
sped on, praying with each clattering hoofbeat that she
might get Stonegate home on time, cursing her own stu-
pidity for not seeing the truth before her eyes and arriving
too late.

Her control over her sense of panic had almost dissipated
when she finally reached the corner of South Audley and
South Street. Slowing only for Stonegate's sake, she feathered an exacting turn past a tall, spreading plane tree and
aimed her hansom like a weapon down the street's wide
length, launching herself like a bullet until she arrived with
clattering commotion outside Stonegate House. A low bank
of clouds shuttered the morning sun. Melanie did not notice
the change. Not even pausing to tie off the lead, she jumped
down from her high perch and stumbled up the walkway
to the door. Then, doubling up both fists, she pounded with
all her strength upon the polished mahogany.

"Oh, Weems!" she gasped when the door finally opened and the butler stood before her, his eyes round as saucers, horrified.

"Dear God, miss, you are covered with blood!" the man exclaimed, stepping back a pace.

Melanie glanced down, then, realizing for the first time the gruesome sight she presented.

"Never mind that," she said brusquely. "I need your help. Stonegate is in my cab, Weems. He has been badly shot."

"Dear God!" the butler repeated, craning to look past Melanie toward the cab. Immediately, he wheeled about and called into the house, "Bateman . . . Grimes! Attend me instantly!" And then he brushed past Melanie and hurried to the aid of his lord.

It took little time for the butler and two footmen to transport the unconscious earl into the house and up to his bed, and then for Bateman to be dispatched for the doctor. Melanie remained at the head of her hack, stroking his nose anxiously while, one by one, neighbors and curious passers-by collected between her and the wrought-iron fence, speculating upon what might have happened and murmuring to each other of what they had seen. A short time later, the doctor arrived. The crowd separated to allow him entrance, and he was quickly ushered through the door and into the darkened hall as if he were royalty.

The street outside grew quiet, then, as if sensing that inside the great house a life hung in the balance. Melanie's gaze fixed on the earl's windows, sensing the tightened connection between them as never before. Bending her thoughts into the sensation, she willed him to receive her strength.

She realized, then, that there was yet another thing she

could do. Unobtrusively, she separated herself from the collecting crowd, mounting her hansom and gently urging her hack into motion. She rode down the remainder of South Street until she reached the boundary of Hyde Park and Park Lane. Then she turned north, touched her whip to the side of her horse's shoulder, and sent him at a brisk trot toward Green Street.

The door to the Palmerton mansion again opened immediately after Melanie had knocked. She stood quite still while the footman perused her, watching his arrogance build.

"I wish to see Miss Parkes," she finally stated in an unwelcome bit of *déjà vu*. Suddenly self-conscious, she folded her arms across her breasts in an effort to hide the bloodstains.

The footman's eyes widened with dislike and grew resolute. He stepped forward, his large body filling the entry space.

Melanie patted her pocket.

The footman heaved a shoulder-slumping sigh. "In the drawing room," he responded, stepping out of the way. "Please follow me."

Melanie trailed behind the footman as he took her up a flight of stairs covered with runners of Oriental carpeting. At the head of the flight, and just to the right, was the doorway leading to the drawing room. She paused when she reached the top and heard the footman announce her to the family as "that cabbie again," and drew in a steadying breath. Then, squaring her shoulders, she stepped forward into the room.

The earl was already in his battle stance, hands fisted at his portly sides, waiting for her. "If you think to wrest more concessions from us—" And then he halted, looking closely at her. "My God! What the devil has happened to you!"

"Papa, her coat is covered with blood!" Eunice added unnecessarily.

"It is not my blood," Melanie said, her reassurance tinged with a tone of urgency. "It is Stonegate's. He was shot this morning by the assassin."

Nesbitt was instantly on his feet. "You see, Papa! I was telling you the truth." Then he rounded on Melanie. "Only this morning you accused me!"

"Is he all right?" Eunice asked with genuine concern.

"I cannot say," Melanie told her, ignoring the viscount temporarily. "I was not there when the doctor saw him. I do know that his wound is severe."

"Who was his assailant?" Nesbitt asked intensely.

"His mistress, Clarisse."

"Ha!" he said, spinning away. "And to think that you dared to accuse me!"

The earl moved toward her, then, studying her face. "You knew all along that she was the one, did you not?" he accused in return.

"Of course not," Melanie replied, trying to keep the urgency and exasperation out of her voice. "If I had known Stonegate was being threatened by his mistress, she would have been put in jail immediately."

"But you did know that it was not Stanley," the earl insisted, coming to a menacing halt directly in front of her. "I can see that much in your eyes."

"Yes, that much is true," Melanie admitted, "but that has nothing to do with what I wish to see you about now."

"I beg to differ," the earl stated with a glacial smile. "Your beastly blackmail now has no teeth."

"I am aware of that," Melanie stated evenly, "and I know

that I have taken a great risk in coming to see you again today. But I could do nothing else. Stonegate needs Miss Parkes now. He is wounded very badly. I am sensible of the fact that I can no longer force your compliance in doing what is right for that innocent family, but I can, and am, appealing to your sense of humanity."

"What is it you ask?" Miss Parkes queried softly as she came to stand beside her father.

"That you come with me now, and let me take you to him," Melanie responded, letting go of her pride to plead into the other woman's eyes. "He meant to ask for your hand this very day, Miss Parkes. If he had not been shot, you would even now be his betrothed. It can only do him good to know that you are there, that he has your support, when he awakes."

"This is preposterous!" Lady Palmerton exclaimed from her seat by the fire. "You said yourself that you had nothing with which to threaten us anymore. Why should we link ourselves to Stonegate when there is no need?"

"Because it is right! Because he has done nothing more appalling than trying to take care of his family!" Melanie cried, her control snapping. "He did not make me what I am. He did not even know of it. And when he learned of it, he only tried to help me. Tell me, my *lady,* are kindness, loyalty, and responsibility qualities the *ton* now scorns?"

Palmerton glanced at his stunned wife. "No, indeed," he replied more moderately, feeling somewhat chastened.

"Then can you not bring yourself to support him? Not because it is the comfortable thing to do, but because it is right?"

Silence absorbed the thickness of consideration and thought. The earl drifted toward the fire.

"Papa?" Eunice called softly.

After a deep sigh, the earl replied, "Yes, my gel?"

"I should like to go," she stated with quiet firmness.

"But why?" her mother cried.

The earl held up a silencing hand. "Answer your mother's question," he ordered gently.

"Because I do so want him, Papa," she said, her eyes flickering toward Melanie, a flush settling upon her lovely features. "And Miss Baxter is quite correct, is she not? Your support could restore him."

"I believe it is not overstating the case to say that I could," the earl responded arrogantly, "but, my dearest, is this truly what you want?"

"Oh, yes, Papa," she cried softly, "I never . . . that is, I am most deeply distressed that he should be cut for only trying to do good. And he is so very handsome." Again her glance skittered toward Melanie.

"Oh, darling, are you sure?" Lady Palmerton asked again, rising to walk to her side.

"I should like it above all things," Miss Parkes uttered sweetly.

Palmerton turned, then, toward Melanie. For long moments he studied her, the resolve that firmed the delicate line of her jaw, her unusual eyes which shone with sincerity. At last he made his decision.

"Very well, Miss Baxter, Stonegate shall have our support. As a matter of fact," he added as his fingertip came to rest upon his chin, "I believe that I might just be able to use the events of this morning to turn the man into quite a hero."

Tears clouded Melanie's eyes. "Thank you, my lord," she told him, unobtrusively whisking them away.

"Yes, well, get your bonnet, Eunice," the earl commanded gruffly. "When Stonegate is lucid, you will wish for him to know that you are there. I shall have your maid pack a bag and bring it to you later in the day. You will, of course, wish to stay close beside him until he is fully recovered."

"Yes, Papa," Miss Parkes replied, her eyes growing vibrant as she eagerly turned to glide from the room.

When she had left, the earl turned toward Melanie. "Shall you still be leaving, Miss Baxter, or have your plans now changed?"

"I shall go after I see Miss Parkes safely inside Stonegate House," she answered, elevating her chin.

Palmerton nodded, staring at her intently, his eyes comprehending her sacrifice, growing warm with admiration. "That is as it must be, my dear," he told her gently.

Melanie smiled and extended her hand. "I know," she murmured. "Thank you." And then she turned to meet Miss Parkes at the head of the stairs, and quickly followed her down.

A soft rain had begun to fall by the time Melanie once again came to a stop before Stonegate House. Using the levers near her seat, she opened the passenger door for Miss Parkes, assured that one of the gentlemen bystanders would take her hand and help her past the huge wheel to the cobblestones. Miss Parkes gave her only a cursory glance as she stepped into the street before turning and hurrying up the walkway. Melanie watched her knock, speak softly to Weems, and then slip quickly inside.

She let her gaze drift upward, then, to the row of Stonegate's windows, acknowledging that there was nothing more for him she could do. Drawing in a shuddering breath, she slapped the ribbons against her hack's flanks before she could think better of it and levered her way into the traffic headed toward South Audley Street.

She sobbed the entire distance to Portpool Lane.

# *Fourteen*

"Deuce take it, Simon, you are her brother!" Justin spat out from a comfortable chair before the fire in his bed-chamber. He had not been many days out of his bed and the hollowness surrounding his dark eyes spoke of it. Dressed in a sapphire velvet dressing gown, black pegtop trousers, poet-collared shirt, and loosely knotted black silk muffler, his slouch was brooding, puissant.

"Justin, you can ask me the same question every day for the rest of your life, and I still will not be able to give you the answer," Simon returned softly from a companion chair, stretching his pale blue trousered legs toward the slow flames. "I am just as blue-deviled as you are about Melanie's leaving, but what can I do? I have no idea where she has gone. She refused to tell me."

"I am not blue-deviled, Simon," Justin insisted, recalling yet again as he stared into the flames exactly how he had felt when he had finally awakened after surviving a ravaging four-day fever to find that she had left him. "I am furious."

"Why?"

Justin's gaze slewed to his cousin's. "What kind of question is that to ask me?" he growled tersely.

"A good one, I think," Simon replied evenly. "Or should I put another interpretation upon your continued avowal to ask for Miss Parkes's hand, not to mention her constant presence in your home for the last three weeks."

The earl pierced his cousin's gaze with a speaking glance before dropping his freshly shaved chin into his palm on a heavy sigh. "God, Simon, I feel as if I am being drawn and quartered," he murmured tiredly. He straightened somewhat, then, rolling one shoulder to gingerly test his healing wound.

"I shouldn't wonder," Simon commented with a soft half-smile, ". . . feeling duty-bound to offer for a vapid marionette when you are top over tails in love with my sister."

Justin's eyes rounded as his gaze jerked back toward Simon's. "How did you—? Devil a bit! Did Melanie keep nothing from you?"

Simon chuckled then. "Be at ease, mutton-head. She didn't have to. I was present on the night of her ball, if you recall. Bloody hell, Justin, I saw the way you kissed her!"

Justin's sallow complexion quickly flooded with color. His gaze again sought the soothing flicker of the fire. "It does not signify," he said huskily. "It cannot."

"Well, the two of you certainly agree on that point," Simon commented softly. "And that, of course, is why my sister no longer exists in our lives."

"Damnation, I couldn't, Simon," the earl murmured, clenching his fists. "Melanie understood that."

"Mmm . . . and, as usual, she has taken the burden of it from you at her own expense, and without bothering to ask if you even wished such a noble sacrifice, has she not?" Simon observed with a slight smile. "Oh, do not start feeling as if you must shoulder part of the blame for it, cousin," he chided, holding up an arresting hand. "If you remember, eight years ago she did exactly the same thing for me. She always has done. It is her way."

Justin seethed with frustration. The weight of his obligation to his title and Melanie's disappearance twisted inside him, overflowed. Growling angrily, he shot an arm out and swept a vase of pungent roses from the table between them, sending the fragile Wedgwood porcelain crashing to the floor. "Deuce take it, Simon, she is all alone. Anything could be happening to her! By God, if I ever get my hands on that damnable woman again, I shall—"

A soft scratching at the door interrupted Stonegate's telling of the indecorous detail.

"Enter!" he commanded brusquely.

"Justin?" queried Miss Parkes anxiously, peeking her head around the door. "I thought I heard a crash. Oh, I do beg your pardon," she pleaded, seeing Simon, "I see that I am interrupting you."

The earl's next breath was deeply drawn, settling.

"No, indeed," he countered in a controlled voice, gathering his discontent and shoving it away somewhere inside him like dirty linen into a wicker hamper. "After your weeks of attendance upon me, my dear, how can you think I would consider your presence an interruption? Do come in," he invited with a warm smile. "I am afraid I have clumsily knocked the vase of flowers you brought me yesterday to the floor."

Eunice returned his smile solicitously. "Give it no further thought," she said, gliding across the room in a blue taffeta morning round gown whose draped, V-shaped bodice folds, long sleeves gathered *à la mameluke,* and three flounces of crimson lace accentuated her abundant figure enticingly. As she bent to pick up the broken pieces of the vase, her blond hair, which had been parted in the middle and smoothed toward three clusters of sausage curls, one over each ear and the other at her nape, exuded the scent of jasmine.

"I have my favorite of Miss Austen's works with me this morning," she told him with soft delicacy as she straightened, showing him the book before carrying the shards to the waste can. *"Pride and Prejudice.* I thought that you might care to have me read to you again."

Pride and prejudice. Justin almost choked on the irony.

"Actually, my dear," he said, his smile becoming a bit more strained, "I believe I should rather forgo that pleasure this morning and enjoy a conversation with you instead. Perhaps another time."

"Of course," Miss Parkes responded, concealing all show of reaction beneath serenity.

"And I must be on my way," Simon inserted, rising to his feet. "Morty has finally persuaded me to play cricket with his team this morning. I told him it was a maggoty notion," he continued, glancing defiantly toward Miss Parkes. "Pitching pennies and mumblety-peg were our only sports in Portpool Lane. But he insisted, and it keeps my mind off . . . er, occupied."

Justin's gaze narrowed at the surprising undercurrent in the room between the two of them, but nodded his dismissal. "Off with you then," he ordered in spite of his curiosity. "We shall talk again."

"Oh, I am sure of it," the young man nodded, letting his gaze rest for a moment upon the earl, "but it shan't change anything."

Justin propped his elbows upon the arms of the chair and cupped the tips of his touching index fingers with the small dent in the center of his chin.

As soon as the door had closed behind Simon, Miss Parkes moved forward to take his vacant chair, passing close enough to Justin for her skirt to brush against his trousers and his nostrils to be filled with her perfume.

When she had seated herself across from him, she slowly, tantalizingly, lifted her blue gaze to his.

"Shall you care to hear the latest in the Court Scandal?" she inquired softly with a rather impish smile. "I have just had a visit from Miss Elizabeth Wilmington and she has told me all."

"Indeed," Justin commented, allowing his head to once again sag against his palm. "The whole scandal broth seems to me nothing more than a tempest in a teapot."

He smiled slightly over Eunice's attempt to flirt with him and, for once, was not vexed by a woman's blatant wiles. The discovery cheered him somewhat. It seemed a rather positive development for their future together that he seemed to be able to inspire a good, healthy case of lust in the decorous girl, but then his spirits drooped. Unfortunately, as far as he was concerned, he felt nothing at all.

"Surely not, sir," the lady countered quite genteelly, smoothing her skirts. "The Queen's own lady-in-waiting has been accused of being . . . well . . ."

*"Enceinte?"* Justin suggested disinterestedly, allowing his gaze to drift over the objects on the mantel.

"Er, yes," Eunice stated through a pretty blush. And then her eyes brightened. "Supposedly it was by the Duchess of Kent's confidant, Sir John Conroy! Just imagine it. She is the Queen's own mother!"

Justin did not comment. His gaze had dropped to ride upon the rise and fall of the flames. He saw Melanie's molten eyes shimmering within the fire.

"You know that Lord Melbourne asked the Queen's physician, Sir James Clark, to determine if it were true, do you not?" Eunice continued, her voice becoming charged with intrigue as if planning treason. "Well, Miss Wilmington just told me that the examination proved that Lady Hastings was suffering from a growth in her abdomen, not a preg—that is, an *accouchement*. Is that not the most astonishing thing?"

"Mmm," responded Justin, seeing Melanie's lips begin to take shape.

"The Queen has asked her forgiveness, of course," Miss Parkes continued obligingly, "but Miss Wilmington told me that Lady Hastings had written of the whole bumble-broth to her brother. He has now arrived in Town and is bruiting it about that his sister's honor has been irreparably impugned, and that it is all the Prime Minister's fault. He is demanding that the Queen dismiss Lord Melbourne!"

"A tempest in a teapot," Justin repeated in a murmur, remembering the first touch of his lips upon Melanie's at the ball, the feel of her against him, the way she so easily stole away his sober pomposity and replaced it with laughter. The connection had not broken with her absence; it had intensified. He felt it now. It pulled at his soul with a constant ache. Remembering, he let his head roll back against the comfortable cushions of his chair and closed his eyes.

"Oh, Justin, forgive me," Eunice said solicitously, placing warm fingers upon his arm. "I am tiring you with my chatter, am I not?"

"No, of course not," Justin reassured her politely. "The fault is mine, my dear. My mind is on other things, I am afraid."

Eunice lowered her lashes before her gaze could reveal her sudden ire. When she had again raised them, she was smiling at him warmly. "Perhaps, then, you would care to speak of more pleasant subjects," she suggested, fingering a curl before letting her hand slide slowly, gracefully, down to her bosom to touch absently at a pleat covering her breast.

Justin followed the movement with his eyes, knowing what she was doing and trying to react, trying to visualize himself sitting with her like this for the remainder of his life. He could not. Panic nudged at the edges of his mind.

"Perhaps," he replied.

"Miss Wilmington said that Albert of Saxe-Coburg is to pay another visit to the Queen," she told him, smiling as she again lowered her lids demurely.

"And have they arrived at a date for the wedding?" Justin asked, imagining Eunice gliding down the aisle toward him at St. George's. The image would not remain. When he mentally raised his bride's veil and cradled her face between his hands, his fingers were ensnared by short, midnight curls and he was adrift in a copper-colored sea.

"It is to be in February of next year," Eunice answered, her lashes fluttering appealingly. "I shall be *aux anges*."

"Will you?" Justin queried in what he hoped was a show of interest.

"Oh, yes," she breathed. "It is all so exciting, is it not? All of London seems to be caught up in Her Majesty's obvious *tendre* for Prince Albert. Mama says that couples are having the banns read all over Town."

Justin's heart began to beat arhythmically. He knew exactly why she had spoken of the Queen's upcoming marriage. She could not have hinted more broadly and still called herself a well-bred lady. He had to do it . . . for the sake of his family, his title, his honor. He would never have a more perfect opportunity. His lips parted as he looked at her; he drew in a deep breath . . .

Nothing came out.

Miss Parkes waited, smiling at him patiently, expectantly.

He could not speak the words.

Miss Parkes clasped her hands together on her lap, her smile waning as she studied the neatly rounded tip of one thumbnail. Moments passed as she summoned her courage, gathering it about her, weighing the risk. When she was prepared, she looked up.

"You cannot stop thinking of Miss Baxter, can you?" she queried softly.

Justin started slightly, but held himself calm. So she knew. Yet perhaps that was not such a bad thing. Perhaps the time had come for the truth. Perhaps if there were complete honesty between the two of them, his offer of marriage would come more easily.

"No," he finally answered.

"I knew that you could not," she told him, again studying her hands. "I know that you love her."

"How . . . ?"

"I saw you kissing her on the terrace at the Fremonts' ball," she whispered.

Justin's lids shuttered briefly. "I am sorry for that," he told her, meaning it wholeheartedly.

"I could be everything you need in a wife, Justin," she whispered plaintively.

The earl's gaze grew tender. "I know," he replied.

"I was raised to it," she continued. "She was not."

"I know that, too."

"Then why . . . ?"

"Please do not make this awkward for yourself, Eunice," he interrupted gently. "How can I speak to *you* of the reasons?"

"Because you must," she insisted, her voice, for the first time since he had met her, tinged with anger. "Because until she came into your life, you had made your intentions toward me clear . . . if not by your words, certainly by the press of your courtship. Because of that, I have a right to know."

Stonegate sighed, suddenly overcome by weariness. "Because I love her," he said gently, his mind seeing

Melanie's flame-colored eyes, hearing her husky voice. "Because, I have discovered, love makes no allowances for what is politic or socially correct. She is my own heart, Eunice."

Miss Parkes inhaled audibly and rose quickly from her chair. Stepping toward the fire, she stared into it. Suddenly she turned, her face tense with emotion. "But you would never be happy with her, Justin," she exclaimed. "Can you honestly tell me that you would ever be able to control her . . . to trust her? Think of her past duplicity! No one in Society will ever be able to countenance it, or her, my lord. Why, the first time I discovered it, I was so shocked that I pricked myself quite painfully!"

A sudden stillness rested upon the earl.

"What?" he finally queried quietly. "You pricked yourself?"

"Yes," Eunice responded without thinking, breathing rapidly, "but do not overset yourself, Justin. It was only upon a small thorn on the rose cutting."

"The cutting my mother gave you?" Justin asked again, recalling the day, his eyes narrowing slightly.

"Yes, of course," Eunice cried dismissively. "Justin, please try to see reason. Miss Baxter will not be able to entertain as it should be done for a man of your stature. Can you picture her giving a dinner party? Has she any idea of the proper order of progression into the dining room so as not to give persons of rank offen—"

"Mother gave the cutting to you the morning of Miss Baxter's ball, did she not?" the earl interrupted, piercing her with a rapier gaze.

"Yes," Miss Parkes replied anxiously, "but what does that have to do—"

And then she stilled, realizing with anguish what she had just revealed. Her eyes closed briefly.

"You saw Miss Baxter dressed as a cabbie outside my house that afternoon," he stated, already knowing that it was a fact.

Miss Parkes began to tremble. "I . . ."

"You were the one who bruited her past about."

"If you will let me explain . . ."

"Explain what?" Justin asked atonally. *"Your* duplicity?"

Eunice rebounded as if she had been slapped. "Very well!" she snapped, angrily accepting that the situation had passed beyond the point of denial. "It is exactly as you have said. I made sure she would be ruined for her impertinence in thinking she could insert herself into the *ton,* and humiliated at her ball."

"And in the process, ruined me," Stonegate added coldly. "Not a very self-serving move, my dear."

"I had hoped that you would not be hurt by my actions, of course," she said with heat.

Odd occurrences suddenly began to make sense to Justin.

"There was no tainted meat," he realized. "Once your family had seen that my reputation was suffering, you had no intention of maintaining the acquaintance with my family or accepting my suit, did you?"

"No," she responded petulantly.

"And yet your father has been working ever since the shooting to redeem me in Society's eyes. Why?"

"Because of her," she snapped.

"Melanie?"

"Yes, your precious Melanie!" Eunice answered. "She came to Green Street on the morning you were shot and convinced my father to help you, and me to give you my hand." And then she laughed, short and mirthlessly. "Should you ask, of course."

"How the deuce did she do that?" Justin wondered aloud, truly amazed.

"Blackmail," Eunice spat out, spinning again toward the fire.

After a split second of astonished silence, Stonegate shouted with laughter, rocking against the soft arms of his chair until his sides ached and his wound began to throb.

"B-Blackmail?" he burbled when he could at last control himself.

Eunice threw him a disgusted look. "She said she would tell Scotland Yard that Stanley was the one trying to murder you."

Again the earl's eyes widened and he laughed with unconstrained joy. "Dear God," he finally managed, "that's my cabbie."

"Justin, darling, are you all right?" Lady Stonegate said, bursting through the door. "I heard loud shouting—"

"Merely laughter, Mama," Justin interrupted on a chuckle. "Do come join us. I am having a wonderful time."

"Well, I am pleased, I'm sure," the countess told him with a befuddled smile as she did as she was bid. "But you must not tire yourself, my love," she scolded. "And Eunice, dear, as long as I am here to keep my son company, I insist that you also get some rest. You are not looking at all the thing."

"Miss Parkes will be getting all the rest she needs from now on, Mama," the earl announced, looking pointedly at Eunice as his mirth took second place to his need to rid himself of the duplicitous young woman forever. "As much as I have appreciated her tender concern for me over the past three weeks, she has now found it necessary to return to her own home."

"Oh, surely not!" the countess exclaimed, intently examining the young woman's rigid features with gleaming eyes that were not quite filled with disappointment.

"Yes, I fear that I must," Eunice said tightly. "My father has sent for me. By your leave, Lady Stonegate, I shall ask my maid to pack my things now. It seems I am needed at home right away."

"Of course, dear, if you truly must," the countess sympathized pleasantly. "And, of course, Stonegate and I cannot begin to express our gratitude."

"No expression is necessary, ma'am," Eunice replied. Then, swinging her gaze back to Justin for a long, lingering moment, she made a deep curtsey. "If I may be excused . . ."

With hurt, haughty arrogance, she turned and left the room.

"Goodness, dear, what was that all about?" the countess asked when the door had closed behind Miss Parkes.

Slowly, painstakingly, Justin rose from his chair and stepped toward the fireplace. "Just before you came in, Eunice confessed that she was the one who spread about the tale of Melanie's past."

"Never say so!" the countess exclaimed, moving to stand beside her son before the fire. "But, darling, that is an appalling deed. Whyever were you laughing when I passed by your door?"

Justin started chuckling all over again. "Apparently Melanie must have known that Eunice was the one who brought about her ruin. When she saw that all of us had been harmed by the gossip as well, she must have determined to do something about it. She went to Palmerton and forced him to use his influence to help us."

"Darling, I still fail to see the humor," the countess said with a shake of her head.

"It is in how she secured his help," Justin told her, chuckling harder.

"Well, how did she?" Lady Stonegate asked, unable to control the escape of a few wayward giggles.

"She used blackmail," the earl replied, again laughing out loud, leaning against the mantel for support.

"Never say so!" gasped the countess, bubbling over with mirth. "Whatever did she threaten them with?"

"Telling the police that Stanley plotted my murder," he chortled, wiping his eyes.

The countess giggled helplessly. "Oh, darling," she gasped, as soon as she could catch her breath, "only our Melanie would think to do something as audacious as that! How shall we live without her?"

Justin's joy ended even as his laughter suddenly died.

"I don't know, Mama," he breathed bleakly. "Somehow, we shall just have to, I suppose."

"Oh, Justin . . ." the countess said with a gentle smile, resting her warm palm upon her son's face. "Why?"

The earl's dark eyes found hers. "Because nothing has changed, Mama," he told her with resignation bulging at the corner of his chiseled jaw. "She has a tainted past. It has put her beyond the pale forever. Can you not see Papa's face if he were here right now? He would be livid with indignation and outrage that I would even conceive of such a notion as to sully myself with her."

"Oh, darling, you are so like him," the countess stated with a loving smile, "so proud, so unwilling to follow your heart instead of your perceived obligation to your family and title. And yet your father betrothed you to her. Do you not wonder at life's ironies?"

Justin's startled gaze narrowed. "The obligation exists, Mama," he said softly. "It cannot be denied."

"Ah, and yet your father . . ." She stopped abruptly then. "Justin, let me ask you . . . do you love her?"

The earl's whole stance softened as he closed his eyes.

"Oh, God . . . yes!" he told her.

"And she, of course, loves you."

Swallowing thickly, Justin nodded. "She has told me that she does."

Lady Stonegate's smile intensified. "Darling, do you remember my telling you that your father had a mistress before we were married?"

"Yes, of course," he replied, looking curiously at her. "But, Mama, what does that have to do—"

"Just listen to me," she commanded. "This has been held in your father's heart, and in mine, for far too long, I think. It is time that it should be said."

"Very well," Justin acceded. "I am listening."

The countess's expression softened; her eyes reflected her remembrance. "Your father wished only the best for you, dear," she began, taking his face between her palms. "He wanted so very much to assure that your life would never know the kind of unhappiness that marred the early years of his."

"Unhappiness?" Justin asked, mystified.

"Yes. That is why he was so strict with you, my dearest son," she continued, "so rigid. He did not want you to make the same mistakes. It was the only thing we ever argued about. He was so adamant that you never suffer as he did, and I, being of a brighter spirit and so willing to blind myself to every unpleasantness, argued that nothing was as bad as it seemed . . . that you should be allowed to live free. I know now that, because he loved me, he shielded me from the worst of it."

"Mama, what . . . ?"

". . . You see, your father could never forget the sting of societal censure so early in his manhood, whereas I . . . I only saw our great success. And our marriage was a success, Justin, make no mistake about that. Your father and

I loved each other with a passion that lasted until the last day of his life." Suddenly, the countess's eyes puddled with tears. "But I did not want to admit to the hurt of the early years, and so we argued, and loved, even as your father did his best to shield me from it."

"Mama, why are you telling me these things?" Justin tried to insert.

The countess ignored him, caught in the momentum of confession, lost in memory. "The truth, of course, is somewhere in between. One cannot blind oneself to reality, but neither can one refuse to acknowledge the happiness that will surely exist. Never doubt for a moment that there will be pain and rejection, Justin. There will be. But if you accept it, and face it together, you will be the better for it, for there will also be unbounded joy. So much that nothing else will matter. And friendships, too, in time, if you are patient, with those who are not so narrow of mind. And then, one day there will be complete forgetfulness. Oh, Justin," she whispered as a tear slid down her channeled cheek, "that is perhaps the greatest lesson I have ever learned. The *ton* is such a mindless, petulant child."

"Mama . . ." Justin began, not comprehending.

''Oh, darling," she smiled gently, focusing upon his face, "do you not understand yet? Your father once stood exactly where you now are. He once had a mistress whom he loved more than his own life. His family had selected a bride for him, a woman who would have taken him into the highest circles of the *haute monde* . . . the perfect wife. And yet he could not give up his mistress. His whole heart belonged to her."

"What did he do?" the earl husked, stunned.

Lady Stonegate shook her head and grinned at her thick-witted son. "The earth trembled a bit, but did not fall apart. Justin, darling . . . he married her."

# Fifteen

A cold mist of rain pearled upon the slick, black hood of the hansom as Melanie turned her hack away from York Minster toward Young's Hotel, where she deftly pulled to a stop next to the entrance. Using the lever near her seat, she opened the passenger door and waited until the gentleman she had been carrying stepped outside.

"My thanks, lad," the gentleman said, probing his pocket until he came up with sufficient coins before pressing them into her hand.

Melanie smiled and nodded, watching as he turned and strode briskly into the ancient hotel. And then her shoulders sagged. This was going to absolutely, positively, without any question, be her last fare for the day. Before anyone could make demands upon her to the contrary, she touched her whip to her horse's flank, traveling only a short distance before turning right into Stonegate.

She smiled once again, as she always did, when she thought of the street's name. When she had first come to York almost a month ago, it had seemed like a sign. She had learned since then that the suffix gate was a holdover from the time when the Vikings controlled the area, and that it meant merely street, but that did not signify. She had known from the moment she saw it that she had found her

new home. She had determined instantly to settle somewhere in the vicinity.

Very carefully, cautiously, because the ancient streets
were so narrow one could almost stand with arms out-
stretched and touch the buildings on either side, she swung
wide and directed her hack into one of the even more
threadlike alleys, or snickelways, that branched off Stonegate, weaving between the half-timbered overhangs until
she came to a small stable tucked next to a long-forgotten
carriageway. Feathering another exacting turn, she drove
her hansom inside.

Due to the extra accumulation of mud created by the
weather, it took longer than usual to rub down her horse,
feed him, and then dry and clean the carriage. Therefore,
when Melanie finally was able to drift wearily up to the
back entrance of the narrow slit of a house she had rented,
she was thoroughly exhausted. Slipping her rain-darkened,
wide-brimmed leather hat from her dark curls, she slid the
soles of her shoes over the scraper just outside the door to
remove the day's mud, inserted her key into the cranky lock,
and stepped into the scullery.

Thankfully, it was warm and dry inside. Melanie hung
her cloak and hat on a peg just inside the door, then strode
over to the sink where she carefully washed away her latest
collection of grime, finishing her ablutions by briskly
abrading her face and hands with a rough towel before
ruffling it back and forth over her rain-dampened hair.
Then, her stomach rumbling noisily, she stepped through
the adjoining door into her kitchen.

Stonegate's tall, broad body filled the tiny space.

Melanie's mouth dropped open; she stared, her full lower
lip trembling its way up to wedge itself between her teeth.
Tears of astonishment and pure joy leaped into her eyes,

giving them an aspect of liquid fire in the waning daylight as she stood unmoving, disbelieving.

He was really there. Dressed in a dove gray, single-breasted frock coat, charcoal peg-topped trousers, and a black silk cravat, he was the most splendid, most welcome sight she had ever seen. Her heart began thudding against her throat.

Logic suggested to her that sooner or later she had to shake herself out of her foolish stupor and say something to him . . . anything! . . . yet she could not. Her bubbling emotions prodded her to tearfully confess to him how glad she was to see him, how much she had missed him, how the bond still pulled, but her jaw refused to cooperate. Growing increasingly discomfited, she forced her mouth to move. What came out from between her lips when she did caused a radiant blush to tint even the tips of her toes.

"Bloody hell, Stonegate. It's you."

Recalling very well that he had said almost exactly the same thing to her when he had first seen her dressed as a woman in her Rookery garret, Justin burst into laughter.

"I am relieved to know that you haven't forgotten me," he said over his chuckles. "You look like a hedgehog, Melanie."

"Oh!" she gasped, suddenly remembering how she had carelessly toweled her hair. Her eyes flew up, nearly crossing as she tried to assess the damage, then she abandoned that effort and began to tunnel frantic fingers through the tangled midnight mess.

"Leave it, scamp," the earl commanded, a touch of belligerence gleaming in his laughing eyes, "and stand very still. I intend to do now what I have wanted to do for almost a month."

Melanie's eyes grew round. "What is that?" she asked,

her fingers halting in mid-stroke, then sliding from her curls to rest at her sides.

"Strangle you," Justin answered, and he started forward.

Melanie's eyes suddenly sparkled with challenge. "I think not," she responded, crouching slightly. Instantly her sling was in her hands, a pebble fitted into its well-shaped groove. "You shall never get close enough."

The earl's left eyebrow soared above his widening smile. "Go ahead," he dared her, his voice softening almost to a whisper. "If you strike me hard enough, I may yet have one last chance to hear you call me Justin."

The sling slipped from Melanie's fingers to softly thud against the flagstone floor. Her breath left her on a silent sigh.

Justin had her mouth crushed beneath his before the pebble in her sling had had a chance to bounce twice. "Damnation, Melanie," he sighed against her, tasting each corner of her lips with the tip of his tongue, polishing each tooth. "You smell like roses and horse." Again his lips descended, more gently this time, moving over hers with insistent sensuality, telling her as nothing else could how much he had missed her, of his poignant, pressing need.

"How did you find me?" she finally managed to ask, her voice low and husky, its timbre vibrating against the sensitive tips of every single one of Justin's nerves.

The earl's eyes darkened under a chiding frown as he pulled back slightly. "After I was finally able to put aside my anger at finding you gone when I awoke from my fever—"

"You had a fever?" Melanie interrupted, tears again springing into her eyes.

"Yes, I did," Justin told her, pouting just the tiniest bit, "for four days. And there was not one swallow left of your catnip and meadowsweet."

Melanie unsuccessfully tried to bite back her smile. "How remiss of me," she commented, sliding her warm palms down beneath his crisp lapels. "Have you fully recovered?"

Justin's face stretched into an impish smile. "Every part of me."

Melanie's head tipped to the side in question, and then she dropped her gaze, flushing. She was not entirely sure what his response had meant, but she knew of a certainty from the look in his eyes that she definitely should not ask.

"I am pleased to hear it," she told him sincerely, "but you still have not told me how you found me."

"It was quite simple really," the earl stated arrogantly, loosening his hold so that they might look at one another more easily. "Once I had stopped wishing to shake you until your eyes rolled around inside your head, I realized that you could never have passed the remainder of your life without knowing at least something of what was happening to Simon. That meant that you would have to have arranged for someone to keep an eye on him over the years, and to report anything he might have learned to you. Obviously, there was only one place you could ask for a favor as involved as that."

"So you spoke with Gran," she concluded softly.

Justin nodded. "But only briefly, Mel. She was very ill."

Immediately Melanie's eyes glittered with worry. "How is she?"

"Better," he smiled, leaning back against the door frame in the opposite wall from the scullery, and quite pleased with the effect the action had on Melanie's proximity. "She is in hospital and recovering nicely."

"But, Justin, they cannot afford—" And then she paused, her gaze growing tender and warm with understanding. "You are paying for her care, are you not?"

Justin shrugged. "The cost is negligible, Melanie. But the benefits . . . mmm, the benefits are worth a thousand times more."

"What benefits?" Melanie asked suspiciously.

"Well, for one thing, when I take care of your Pollards and Hickses, I have discovered, you call me Justin without my having to suffer a mortal wound first," he told her, grinning broadly.

Melanie could not stop herself from joining him. "What else?" she asked, her gaze becoming playful.

Justin's countenance grew very hungry. "That, cousin, is something I intend to discuss with you in great detail later."

Melanie's smile melted under the onslaught of Stonegate's heat. She trembled slightly at the leashed power she saw shimmering in his intent gaze.

"Why have you come?" she finally asked quietly when their eyes had lingered too long upon each other's and the bond between them had contracted into an insistent yearning that electrified the short distance between their bodies.

"Ah, well," the earl replied softly, "as to that, I have come to offer you two choices pertaining to your future. When I have explained them, you, of course, may make the decision as to which one you will take."

Melanie straightened slightly and drew away, raising one finely sculpted eyebrow. "I believe that the choice has been made," she informed him firmly.

"I have just unmade it," Justin countered with a grin. Then, stepping aside, he motioned with a sweep of his arm that she should precede him into the hall. "And now, if you will lead the way to your dining room, I shall begin my explanation."

Melanie's gaze flickered over every plane of the earl's face, searching for a clue to his odd behavior and the even more bizarre gleam in his dark eyes, but she could discern nothing. Nodding once in brisk acquiescence, she brushed past him and stepped into her narrow hall. Almost immediately, as the house was very small, she came to the door leading to the dining room and entered hesitantly. To her astonishment, two distinguished, expensively dressed gentlemen scraped back her two second-hand chairs and rose instantly to their feet.

"Gentlemen," Justin greeted, giving the astounded woman a gentle nudge so that he could also enter the room, "may I present Lady Melanie Baxter . . . my betrothed."

Melanie whirled around to face him, unable to keep her breasts from brushing against his claret silk waistcoat, or her forehead from clacking against the dent in his chin, as he inundated the tiny space.

"No . . ." she breathed, shaking her head slowly as she again stared into his eyes.

"Yes," Justin whispered, smiling with a combination of tenderness and mischief.

"But you were only eleven," she hissed in return, quite quietly, actually, for a hiss.

"And you were a babe," he replied tenderly, lowering his mouth to within inches of hers, "with the most extraordinary copper-colored eyes. But what of it? It does not signify."

"But you cannot—"

Suddenly, Justin caught Melanie's lower lip between his teeth in a gentle bite, a stallion gentling his mare. "Yes, I can," he told her on a soft breath before his tongue flicked out and licked her upper lip's soft inner lining.

Melanie was felled by a bolt of inner electricity. She slumped on gelatinous legs, reaching out to clutch at the earl's dove gray lapels with fingers still trembling from the sensual charge. Instantly, Justin's hands were at her

waist, supporting her, turning her away from him to face
the two men. One strong arm slipped around her, pressing
her back against his strength, while the other hand rose
to rest spiderlike upon the top of her head, nesting among
her clinging curls.

"Make your curtsey, Melanie," he commanded into her
ear, pressing down upon her curls, his warm breath skit-
tering over her skin like the touch of butterfly wings.

Melanie did as she was told, except, of course, that the
earl was holding her against him quite firmly, so she did
not go anywhere. Her legs rose up, though, as if she had
performed a proper stoop. She looked down, amazed that
she was hanging suspended against the earl. After blushing
like a fresh burn, she allowed her feet to return to the floor.

"The gentleman on the left is Mr. Clyde Gorton," Justin
informed her with a well-controlled grin, "my barrister."

"How do you do, my lady," Mr. Gorton responded with
a commendable bow.

"I am quite well, thank you," Melanie answered, feeling
quite at sea. Surreptitiously, she dug back a bit deeper into
Justin's masculine heat.

"The gentleman on the left," Justin continued quite happily, "is my godfather, the Archbishop of York."

Instantly, Melanie's eyes grew round. "Oh, my goodness! Your grace," she breathed, dropping into another of
her suspended curtseys.

"Delighted to meet you, my dear!" the Archbishop exclaimed with deep, hearty exuberance. "Justin has told me
a great deal about you. Extraordinary . . . quite extraordinary."

"Well, I am pleased that you are delighted, I am sure,"
Melanie responded, feeling the veriest clodpole the second
the inanity left her mouth. "Justin?" she whispered des-

perately, turning her head back so suddenly to speak with him that her curls brushed his mouth.

"Yes, my betrothed?" he whispered back after he had untangled several of his teeth.

Melanie scowled at him chidingly. "Stop saying that! Deuce take it, Justin, why are they here?"

"They are here at my request, of course," he told her with another wicked smile, "to help in your choices."

Melanie heaved a frustrated sigh. "Very well," she said tartly, "suppose we get right to the heart of the matter. What are these choices you keep referring to, Stonegate?"

Justin's features creased with the struggle to contain his triumphant grin beneath a facade of arrogance. "Your choices for your future, of course," he told her casually. "You see, Melanie, as much as you and I may have wished, for our own reasons, to ignore the document signed all those years ago by our fathers, it is still quite legal. You are most definitely my betrothed. And, being a high stickler of the utmost propriety, I find that I simply cannot brush the fact aside and still maintain my sense of honor."

"What does all this mean?" asked Melanie, shaking her curls in confusion.

"It means that I am holding you to our betrothal, my dear . . . and if, knowing that, you still choose to ignore it, well . . ." he told her, motioning toward Mr. Gorton with his chin, "I shall sue you for everything you possess for breach of promise."

Melanie gasped in astonishment.

"Or," he continued, gesturing toward the benignly smiling Archbishop while his eyes sparkled triumphantly, "you may choose to marry me."

"What?" Melanie cried, beginning to struggle against him.

"My, my, Justin," the Archbishop said watching

Melanie's thrashings with intent curiosity, "you were indeed correct in your conviction that she would have to be restrained."

"You bounder!" she continued, shoving at the viselike clamp of his arm. "I did not even sign that betrothal agreement!"

"Nevertheless, it is legal, my lady," intoned Mr. Gorton nervously, backing away a bit. "Upon the earl's request, I have looked into it extensively."

"Watch for the sling," Justin warned, scooping his powerful arm under her knees before it occurred to her to start kicking, then lifting her against his chest. "If she pulls that out we haven't a chance."

"It . . . does not . . . signify," gasped Melanie, wriggling against the earl to free her hands. Suddenly she stilled and pierced him with her troubled gaze, her breath gusting in heavy pants against his face. "I cannot . . . marry you," she breathed between gasps. "You must marry Miss Parkes. I heard what you said to the countess and Angela after I was sent to my room the night of my ball. I know you must marry her to restore your name."

"Actually, no," Justin countered softly, reaching up to tenderly stroke her cheek. "Lord Palmerton is doing that for me."

Melanie's brow grooved with consternation. "What?"

"He agreed to the task, it seems, because a certain rag-mannered cabbie blackmailed him into doing it," Justin revealed, his dark gaze dancing with humor, "but he is continuing to do so now, even after I made it clear to his daughter that I would not marry her, because he felt very badly about what she had done."

"What she had done?" Melanie echoed in a whisper.

Justin nodded and smiled. "I know everything, Mel," he said nudging her chin with the edge of his finger until her eyes surrounded him with their molten depths and her mouth was only a breath away. "Marry me, Melanie," he demanded into her mouth. "Marry me."

"No."

"Clyde, go file those papers," Justin ordered, dropping Melanie's legs to thump against the floor as if they had been hot coals.

"Justin, listen to me," Melanie pleaded after she had regained her balance. "I am glad for you . . . that you have discovered Miss Parkes's true nature, and that her father has agreed to continue to help you. But none of that signifies."

"No?" he challenged, fisting his hands on top of his hips.

"No!" she declared hotly, copying his action until the two of them looked like combative book ends. "Look at me, Justin! I am still a cabbie!"

Stonegate straightened and let his hands drop to his sides. Then, in one swift movement, he yanked Melanie back into his arms.

"Now you listen to me," he commanded, his gaze stabbing into hers with sweet intensity, "I have learned a great many things since the shooting, Melanie, not the least of which is that very little in life is black or white. My mother brought that truth home to me most effectively. She also convinced me that people *can* do what is unthinkable in Society's view, and survive. I shall tell you all about it sometime, but for now, please know that my standing in the *ton* is no longer the most important thing in my life. You are . . . and you always will be."

"But, Justin," Melanie whispered, her molten eyes flooded with tears, "I cannot erase the past. How can I go back again?"

"We do not go back, my love," he told her tenderly, "we

go forward . . . together . . . from here. It shall not be easy, but we shall eventually overcome. And Mama is especially well suited to help."

"Still, I—"

"Darling, listen to me," he insisted, shaking her against him slightly. "Both of us have allowed ourselves to become mortared to the past . . . I in my insistence upon unreasoningly following my father's dictates even though I knew they were causing my unhappiness, and you in your dogged determination to live up to a decision you made when you were fifteen years old. We were both wrong."

"Are you saying I was a fool to choose as I did?" she queried more warmly.

"No, of course not," Justin soothed, "but, Melanie, don't you see? People of that age are so idealistic, so noble in their passions. Your decision eight years ago to forgo a life of your own—with all the rigid self-denial that went along with it—is perfectly in keeping with what someone of that age would resolve. But life is not so rigid, Melanie. It allows for a little give and take. You are now three-and-twenty, and it is time to let go, my love. It was right and honorable for you to provide for the future of your brother for all those years, but it is also right and honorable for you now to seek your own happiness."

"Oh, Justin," Melanie sobbed as she leaned against his strength and slipped her arms around his neck. "I love you so much."

Justin squeezed her bruisingly. "I love you, too," he murmured against her soft hair. "Now," he said, running his thumbs beneath her eyes to scoop away her tears, "do I send Mr. Gorton on his way to file the papers, or does he remain to serve as our witness?"

Melanie turned shakily toward the two broadly beaming gentlemen. Drying her eyes on the wrinkled sleeve of her faded cutaway, she caught the barrister's warm gaze and said, "I should be most grateful, sir, if you would stay."

Behind her, Justin let out a most unlordly whoop.

Melanie jumped straight into the startled Archbishop's heavily padded arms.


"Gentlemen, I believe our next destination is the parlor," Stonegate uttered with sudden detached hauteur as if he had not just frightened everyone in the room into a head of gray hair. "If you will precede us and take your places, I shall shortly bring you my bride."

"Justin, you cannot mean to marry me now!" wailed Melanie as the two gentlemen slipped past her and entered the hall.

"Of course, I do," he said evenly, taking her back into his arms. "What good does it do to have an archbishop for a godfather if one cannot depend upon him for a special license and a hasty wedding?"

"Justin, that is not what I mean, and you know it!" the lady groused.

"I know no such thing," the earl told her in bafflement. "Explain."

"Stonegate, really," she uttered in exasperation. "Look at me!"

The earl did . . . from head to toe . . . very slowly . . . very thoroughly. When at last he sought her eyes again, he was grinning irrepressibly.

"Yes?"

"I am in my cabbie's clothing, you impossible man!" she scolded. "I cannot be married in them. Let me go so that I can run up stairs and change into my blue dress."

"Not for the twentieth part of a moment," Justin told her with a gleam of challenge in his eyes. "You disappear far too easily. I am not letting go of you until you are legally mine."

"But, Justin—" she sputtered.

He silenced her objection with a swift, hard kiss. Grinning arrogantly, he immediately propelled her into the hall.

Melanie struggled against his tight, proprietary grip upon her elbow, then decided she was more vexed with his self-satisfied, peremptory attitude. It was the outside of enough. Twisting her arm against his fingers, she glowered up at him. In return, he smiled down on her as would a complacent, beneficent god. And then he turned her toward the parlor door, slowly swung it open, and gestured for her to enter the small room.

Nothing could have prepared her for the sight she then beheld. The surface of every table was covered with arrangements of pink roses, dozens and dozens of them. Garlands of greenery and Queen Anne's lace draped gracefully over the curtain rods, their delicate strands broken at pleasing intervals by more roses, gathered into elegant clusters of blooms. Directly across from her, a wide, lattice arch, entwined with even more blossoms, stood between her two small windows, sheltering Mr. Gorton and the Archbishop, who had somehow contrived to be dressed in all the splendor of his vestments. And, gathered around the arch, smiling at her warmly, were Simon, the countess, Angela and her husband, Viscount D'Antry, who had come in from their home in the country for the occasion, Fanny and Edward, and, with the exception of Gran, every single one of the Pollards and the Hickses.

"Ohh," Melanie peeped, placing her trembling fingertips against her lips just before the first of her tears splashed over them. And then she turned away suddenly, and threw herself into Justin's arms.

"Justin . . ." she breathed against his corded neck.

"Surprised?" he whispered in return, his voice a smile.

"Oh, Justin . . ." she repeated, squeezing herself even more tightly against him.

"I love you, too, Melanie," Stonegate replied.

# Sixteen

The Earl of Stonegate closed the door on the last of his wedding guests and turned slowly toward his wife. An odd look crept into his eyes as he regarded her, a look that was both calculating and raptorial.

"Justin?" Melanie questioned from farther down the hall, suddenly wary of the strange mood that had come over him. "Is something wrong?"

"I am not sure," he told her as he began a slow stalk toward her. "I have never felt quite this way before."

"What way?" she asked, trying for a bright smile as she began to awkwardly retreat before his steady advance.

"Unsure as to what to do first," he responded, his gaze intensifying. "I do not know whether to kiss you until you are mindless, or shake you until every one of your teeth fall out."

"Goodness!" she laughed nervously, feeling her heels come into abrupt contact with the foot of the stairs. "What a choice!"

There is nothing amusing about this," Justin declared with heat. "Wife, do you have any idea of the month I have just endured? I swear, Melanie, if you ever put me through such a thing again, I cannot be responsible for what I might do!"

A sweet smile touched the edges of Melanie's mouth.

"Justin, you called me wife," she declared softly, ignoring his pique, her eyes sparkling with gold chips.

Disconcerted, the earl's attention was diverted momentarily by the pleasant thought, not to mention the tantalizing sight of her hypnotic eyes, but then he gathered himself again behind a sturdy frown.

"Do not think to run away again," he continued scolding, backing her up the stairs. "If you do, I shall move heaven and earth to find you, and then I shall lock you away for the rest of your life!"

"I think I have never heard such a lovely sound, have you?" the new countess whispered huskily, her gaze growing soft, her eyes warm and molten. "Wife."

Justin's heart settled into a heavy rhythm that pounded down into his abdomen as her voice thrummed against his senses. He chewed on his inner cheek, his fingers tingled. Mentally shaking himself, he summoned every mote of his willpower and continued on.

"Do you have any idea what I felt when I found out you had gone?" he grumbled as he backed her up to the second-floor landing, refusing to be dissuaded by the scent of her, the thought of her filling his arms. "There was no way for me to protect you, deuce take it! Anything might have happen—"

"Justin," Melanie sighed, her eyes sparkling with joy as she reached up to touch her fingertips to his lips. "If I promise never to leave you again, will you be satisfied?"

The earl's rigid posture slowly, unwillingly, relaxed, softening beneath her touch.

"Yes," he growled as she trailed her fingernails down to the dent in his chin. "Besides, you cannot run away, can you?" he said, as if the thought had just occurred to him. "You are my wife."

"Yes, I am," she whispered, backing toward the bedroom. "And since we now have that point nicely settled, would you mind concentrating on the other part of your impulse?"

"Other part?" Justin asked, puzzled.

"Yes, you remember," Melanie reminded him, her eyes darkening into rust. "The part where you wanted to kiss me mindless."

"Ah, that part," the earl recalled, his gaze heating markedly.

He frowned slightly then, trying most studiously to recall what the devil he had just been cutting up stiff about, sure that he should make at least one more attempt to finish staking out his wife's new set of behavioral parameters, but just then the sun broached the gray canopy of clouds outside the bedroom window and set fire to Melanie's copper-colored eyes. The earl decided quite quickly that he could belabor the point later. Besides, Melanie had just unbuttoned the top button of her shirt and he had become rather intently absorbed with the novel idea of divesting his new bride of a set of men's clothing . . . so sensibly quick and easy to get out of, devoid of all those rows of buttons, ties, and tabs.

His fingers twitched; his mouth quirked into a half-smile of anticipation as he watched his wife slip the second button from its mooring, revealing the secret, shadowed valley between her breasts to his appreciative gaze. He swallowed thickly; his blood surged.

Deuce take the bloody parameters, the earl decided as his body clenched. Tearing at his silk cravat, he followed his countess into the room, pausing only long enough to quietly kick the door closed.

* * *

Much, much later, the Earl of Stonegate slipped contentedly from his wife's body and gathered her close.

"Are you all right, my love?" Justin whispered against the top of her head, his heart still shoving his blood through his heavy, sated limbs with frantic thuds.

Against his warm neck, Melanie nodded, still unable to speak.

"Did I hurt you?"

Midnight curls shook against the pillows, sending a trembling tendril to twine around his nose.

"It was wonderful," she finally breathed, gripping her arms around his chest more tightly.

"God, yes," Justin agreed, kissing her forehead.

The bond . . ." she whispered with wonder, slipping her bare leg up over tangled bed linens to come to rest between his, "the connection between us. It was leading to this, was it not?"

Justin nudged her face up to his with the edge of his hand and tenderly kissed her damp upper lip. "Yes," he replied with a soft smile. "And everything that goes along with it."

"Such as love?" she suggested, using one finger to make a path through the crisp hair covering his chest.

"More . . ." he breathed against her mouth before he again captured it for a lingering kiss. "All the ways in which a man and a woman truly become one. I must admit, however, that this part of our connection is the one I particularly enjoy."

Melanie laughed softly. "The other part of the benefits you spoke of, I assume."

Justin nibbled on her soft, fragrant ear, drawing the lobe into his mouth where he suckled it tenderly.

"Damned right."

"Justin?" Melanie asked him, leaning back slightly. "What will happen to us now?"

The earl heard the worry in his wife's voice and responded to it. Tucking an arm behind his head, he gazed at her warmly, letting her see the new confidence, the reassurance, that had filled him since his mother's incredible revelation to him earlier.

"We shall take one day at a time, my love," he told her, "and make each one a treasure. And whatever happens to either of us, we shall face it honestly and together."

"Yes," Melanie breathed, smiling her consent.

"For the nonce, I believe it will be best to spend much of our time in the country . . . at least for a while, until Society has time to forget and another scandal has arisen to occupy it. But you will not be lonely, love," he added, looking at her. "You will have your family with you."

"Simon will stay with us?" she cried, sitting up abruptly, her small breasts suddenly bared to her husband's delighted, and certainly most avid, gaze. "What about Oxford?"

"Melanie, you misunderstand," Justin corrected, reaching out a long, tapered finger to circle the puckered tip of one soft mound, his eyes becoming riveted to his delicate, consuming work. "Simon shall still attend Oxford. He shall visit us on holidays and between terms. Dearest, the family I referred to are the Pollards and the Hickses."

"Justin, what do you mean?" Melanie cried, sitting even straighter, unknowingly thrusting her breasts into greater prominence. "Shall they live with us in the country?"

The sight was more than the earl could be expected to ignore. Growling low in his throat, he reached for her.

She pushed aside his hand. "Justin, answer me," she commanded, rising up to sit upon her heels.

The earl groaned and passed his rebuffed hand over his

face to block out the enticing view of his wife's newly revealed, and delicately flared, hips. "My love, if everything has gone as planned, they are already on their way." Again, hungrily, he stretched out his arm.

She caught his wrist and set it back against his hip. "But how shall they all be occupied?" she asked with concern.

"Melanie, for the love of—"

Justin gritted his teeth in frustration and pushed the sheets aside so that the temptress could witness exactly what she was doing to him. Earlier, she had been most concerned to know if it hurt. Well, let her take a good look. He had no qualms whatsoever against playing upon her sympathies . . . or seasoning them with a goodly dose of guilt, either, for that matter.

"Con is to work with the gardener and Maeve in the dairy," he explained through his teeth. "Maudie and George . . . oh, deuce take it, wife, they shall all have work, cottages, a decent living, and, if the boys show an aptitude, I shall send them to good schools. There now, are you satisfied?"

"Oh, Justin, yes!" Melanie gasped happily, seizing his hand and pressing it against her lips, inadvertently brushing her husband's long, furred forearm against the tightened tip of her breast.

Justin stiffened, groaned, and in a swift movement, rolled to his side, bringing his thick erection into prominence. Pulling his hand from her grasp, he shaped it into a hook and tried to snare her slender neck.

Melanie skittered playfully out of the way just as his hand swiped past her. And then she stilled, at last noticing his rather pointedly obvious condition. She stared.

"Oh, goodness, Justin, is *that* why you have been reaching for me?" she said, jabbing a delicate finger toward the evidence of his desire with rounded coppery eyes. Suddenly, her gaze widened even more. In a whisper she asked, "Never say you mean to do it again!"

The earl grimaced. "Get this straight in your mind right now, my love," he snarled, his eyes stabbing into hers with sensual purpose, "I mean to stay very busy 'doing' things with you over the span of our lives, and, believe me, we shan't be doing embroidery!"

A pert, impish grin suddenly spread across Melanie's kissable lips. Then, not quite containing it, she sobered, regarding him with owlish eyes.

"Cor, milord," she whispered, blinking innocently, "when does ye 'ave time to go to the bleedin' privy?"

Justin groaned his laugh as he fell back against the pillows and opened his arms.

"Hush, scamp, and come here," he commanded softly. This time, his lady complied.

## *About the Author*

Jenna Jones lives with her family in Phoenix, Arizona. She is the author of two Zebra regency romances: *A Merry Escapade* and *A Delicate Deception*. Jenna is currently working on her third Zebra regency romance, *Tia's Valentine* which will be published in February 1997. Jenna loves hearing from her readers and you may write to her c/o Zebra Books. Please include a self-addressed stamped envelope if you wish a response.

# WATCH FOR THESE ZEBRA REGENCIES

LADY STEPHANIE                          (0-8217-5341-X, $4.50)
by Jeanne Savery
Lady Stephanie Morris has only one true love: the family estate she
has managed ever since her mother died. But then Lord Anthony Rider
arrives on her estate, claiming he has plans for both the land and the
woman. Stephanie soon realizes she's fallen in love with a man whose
sensual caresses will plunge her into a world of peril and intrigue . . . a
man as dangerous as he is irresistible.

BRIGHTON BEAUTY                         (0-8217-5340-1, $4.50)
by Marilyn Clay
Chelsea Grant, pretty and poor, naively takes school friend Alayna
Marchmont's place and spends a month in the country. The devastating
man had sailed from Honduras to claim his promised bride, Miss
Marchmont. An affair of the heart may lead to disaster . . . unless a
resourceful Brighton beauty finds a way to stop a masquerade and
keep a lord's love.

LORD DIABLO'S DEMISE                    (0-8217-5338-X, $4.50)
by Meg-Lynn Roberts
The sinfully handsome Lord Harry Glendower was a gambler and the
black sheep of his family. About to be forced into a marriage of convenience, the devilish fellow engineered his own demise, never having
dreamed that faking his death would lead him to the heavenly refuge
of spirited heiress Gwyn Morgan, the daughter of a physician.

A PERILOUS ATTRACTION                   (0-8217-5339-8, $4.50)
by Dawn Aldridge Poore
Alissa Morgan is stunned when a frantic passenger thrusts her baby
into Alissa's arms and flees, having heard rumors that a notorious
highwayman posed a threat to their coach. Handsome stranger Hugh
Sebastian secretly possesses the treasured necklace the highwayman
seeks and volunteers to pose as Alissa's husband to save her reputation.
With a lost baby and missing necklace in their care, the couple embarks
on a journey into peril—and passion.

---

*Available wherever paperbacks are sold, or order direct from the
Publisher. Send cover price plus 50¢ per copy for mailing and
handling to Penguin USA, P.O. Box 999, c/o Dept. 17109,
Bergenfield, NJ 07621. Residents of New York and Tennessee must
include sales tax. DO NOT SEND CASH.*

# WATCH FOR THESE REGENCY ROMANCES

# LOOK FOR THESE REGENCY ROMANCES